CAPTURE MY DESIRES
MALCOLM & STARR PART I

STEELE INTERNATIONAL, INC. A BILLIONAIRES ROMANCE SERIES BOOK 7

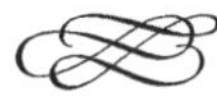

CHARMAINE LOUISE SHELTON

CONTENTS

FREE BOOK

Get the start of the STEELE International, Inc. A Billionaires Romance Series with *Discover My Desires Sebastian & Lola Prequel* FREE!

Click Cover Below or visit **bit.ly/CLBooksNewsletter** to subscribe to my newsletter for latest news and launches, books from my author friends, and sizzling reads in book promotions. Plus, start reading the steamy billionaire romance *Series Prequel* of Sebastian Steele and Lola Lewis.

Their stories. Their discovery of unknown desires…

ALSO BY CHARMAINE LOUISE SHELTON

STEELE INTERNATIONAL, INC.
A BILLIONAIRES ROMANCE SERIES

Discover My Desires Sebastian & Lola Prequel
(Available Exclusively to Subscribers)

Fulfill My Desires Sebastian & Lola Part I

Heighten My Desires Sebastian & Lola Part II

Ignite My Desires Roger & Leonie Part I

Stoke My Desires Roger & Leonie Part II

Justify My Desires Roger & Leonie Part III

Deepen My Desires Sebastian & Lola Part III

Capture My Desires Malcolm & Starr Part I

Embrace My Desires Malcolm & Starr Part II

Cherish My Desires Malcolm & Starr Part III

A Trilogy of Desires Sebastian & Lola Parts I-III

A Trilogy of Desires Roger & Leonie Parts I-III

A Trilogy of Desires Malcolm & Starr Parts I-III

Series Extras

Series Playlist

STEELE INTERNATIONAL, INC. - JACKSON CORPORATION
A BILLIONAIRES ROMANCE SERIES CROSSOVER

Tempt My Desires Lachlan & Haley Part I

Tease My Desires Lachlan & Haley Part II

Grant My Desires Lachlan & Haley Part III

Intrigue My Desires Harris & Kat Part I

Decode My Desires Harris & Kat Part II

Honor My Desires Harris & Kat Patt III

A Trilogy of Desires Lachlan & Haley Parts I-III

A Trilogy of Desires Harris & Kat Parts I-III

Series Extras

Series Playlist

ABOUT STEELE INTERNATIONAL, INC. A BILLIONAIRES ROMANCE SERIES

Welcome to the titillating world of the multibillion-dollar global company and the love affairs of the family that controls it.

STEELE International, Inc. is a series of interconnecting Billionaire romance. Follow the Steele family as they fly around the world chasing the women they love and their happily ever afters. Get ready for glitz, glamour, and steamy romance books. What's better than that? The Jet-set Lifestyle has never been hotter...

The Desires Series is not for the tea set; it's for the top-shelf vodka straight up in a pretty crystal glass coterie!

Don't miss any of the sizzling romance books in the STEELE International, Inc. A Billionaires Romance Series:

Discover My Desires Sebastian & Lola Prequel
(Available Exclusively to Subscribers)

Fulfill My Desires Sebastian & Lola Part I

Heighten My Desires Sebastian & Lola Part II

Ignite My Desires Roger & Leonie Part I

Stoke My Desires Roger & Leonie Part II

Justify My Desires Roger & Leonie Part III

Deepen My Desires Sebastian & Lola Part III

Capture My Desires Malcolm & Starr Part I

Embrace My Desires Malcolm & Starr Part II

Cherish My Desires Malcolm & Starr Part III

A Trilogy of Desires Sebastian & Lola Parts I-III

A Trilogy of Desires Roger & Leonie Parts I-III

A Trilogy of Desires Malcolm & Starr Parts I-III

Series Extras

Series Playlist

Capture My Desires Malcolm & Starr Part I

Capture My Desires Malcolm & Starr Part I is Book 7 in the STEELE International, Inc. A Billionaires Romance Series

I'm the second son; the rebel; the bad boy billionaire playboy of the family. The one others come to for solutions—The Enforcer. My wild, reckless days help me to make my Entertainment Properties Division of STEELE International, Inc. the highest generator of revenue. I'm Malcolm Steele and I always get what I want. And I want the brown-eyed beauty.

I'm the laid-back LA girl who owns a luxury yoga and wellness center; the one with the hippie parents who named her Starr Knight; the one who on a chance encounter meets a sexy as sin man when she closed her heart to love. He brings out a wildness in me I never knew existed. And now fear.

Can the Powerful Billionaire capture the heart of his free-spirited Independent Woman or will one of his former lovers make their fledgling romance collapse?

Travel with Malcolm as he chases his Starr around the skies in private jets, wingsuits, and water jetpacks from Beverly Hills to Rishikesh to St. Barth's in this love triangle steamy romance story.

Anthem: "Gypsy" Fleetwood Mac
https://www.youtube.com/watch?v=mwgg1Pu6cNg

Playlist:
https://www.youtube.com/playlist?list=
PLXwYvn0e218Bkvniy3AAnyw7o8DMj0geb

Visit CharmaineLouise.com The Sensual Lifestyle for CharmaineLouise Books Sexy Fantasies and CharmaineLouise Intimates Sexy Under Things & Loungewear to keep you in the mood.

PROLOGUE

1 *8 Years Ago*

Starr — 13, Beverly Hills, CA

"—Yeah, right! What makes that loser nerd think anyone wants to go to her corny birthday party?"

"Right! And with her weird hippie parents, too! What'll she have there? Unicorns and rainbows?!"

"Did you get a glimpse of her face when we told her we'd go? She grinned ear to ear with happiness braces on full blast... SIKE!"

"With a name like Starr, she's not very bright, is she?"

"That's the problem she thinks she's so smart, knows more than the rest of us—"

My mind reels as their voices fade out behind the

closing bathroom door. I hug my knees to my chest while I rock on the toilet's lid. Tears stream down my heated cheeks, blurring my vision.

I don't need to see clearly to know the voices of Sally, Laura, Gail, Connie, and Jessica—the It Girls of Beverly Hills Junior High School. I could envision Sally, their leader tossing her silky blonde hair over her shoulder as she mimed my glasses. Gail, her main sidekick would have fluffed her curly afro to copy my naturally curly hair.

Obviously, I'm not so smart to have fallen for their easy yeses to attend my thirteenth birthday party this weekend. The It Girls at my simple backyard barbecue? Too good to be true.

For a moment I thought their teasing ways were over since we're in the seventh grade now. Who knew they'd carry over their mean-girl antics from fifth and sixth grades to a new school?

Duh!

A drawn-out sigh slips from my lips when I tilt my head back to stare at the ceiling, hoping to stop the flow of my tears. I'm so tired of them being so nasty to me. And for no reason!

Sure, I like to excel in my classes, and I answer the teachers' questions happily—and correctly. But that doesn't make me a nerd. Just interested in my schoolwork.

The whole braces thing is messed up too. I got them this past summer and grew five inches. So along with a mouth full of metal, thick-lensed glasses, and unruly curls, I tower over the other girls in our class.

Gawky much?!

It was bad enough they teased me ruthlessly about my "hippie" parents, clothes, and crystals in elementary school.

So what if my parents changed their names from Jordan and Belinda to Peace and Sun years before I was even born?! I like my name, Starr Knight. And doggone it, I am bright, and I love my parents—hippies and all!

They're brilliant environmental law attorneys who take on the most challenging cases against big businesses and win billions! The law firm—Knight & Knight LLP—my parents founded years ago after they met at a music festival while at Stanford Law School ranks in the top five of the United States. With offices in LA, Seattle, Denver, Chicago, Houston, New Orleans, Miami, New York City to represent cases in the top environmentally focused cities. They may be hippies, but they're sharks in the courtroom.

And so am I!

After a sniffle, I rise, shake out my vintage, glittery matchstick midi skirt so the layers fall to my Doc Martens' eight-eye, patent leather boots on a whisper. I smooth my off-the-shoulder ruffle top over the white camisole before I grab my well-worn leather crossbody bag.

Loose tendrils of curls fall over my eyes as I bend over. I sweep them back into the big bun at the nape of my neck with a resigned huff as my rose quartz pendant slips along its leather cord. Determined, I straighten my spine and leave the bathroom.

Time to face the music on the school bus ride home.

"Hi, sweetheart, how was school?"

I lift my head from my notebook and smile at my mother. We look exactly alike. Sorrel brown eyes full of love as she peers at me. Smooth chestnut-colored skin glows from healthy eating and regular exercise. Long, curly, dark brown hair pulled up in a topknot. Dimples highlight her sculpted cheekbones when she returns my smile. She's a beautiful woman in her late thirties.

"History class was interesting, and I loved art," I answer as I stand three inches taller than her petite feet-foot-three-inch frame. "But the crew siked me into believing they were coming to my birthday party."

I raise my hand when she speaks. A scowl settles on her pretty face.

"Hey, no worries. 'Be equally thankful for what you perceive to be good and for what you perceive as bad. It all happens for a reason. Either way, you don't let it disturb your inner peace. Strive for tranquility no matter the outer circumstances.' Right?" I ask, reminding my mother of her favorite yogic piece of advice.

She cups my face and beams at me.

"Absolutely, Starr!" My mother exclaims.

"What's the 'absolutely' for?"

We turn to see my father stride into the room. His baritone voice booms around us.

I get my height from him being six feet, five inches. He's opposite of my mom and me, with his obsidian eyes and pecan-colored skin. Equally fit and health conscious, he exudes power at forty-one. He's renowned for his command of the boardroom or the courtroom if negotiations reach that extent.

"A bit of a misunderstanding about my party. But no worries!" I respond as I give him a hug.

It's nearly dinnertime, and they make a point of being home as a family each night if possible. Otherwise the chef makes a meal for me.

"Well, perhaps your gift will make up for it," my father says as his eyes twinkle. "How about you open it early?"

With a shriek, I grasp the envelope and rip it open. An itinerary for a two-week stay at an ashram in Rishikesh, India, the world capital for studying yoga and meditation rests in my hands.

I never thought my parents heard me rambling about the center for spiritual studies a few months ago when I found it online.

Another of their traits I inherited is their focus on well-being. Whenever I have encounters with the crew, I practice breathing exercises to brush off their meanness. It takes the focus away from them and brings it back to me, keeping me centered and at peace.

I whoop and throw my arms around my father, then my mother. Yup, hippies and all, I'd have them no other way!

MALCOLM — 15, Southampton Village, NY

"OH SHIT! What the hell is that on your back, Malcolm?! It better not be real, bro!"

My head whips around, my mouth twisted as I glare at my older brother—older than my fifteen by two years barely.

Since we're so close in age, everyone confuses me with

him. We share the Steele clan traits of wavy ebony hair and dove gray eyes. Our olive-colored skin tanned further by the bright sun of Southampton Village, where our family's compound spans for a mile along our private beach.

Baz has a few inches on my six-foot-frame, so I have to look up at him.

But I don't look up *to* him. Hell nah!

He's Mister Perfect. The supposed leader of the Steele siblings. A role he's taken upon himself since forever. That's cool for Roger who's fourteen and the fraternal twins Harris and Haley at eleven. They freaking idolize Baz.

Me? Not so much. I refuse to be in Sebastian's shadow. I make my own way and don't need his interference in my life. My identity is my own. Screw looking alike.

"Oh, screw you, Sebastian! You're not my father! Back off, *bro*!!" I snarl viciously as my nostrils flare and my face reddens.

I storm off from the party we're having on the beach, sick and tired of his crap. I push past the others ranging from my age to twenties.

Of course it's a crowd. Everyone wants to be around the Steeles. Our multibillion-dollar family has deep roots in New York City with our multigenerational luxury real estate development and management company based out of The STEELE Tower.

Even though it's the summer and we're out in the Hamptons for the weekend, each of us interns at the company. Come Monday, we'll be on Fifty-seventh Street and Fifth Avenue in the heart of Billionaires' Row at our respective divisions, learning our family's business from the ground up.

We have our mother to thank for "not being spoiled rich kids who only lounge around the pool all day." Shelley is a native New Yorker who worked as a shopgirl in one of STEELE's retail spaces. She met our father Morgan when he was on a business call to the store. At the time he was President of the Retail Properties Division and our grandfather was the CEO. Now, our Dad is top dog.

Baz assumes he's next in line, so he runs around barking orders at the rest of us.

Well, to hell with that!

I want no parts of STEELE International, Inc. I plan to start my own company for extreme sports lovers like me. Baz can have it all—Favorite Son and future CEO. I'll continue on as the second son; the rebel; the bad boy billionaire playboy of the family. And billions it will be too. Those I make on my own, not handed to me. Thank you very much!

Who the hell does he think he is telling me how to behave and what to do constantly?! He needs to get off my back already, literally.

That's why I got my tattoo. The wings on my back symbolize freedom from family constraints and the flying as I speed along on my bikes. After I won my latest motocross race, I memorialized it forever in ink. The tattoo artist didn't give me any flack since my height and attitude make me appear older than fifteen. Plus, I flirted with her, then backed it up once she completed my tat. She did a damn good job, and I thanked her royally.

So Baz can shut up with his nagging.

I need to feel the wind in my face to cool down. A quick walk to the garage and I'm astride one of my KTMs, ready to hit the dirt trails outside of the ritzy town. Just as I lift my helmet—I may be a rebel who takes risks, but I value my life—a movement to my left catches my attention.

Damn. Belinda Crane.

Belinda *Baz's Girlfriend* Crane, to be exact.

By her expression, she's not thinking of Big Brother right now. Nor does she mistake me for him. Nope. That heat is all for me.

She twirls a strand of her long silky red hair between her delicate fingers as her eyes travel from my boots to my leather-clad muscular thighs and chest to my smirking mouth. When green meets gray, the lust rolls through us in waves.

I may be fifteen, but this isn't my first rodeo, nor will this be my first ride of this little filly. Poor Baz has no clue. Yeah, height and attitude make all the difference in life.

Belinda sashays over to me, her grip-worthy hips sway, making the strings of her white bikini dance. The round mounds of her tits bounce with each step. Her hooded eyes never leave my face, but my eyes travel the curves of her luscious body. She's a true redhead.

"I love your tattoo, Malcolm... A lot," Belinda says breathlessly as her fingertips skim over my back from shoulder to shoulder, sparks reach through the leather to make my cock jump to attention.

"Do you now, B.?" I smirk.

She nods and licks her full glossy lips.

My eyes dart to them, and I chuckle.

The first time her little pink tongue wrapped around my hardness, I nearly came before she even started blowing me.

I've learned more control since last winter's break. And I plan to use it.

"I'm going for a ride. You wanna cum?" I ask, not missing she picked up on my word choice when her pale cheeks flush bright red.

A quirk of my eyebrow has her nodding and scurrying to hop behind me. The warm, wet folds of her pussy press against my ass.

Yeah, I can't wait to bury my thick ten inches balls deep in her greedy snatch.

The purr of the engine is a precursor to the purrs I'll have Belinda moaning as soon as I get her writhing beneath me.

At times, it's good to be a Steele.

But on my terms.

MALCOLM

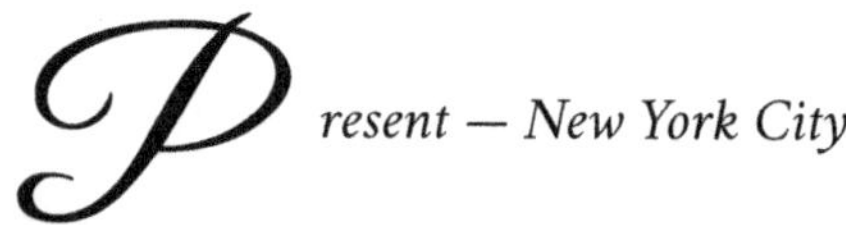

resent — New York City

"GOOD EVENING, MR. STEELE."

On reflex, my gaze travels over the mâitre d' at LEVELS 4 Restaurant as her whisky-colored bedroom eyes drink in every one of my six feet, four inches. Her sultry smile widens with satisfaction. Unmistakably impressed by my bespoke three-piece suit, custom dress shirt with Hermès silk tie and pocket square, and A. Testoni Oxfords.

I run my hand over the five o'clock shadow covering my firm jaw, partially to distract her heated gaze and to hide my delight in her beauty.

Not one to flirt when in a committed Dominant-submissive relationship, even if it has lost its allure. I can still appreciate a gorgeous woman.

The mâitre d's honey-colored skin glows naturally with

minimal makeup. Only ruby-red lips that draw my attention to her lush mouth. My cock—having a head of its own—twitches at the vision of her lips wrapped around my girth as she kneels naked before me.

I incline the head on my shoulders in response to her greeting.

"Your guest has not arrived yet. Would you prefer to wait at the bar, or shall I escort you to your table, Sir?"

This time I can't contain my smirk at her innuendos. Well played.

"The bar will do, thank you... Tabitha," I answer as I read her name on the tag placed strategically on the ample curve of her left tit.

Her eyes gleam after my gaze lingers on the fullness of her breast.

I give her an appreciative nod, then pivot to stride towards my bar.

Yeah, my bar as in part of my global, luxury, members-only BDSM/dance club LEVELS New York in Manhattan's Meatpacking District. Apropos for the flagship location since men pack their meat into willing women and willing men allow women to pack them with their toys, or whatever combination suits members' fancies.

The decorative theme for the club is minimal and industrial in deference to its warehouse history. The fixtures and furniture that appear well worn are high-end, modern replicas used to add authenticity without the grime of old pieces.

My cousin Lucien Jackson cooked up the idea and told me about it. Lucien literally cooked it up since he thought of it as he finished his hospitality and culinary training at Le Cordon Bleu in Paris.

Of course, when we presented the concept to Sebastian for his approval, his response was typical Sebastian. "Who the hell goes through that prestigious training to come up with a titty bar?"

Well, five years later Lucien's idea proves it's bigger than that and has a high profit margin with additional locations in Paris and London. That's all that concerns Sebastian and me, to be honest: will it add to STEELE International's bottom line? Yes, well, it's a go. No, then no go.

LEVELS is one of many business partnerships that STEELE has with Jackson Corporation. World-renown for their award-winning eateries, choice cigars, and distinguished liquors and wines, their products pair well within STEELE's casinos, hotels, resorts, and residential and retail properties.

On the personal side, my mother is best friends with the Jackson matriarch. They spent most of their adult lives together forming a closer bond than they have with their blood siblings and relatives. Not sharing DNA doesn't keep our families from being a close-knit group.

Growing up, Lucien and I were the deviants, the ones who took the most risks—and won. As the second son of the Jackson clan, he relates to my frustrations, especially as teenagers. He set his course to prove himself within their company, just as I did with STEELE.

As the president of STEELE's Entertainment Properties Division, I oversee our casinos, hotels, and resorts.

LEVELS falls within my milieu. I'm the most appropriate sibling to take on the division. My wild ways of pushing the envelope and my love of the challenge extreme sports triggers prepared me for the role to lead our most profitable division focused on pleasure and thrills.

While in my sophomore year at Harvard University—our family's legacy school—I came to terms with my position when Baz saved my ass from being thrown out due to lack of focus. As a Steele didn't get me accepted, I'm smarter than the average guy. But I slipped when once again I was in my older brother's shadow.

My come-to-Jesus moment occurred when Baz laid it all out on the table. He had no interest in competing with me, controlling me, or clashing with me. His purpose being to look after his younger siblings and do well by our family name. He urged me to work with him and not against him as I had for years.

I got everything off of my chest as we shared some Jackson Special Blend Scotch in his off-campus loft apartment one night. The fact he offered the liquor to me despite my age put him in the cool category for the first time in our lives. It loosened my tongue, and we resolved our issues—or rather mine.

The next weekend I flew to New York for a session with a tattoo artist famous for his intricate designs. He morphed the wings on my back into a work of art that wraps around my shoulders to my pecs like a mantle. The wings still represent my freedom and flight, but the additional design elements blend with them to serve as a reminder of my responsibilities to my family and to STEELE International, Inc.

I reapplied myself to my studies from undergrad through Harvard Business School to graduate with honors at the top of my class both times. Combined with my summer internships over the years, I was more than ready to join our family's company upon graduation.

Every one of the successive positions led to my current role, along with being the Second Vice President of the Board.

Each sibling works at STEELE and has board positions: Sebastian, president of the Retail Properties Division and First VP; Roger, president of the Residential Properties Division and Third VP; Harris and Haley, fraternal twins, co-founders of the subsidiary STEELE Technology and Cyber Security and Members.

At the moment, our father serves as CEO and Chairman of the Board. He trusts Baz to carry our legacy into the future and my younger brothers, sister, and I respect him and accept his leadership.

Fortunately, Baz and I grew past my teenage angst to develop a close relationship. We've come a hell of far since my wild days.

Although I still enjoy my adventurous activities. Excursions happen around my work schedule with Lucien, Anton Alexeyev—my Vice President of Development and college friend—and his cousin Borya *The War Defender* Alexeyev, my personal trainer and former MMA champion. Now I control my fighting, no longer chaotic with the MMA fights I take part in regularly to blow off steam.

Harris nicknamed me *The Enforcer* from my lethal fighting skills and for my no-nonsense, take-care-of-it attitude.

So while Baz is the leader and Roger the responsible one, I've become the guy everyone comes to get shit done… Or corrected.

The thought brings my mind back to the present and my reason for being at LEVELS New York tonight and not my usual Dominant/submissive scene with my current sub, Vicky Reynolds. Although who I'm meeting would most definitely be a sub I'd like under my palm.

My guest being Sebastian's former girlfriend/sub Lola Lewis. However, not former in his mind… And I'll use her request to meet as a means of correction for him.

One night six months ago, Sebastian and Lola literally bumped into each other at LEVELS New York. Then by chance Lola turned out to be the owner of the Paris-based luxury lingerie company Baz had a meeting with the next morning at STEELE. Lola's expansion plans for her Lola's Coterie turned into an expansion of her sexual desires with the Alpha Dom.

Yeah, Baz and I have more in common than our doppelgänger looks.

Somehow he fucked up, and here I am to fix things. Naturally.

My chuckle catches in my throat when I glimpse Lola strutting off of the elevator. She captivates more than my attention as several heads—male and female—turn to track her path across the floor.

Lola stuns in a black, long-sleeved mini dress side

knotted with a plunging neckline. Her magnificent tits play hide and seek with the soft fabric. The draping follows the natural curves of her body elegantly. Its hem skims her upper thighs, lengthening Lola's petite frame. Her toned legs end in nude fuck-me sandals.

I slam back my Scotch and rise from the barstool. Time to save the lucky prick's relationship.

"I'm here to meet Mr. Malcolm Steele for dinner—"

"Lola, good to see you," I interject as she speaks to Tabitha, who's eyes dim when she sees my sexy AF dinner guest.

I don't harbor any intimate attraction to Lola. My hard limit of no involvement with my brothers' or friends' partners—current or past—stops my cock from coming to life. Despite Lola's beauty, it's a definite hell no.

She tilts her head back to reach my eyes and smiles warmly.

"Malcolm, good to see you, too," Lola trills.

A less enthusiastic Tabitha leads us to our table in the center of the dining area, perfectly situated with an unobstructed view of the large room and of the bar. A spot from which I can easily observe all the patrons and the staff. I may be here for personal reasons, but I can keep an eye out on my business too.

The bar and dining room bustle as usual with the crème de la crème of society. They hobnob with top-shelf drinks and eat Continental cuisine of pastas, meat, and steaks with favorable sauces crafted by Lucien.

My gaze alights on several recognizable faces enjoying nightcaps at the bar area's high-top tables or savoring the dishes. Tonight, the box office hit action movie actor and his wife, a former senator of Connecticut, and a high-powered female CEO of an online shopping conglomerate represent some members and guests. The club caters to the most wealthy and influential in society. They prefer the relative safety that one can expect from the ironclad nondisclosure agreement that LEVELS requires every member and their guests to sign.

Membership offers two options: Global All Access or Dine/Dance. GAAs can choose from any of the seven levels: 7th Sky Lounge that offers a stunning, 360-degree view of Manhattan and across the Hudson River to New Jersey's shoreline, a bar, restaurant by day dance club by night, a coverable pool that's open during the warmer months, and a glass-retractable roof; 6th and 5th multilevel dance club with two bars and a lounge for food and drinks; 4th Level 4 Restaurant and bar open for breakfast, lunch, and dinner; 3rd has twelve private suites for members to continue their pleasure apart from the BDSM levels; 2nd Peepshow for BDSM with seating alcoves, primary stage, mini-stages, performance rooms, and a bar that serves non-alcoholic mocktails; below ground the Cellar a BDSM dungeon with mocktails bar. The DD members only have access to the party levels—Sky Lounge, Dance Club, and Level 4 Restaurant.

Like the other members, my brothers and I seek LEVELS New York for the solution our bodies crave. We're Global All Access Members. Other than Haley, who we forbid membership. Our baby sister in a BDSM club? Errr… Hell no!

We're all guilty of not having longstanding relation-ships. Our work to increase STEELE International's success as the next generation takes most of our time. All of us, including our sister Haley, commit at least ten hours a day on business. In Sebastian's case, it's fourteen hours. We put pressure on ourselves, but he does it even more. I'm not far behind with thirteen. We're not left with enough time a relationship requires.

Although I make time for my sub. I prefer commit-ments of three to four months at a time or until they get too clingy. As with my current sub, Vicky. Fortunately she's bicoastal, so we see each other a couple of times a month.

Women are more than willing to have a one-night tryst or a few months with one of the STEELE Quaternity, as the media has labeled my brothers and me. They've dubbed us the most sought-after of the world's eligible billionaires. Our near-limitless wealth, power, and good looks attract women like bees to honey. They clamor for a taste, if only for one night.

I dispel thoughts of Vicky to focus on Lola. She slides into the chair I hold out for her, then I sit across the table. We exchange pleasantries before we place our orders.

Once the server leaves, Lola tosses her lustrous ebony hair over her shoulder and leans forward to pin me with her hazel eyes fringed with long lashes.

"I have a business offer for you, Malcolm," she says as her eyes glitter.

For a second, I choke on my sip of Pellegrino. What the everlasting fuck?!

Lola giggles and claps her hands in glee.

"Okay, you have my attention. But do know, I value my life and will not tangle with you, vixen," I tease with a smirk, wiping the sparkling water from my lips. Baz trains with Borya too.

She places a hand over her heart and raises her other hand in the air as she grins.

"I swear to not inflict you with bodily harm by your brother, Captain Caveman," Lola laughs.

We chuckle as the server sets our appetizers on the table between us.

Over our meal, Lola explains her thirtieth birthday trip to Laucala—a private island in Fiji—for a fitness retreat a couple of months ago. She raves about the location, classes, and the instructors.

I listen politely, unsure of the direction she's taking. Does she want me to tell Sebastian to take her back there for a makeup holiday? Does she think I need a vacation? My head nods automatically as I eat my main course.

"—Starr is phenomenal! We're so much alike being driven to succeed with our businesses, in our early thirties, and only kids." Lola gushes.

"Wonderful," I respond, partially in response to Lola and to the delicious Shrimp Oreganata.

Lola narrows her eyes and purses her lips.

"Maybe this will keep your attention, Malcolm," she huffs before she continues. "Starr plans to expand her center, Starr Light Fitness & Wellness Beverly Hills, into international fitness retreats at luxury resorts around the globe and to open a location in the Caribbean to start. She wants a partner. Just like Lola's Coterie did with STEELE International. Get it?"

Lola ends on a triumphant smirk.

Now, she has my attention.

Fitness? Could be conducive to my new venture with Lucien and his older sister Lydie, who is second in command to their father Connor at Jackson Corporation. Our latest project Jackson Hole at STEELE Resorts concept is a members-only, high-end beach clubs for the jet set. It's my second foray with clubs in co-ownership with Lucien. Basically, Jackson Hole is LEVELS on the beach minus the BDSM.

A fitness and wellness center could offer more amenities for JHSR and placed within one of our STEELE resorts, increase activities for guests. Fascinating.

I thank Lola for the introduction, then it's my turn to lean forward.

"You… Sebastian. Tell me how to make the two of you work again?"

Lola crumbles a bit in her seat. Her eyes lose their glitter as she glances down to adjust the linen napkin on her lap. She sighs and raises her gaze back to mine.

By the time she finishes her side of their captivating story and swears me to secrecy, I have the mind to box Sebastian upside his thick head. Seriously, bro? I wonder to myself.

To Lola, I give her tips on how to handle my brother. Tips I learned from years of being around him and the women with whom he's had brief encounters. He's a playboy who never settles with one woman for longer than a night or two.

I can tell his feelings for Lola are on a different level. Now speaking with her and witnessing the gut-wrenching hurt in her eyes, I know she cares deeply for Baz too.

When we stand outside of LEVELS New York, I give Lola a squeeze and promise to not say a word to Baz and to contact Starr tomorrow afternoon. I help Lola into her chauffeur-driven Bentley Bentayga SUV and wave as they pull off.

I duck inside the back seat of my Bentley Mulsanne Duo-tone in platinum and black as my driver Oscar Carrera holds the door open.

As we weave through the evening traffic of Manhattan heading north along the West Side Highway to my penthouse on the fifty-third floor of The STEELE Tower, I stare out the window. My mind goes over the conversation and the emotions that rolled off of Lola in waves.

I sense she loves Baz truly and neither of them know how to deal with their unchartered relationship as they explore D/s for her. But it's deeper.

If Baz is on the verge of love at thirty-five, should I reconsider my relationship status since it's not as fulfilling as in the past?

A vibration and buzz from my trousers pocket bring me back to the sedan. I withdraw my mobile and glance at the screen. The glow in the dim interior reveals a text message from Vicky.

Sir, I miss you.

I click the video link and my lower head takes over.

Vicky lies on her bed spread-eagle with a blindfold over her cornflower blue eyes. Nipples pointed peaks atop her DD mounds. Her soaked pussy glistens with her juices in the candlelight.

"Oscar, change in plans. Take me to Vicky's, thanks," I say into the sedan's intercom as I adjust my burgeoning erection, then type my response.

Do not touch yourself, or I will punish you, Little Pet...

I chuckle to myself.

Nah! I'm good!

STARR

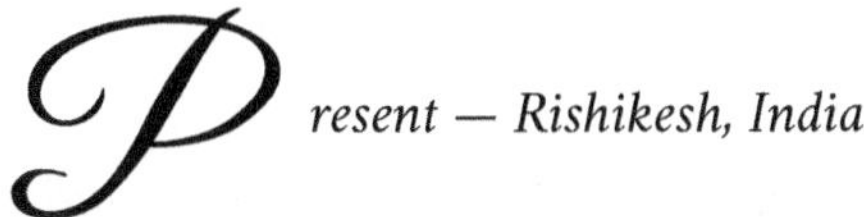

resent — Rishikesh, India

"STARR, you've been distracted since you arrived a few days ago. Do you want to talk about it?"

I lift my gaze from the lunch bowl to Ganika Mishra, my yoga teacher and friend of eighteen years. Her obsidian-colored eyes fill with concern, drawing a frown on her lovely face.

Ganika can read me as clearly as she interprets *The Yoga Sutras of Patanjali*.

We met eighteen years ago when my parents brought me to Rishikesh, India for my thirteenth birthday. Ganika was the youngest teacher at twenty-one years old. So the lead teacher of the ashram thought it best I pair up with Ganika. Since then, we've been close.

Nothing gets past her.

I knew she sensed my concentration was off center. Being polite, she didn't pry.

Now, as we eat lunch on the ashram's terrace overlooking the Ganges River, Ganika peers at me.

My thoughts wander to the night a few weeks ago.

"Damn, Starr, you feel so good, baby. Unh... Unh... Unh."

Quinn Peters, my boyfriend, if you will, of six months grinds and groans on top of me in my bed. His chocolate brown eyes roll back in his head in pure ecstasy.

One-sided ecstasy, that is...

Me? I'm staring at the ceiling praying to God and to every deity in every religion's pantheon Quinn will just cum already.

No matter how many times we've had sex, it's never satisfying for me. Foreplay: kiss mouth, lick one nipple, ram inside my pussy. My barely wet pussy, to be exact.

"Fuuuuck! Yeah, baby! That's how you like it, huh?"

"No."

Holy mackerel, you could hear a dandelion puff drop on the surface of a puddle.

What the heck? Did I just admit it out loud???

Quinn stops in the middle of an unimpressive thrust, the tip of his so-so dick halfway in and halfway out of me. He zooms in on my face with his legal-eagle eyes.

I squeeze mine shut and pray to fall through the mattress. Get swallowed up by the bedding.

A single bead of sweat rolls off the tip of Quinn's nose to land between my eyes.

My lips press together to hold back my groan—not one of pleasure, but one of disgust. Yuck.

After a century passes, more likely less than thirty seconds, Quinn breaks the tense silence.

"What did you just say, Starr?"

He's all attorney in the courtroom with me now.

I take a deep cleansing breath, then open my eyes to face the situation.

"I said, 'No,' Quinn," I respond, staring back up at him. His scowl urges me to continue before he speaks. "I need more. Let's try something different."

Using the strength of my core and leg muscles, I flip us over. I straddle his narrow hips and grind down on his dick. My eyes close as I throw my head back, then pinch and tug the aching nipples of my heavy breasts.

"Drive up into me, Quinn. Hard! I want you to take me!" I tell him, wishing to ease the pressure built up in me after so many nights of dissatisfaction.

After a moment, I notice he's still as a stone statue.

My bouncing ends abruptly. I squint my eyes to peek at him through my lashes. Yup, he's checked out. Great.

With an exaggerated sigh, I roll off of Quinn onto my back to stare at the ceiling... again. This is simply not working for me.

My parents introduced us years ago since he's an attorney at their law firm. They thought we'd have a lot in common.

I finally gave in to his dinner requests, then to spending time with him. Finally, we started seeing each other. The sex began shortly thereafter. Not at all what I expect or want.

I need more, and Quinn can't give it to me.

Without going into the details of my desire for a man who will take me roughly and satisfy my needs, I tell Ganika Quinn and I broke up.

She listens without judgement, then reminds me how everything happens for a reason. I can't allow myself to lose focus by dwelling on what's not meant to be in my life.

As always, she gives me sage advice. The rest of my stay goes smoothly. I enjoy my lessons and time with my friend and others at the ashram. By the end of my stay, I'm back on track and feeling centered.

* * *

"OH, yes, another thing. Anton Alexeyev the Vice Present of Development for STEELE International, Inc.'s Entertainment Properties Division called twice. He wants to schedule a meeting with you and his boss regarding your expansion project."

Adrienne Anthony—my CMO and General Manager of my Starr Light Fitness & Wellness Beverly Hills—tells me with an exaggerated eye roll and air quotes for his title. Mr. Alexeyev must not impress my best friend of eight years.

We met at Stanford Graduate School of Business. Everyone referred to us as Night & Day since we contrasted in our appearances and attitudes. From our long, curly hair with Adrienne's light brown and mine dark brown to her green feline eyes and my sorrel brown angelic eyes to her buttery pecan-colored skin and mine the color of warm chestnuts. I have dimples to her sharp cheekbones. But we're both five feet, six inches with curvy fit bodies from our years of yoga, Pilates, and strength training as certified teachers and students.

Again alike with our hippie vibes, independent nature,

and outgoing bubbly personalities. We're loyal and open to a fault. Resourceful and trustworthy round out our traits.

Where Adrienne has a tattoo of a peacock wrapped around her foot up her ankle to symbolize success, I have shooting stars on the back of my neck for wishes.

We hit it off immediately at Stanford.

I followed my parents' footsteps to their alma mater. Undergrad I received a degree in economics from Stanford University, then continued on to the B-School. Not exactly the Law School. But I wanted to forge my path. Health and wellness became my focus after my first trip to Rishikesh. It helped me to regroup from the taunts of the It Girls in junior high school. Then stayed with me through adulthood.

I wanted to combine my love of wellness with helping others. So I opened my center six years ago at 25. It was my initial goal. Now, I want to expand into international fitness retreats at luxury resorts and add a second center location in the Caribbean. The Fiji retreat was a test run.

And a good thing since I met Lola Lewis. As she promised, she made the connection for me to STEELE. So despite Adrienne's eye roll, I'm super psyched!

"Yeah? Awesome! When is he available?" I ask, clapping my hands.

After Lola told me about STEELE, I Googled the company and understood what she meant about the partnership opportunities. Although everyone knows of STEELE, I wanted to get the details on their resorts specifically.

Besides the opulent properties and their many locations

around the globe, the corporate headshot of the division's president captured my attention.

Malcolm Steele.

I bet he's a man who can take control of the boardroom and of a woman in the bedroom.

His gray eyes zinged me from my tablet screen, setting my nether regions afire. The full lips and angular jaw coupled with his thick, tousled ebony hair had me squirming in my bed. I researched him the night Lola told me she'd make the introduction.

The tropical temperature of Fiji didn't compare to the heat coursing through my body.

Sadly, I noticed he's with different women in every social photo on the Internet. Labeled a member of the STEELE Quaternity didn't help.

At least my libido cooled when I noticed he's a playboy. I've had enough with self-centered men.

Now, I take a deep breath when I feel the heat rise once again at the thought of Malcolm Steele.

Down, Starr!

"Well, the meeting will be with him and his boss… Malcolm Steele," Adrienne says as she swipes her finger on her tablet to retrieve the boss' name. "But he's traveling out of the country now. Alexeyev said something about Positano—"

Adrienne continues on for another hour, catching me up to the happenings at the center while I was in India.

I listen attentively. But on the edges of my mind, I wonder how a man like Malcolm Steele compares to a man like Quinn.

Malcolm Steele has such confidence and exudes dominance and power. Granted, Quinn is a shark in the courtroom and even in the bedroom, just not enough to satisfy me. His needs come first.

Even now, weeks after I broke up with him, he can't let go.

Ego. Give it a rest.

I chuckle to myself when I remember Quinn's reaction to my vinyasa flow class I invited him to early in our relationship. He couldn't get into the asanas like others around him. So he flounced out of the class before it was over.

Ah well. Let it go, like Ganika said.

"—I told her you may be tired from the return flight, but she insisted on coming in for a private session with you. It's in an hour."

I shake my head to clear my thoughts of men to focus on my business. No more salivating over Malcolm Steele or replaying Quinn's antics.

"I apologize, Adrienne. My mind wandered. Who's coming in for a session now?" I ask sheepishly.

"Vicky Reynolds," Adrienne replies with another giant eye roll.

A giggle bursts from between my lips.

Adrienne cannot stand Vicky. She thinks the Hollywood royalty actress is beyond annoying. She tends to name-drop her great-grandfather the founder of a movie studio, her father a major producer, and her mother a screen siren. At all costs, Adrienne avoids Vicky.

After two years of her being a client, to me she's like a little sister. Albeit a petite, blonde-haired, blue-eyed sister from another mother. Four years younger than my thirty-one, her acting career and travels make her worldly. But she appears to look up to me. Often asking my advice. It could be the yogi tenets I share in my dharma talks. I shake my head and tune back into Adrienne.

I'm surprised they even spoke since Adrienne has instructed the front desk staff to handle Vicky's requests.

"Fine, I'll see her in my studio," I respond with a chuckle. "Let me know when she gets here."

"Namaste."

"Namaste."

No sooner than I straighten from my bow to the light in her, Vicky starts in on her latest "scene" with her Dom.

"Oh, Starr! It's just so incredible the way my Dom makes my body tingle and crave his command! I flew back from New York on a pillow from the spanking he gave to me. You know"—Vicky glances around my private studio as though others may overhear her next words—"I didn't obey his command to not touch myself before he made me come on purpose. I just love the way he punishes me! It's the best fuck ever—"

My mind wanders again as I visualize me with a Dom as incredible as Vicky's.

I've never been in a D/s relationship, but after six months of hearing Vicky brag about her latest Dom made me realize that's what's missing for me.

A man who will control me and bring me the maximum

satisfaction possible. The erotic visions that play in my head have a definition. BDSM.

I live vicariously through Vicky since Quinn could never fulfill my desires. She's the only person I know in a D/s relationship. After she told me about it, I had to Google most of the words and activities she spoke about.

My research revealed most active participants in the scene don't discuss their lifestyle with non-players.

But like Adrienne says, Vicky loves to talk about herself. It's all about her.

The one thing she's never disclosed—and she's not in the least bit shy about telling me every minute detail—is the name of her Dom. Vicky told me she had to sign a contract for the terms of their D/s relationship and a nondisclosure agreement. She only hints at him being a powerful multibillionaire who's "to die for" in looks and in the bed. He infatuates her with his "ten-inch cock… The absolute biggest she's ever had."

By the time Vicky finishes, I'm as hot and bothered as she is with her face flushed and blue eyes so dilated they appear black.

However, I dismiss my unrestrained fantasies. No way will I find a man like her Dom. Besides, I'm not so sure I want the commitment she's in. The idea of a contract and an NDA throws cold water over my heated skin.

Vicky and I part ways at the elevator. She heads down to the locker room and spa. I go up to Adrienne's office to close out my day. The jet lag has me ready to crash.

We go over a few more items on her list before I head home for the day.

As I walk through the center, my heart swells with pride at my accomplishments. The classes stay full; clients have standing private sessions; the teachers enjoy being here; the rest of the staff go about their work happily.

The idea of a Caribbean location and regular international fitness retreats excites everyone. Requests for assignments started as soon as I voiced the ideas.

Just as important as my staff's elation, my parents' approval and acceptance of my separate journey ranks high for me.

They would have preferred I studied law and followed in their footsteps, then joined the family firm. But they understand my need to take my path. And my need to seek solace from turmoil when it rears its ugly head; something I carry over from junior high school.

It pleases me to hear clients get their relief through the services my fitness and wellness center provides. To extend my peace to them fills me with joy.

I wave to the front desk staff, concierge, and the boutique consultant before I exit the bliss of the center. The valet smiles and opens the door to my silver Tesla Model X Long Range. I bow my thanks with prayer hands, a custom we do each time.

When I arrive at my Benedict Canyon Drive mansion, I marvel at its brick walls, wood-beamed ceilings, stone-tiled flooring, and wood-burning fireplaces. The elements lend to its concrete and stone rustic appeal. The pool with cabana, tennis court, and manicured lawns appeal to my outdoor nature. My favorite pastime of meditation in the side garden amongst the fragrant flowers relaxes me after a day at the center.

But tonight, I bypass the soothing sounds of the fountain to head straight to my steam shower.

During the drive home, my mind returned to Vicky's boasts about her "Dom to die for." The fever ran through me again as my core clenched at the vision of a Dom capturing me with his silks bound around my wrists and ankles. Spread before his hungry eyes, my body quivers with the thrill of erotic possession.

I take a deep inhale under the rain shower's warm water.

The rivulets glide down my heated skin from my soaked curls, between my heavy breasts, over my bare mound. A trickle touches my folds, adding to the moisture of my needy pussy.

A fingertip brushes my engorged clit when I lift my foot to rest it atop the travertine bench. My eyes flutter closed as I tilt my head back and give in to the vision of the Dom spanking my beaded nipples and swollen lower lips.

My full bottom lip nearly splits as I bite down on it with a throaty moan. My Dom grips my hips as I undulate against the invasion of his rock-hard dick pounding my dripping pussy.

His massive girth and length force me to rise onto my toes. I slap the stone wall of the steamy shower for leverage and buck against him, matching each of his powerful thrusts.

"Take it, take it deep, Little Pet. You... belong... to...

me," my Dom growls against the delicate shell of my ear, driving me closer to the edge.

The warmth of his skin on mine and the slickness of our wet bodies as he takes me roughly from behind makes me cum with a strangled scream.

As I press my forehead against the stone, my pants slow. But my mind still races.

I don't want to live vicariously. I don't want to just fantasize.

What do I want?

My Dom.

What throws me for a loop?

My Dom looks just like Malcolm Steele.

MALCOLM

The late afternoon sun reflects off the windows of the buildings along Fifty-seventh Street as I take a moment between calls to stare out the floor-to-ceiling windows of my office on the twenty-ninth floor of The STEELE Tower.

The modern, gray-tinted glass fifty-seven story mixed-use skyscraper on the southwest corner of Fifty-Seventh Street and Fifth Avenue. I'm on the executive level where my father, Sebastian, Roger, and I have office suites. Our finance and legal departments along with various conference rooms occupy the remaining space. The other divisions have designated floors below along with my younger siblings', twins Harris and Haley, STEELE Technology and Cyber Security.

From my office suite, the view of Manhattan stretches out before me unobstructed. Central Park to the north, the Hudson River to the west, the East River opposite, and the rest of northern Manhattan from Harlem to Inwood. On a beautiful, cloudless day like this morning, the panoramas are riveting.

The interior of The Tower reflects the metal our name represents. The decor—as sleek as the exterior—features platinum silk wall treatments, ebony wood floors, dove gray and white leather furniture, crystal light fixtures, Lucite tables, steel accents, and original artwork. The reception area has a spacious desk. Three attractive receptionists with headsets in their ears and custom-tailored light gray dress suits and skin-tone heels that serve as uniforms sit behind it.

The majesty of our family's power and wealth awes all who enter SI's offices.

After my respite, I swing my chair back to face my desk. Through the glass wall that separates my inner office from my administrative assistant's area, guests seating area, and conference room, I spy Sebastian with Lola as they walk past in the corridor.

Perfect timing. I can update Lola about the fitness center meeting and fuck with Baz.

With a devilish grin, I stand. Then adjust my navy blue striped suit vest and smooth the Full Windsor Knot of my platinum silk tie. A quick finger combing tousles my thick hair the way women adore. All to piss off Baz.

My long legs make quick work of the distance to the corridor, and I call out to my brother and Lola.

They detour into my outer office.

"Hey there, gorgeous!" I greet Lola with an embrace and Baz with a nod. Then wink at him over the top of her head before giving her a squeeze.

A growl falls from Sebastian's lips, and I laugh, releasing Lola from my hug.

"Good to see you again, Lola," I start with a twinkle in my eyes. "I spoke with Adrienne Anthony, Starr Knight's studio manager. Apparently Starr is out of the country at an ashram in India and unreachable. So, we must connect when she returns."

Baz's expression morphs from annoyed to confused.

"It's so good to see you again, too, Malcolm! Thank you for dinner. The—"

"Whaaaat???" Baz yells, his eyes zip between Lola and me.

The cool, in-control Dom now completely off the grid.

Perfect! Just the reaction I wanted from him. He needs to value Lola and not be a giant dick to her. Someone needs to make him see how easily he could lose Lola to another man if he doesn't get his head out of his ass.

While Baz stands gobsmacked, I tell him about Lola's suggestion for me to meet with her friend. It's apparent he's not listening to me, still focused on my hands on Lola and the dinner she had with me. Too bad, bro. That'll learn ya.

He snaps his head in my direction when my words filter through what must be his nightmare—Lola as my sub.

I plow on, behaving obtuse on purpose. Maybe he'll catch up.

"—concept could fit well with our latest Jackson Hole venture. New amenities attract unique guests, while the regular ones find more reasons to keep coming back to stay. Once I meet with Ms. Knight, I'll fill you in."

Since a baffled expression lingers on Baz's face when I finish, I sigh dramatically, realizing that he wasn't paying him the least bit of attention after all.

"Get your head out of your ass, Baz. Lola and I had dinner last week to discuss business. B-U-S-I-N-E-S-S. Got it?" I admonish him "Lola met Starr Knight, the owner of the Beverly Hills-based fitness studio and wellness center Starr Light Fitness & Wellness. She plans to expand into international fitness retreats at luxury resorts and to add a second center location in the Caribbean. Lola told me about Starr since she had an exceptional experience at her first retreat in Fiji on the private Laucala Island. Are we clear?"

Sebastian appears chastened and risks a peek at Lola to find her hazel eyes glowing warmly with suppressed laughter.

To add to his unease, I drape my arm around her shoulders as I join in her glee. How low can the Alpha male sink? I chuckle.

"Crystal clear, brother. Now, back off my girl. We're going to dinner," Baz chides to regain control.

Lola's eyes widen.

He frowns at her, then realizes he referred to Lola as his girl.

Oh boy.

Instead of addressing the term of endearment, Baz grasps Lola's hand and pulls her from my office.

"Have fun," I taunt with a mocking wave.

Baz throws a glare over his shoulder at me as he ushers Lola through the door.

I can't help myself. My booming laughter carries across the office suite.

Gotcha, big bro!

"READY FOR THIS ONE, big guy? Or do you want to pussy out for the nine-thousand-foot jump instead?"

A sound that one may consider a laugh rumbles deep in Borya's chest in response to my taunt.

"*Da. Posmotrim, kto takaya kiska.*" He sneers as he slams his massive hands in front of his broad chest.

Anton chuckles and adds, "We all know it'll be Lucien who's the pussy in the end."

I glance over at Lucien *The Sexy Chef* as he's known by his millions of social media followers. He does seem a bit green around the mouth and his eyes widen at the jabs.

Our crew sits aboard the skydiving plane over Fox Glacier in New Zealand. We're going for a twenty-thousand-foot jump. A glance out the windows and door offers stunning views of rainforests, lakes, mountains, glaciers, snowfields, and the Tasman Sea. The Westland National Park appears in the distance as we make our way to the jump point.

It's been six weeks since the four of us met up for one of our escapades.

The adrenaline pumps through my veins as I check my safety gear. I may be a thrill seeker, but living is my top priority.

The guide gives us last instructions. Then we line up to

exit the plane one after the other for the drop zone 300 feet above sea level.

"Yeah, baby! Let's rock!" I yell as I fist bump Anton before he jumps out the door.

I turn to Lucien and give him a thumbs-up to check on him. No need to do something that will cause anxiety beyond the rush.

He nods and gives me the signal he's ready to go. Then gets in position.

Borya jumps next and does a crazy flip in the air. The wild Russian's laughter floats back as he soars through the clouds.

Up next, I go through my ritual to give thanks for my fearless friends, love to my family, and my safe finish. It's what I do before any of my extreme activities, even when I was a pain-in-the-ass teen. My rebel spirit still exists, but it's alongside my duty to family and self.

A thumbs-up to the guide, and I take my jump.

The air rushes past me as I hurtle through the clouds. My blood races through my veins as my heart pumps with exhilaration.

A shit-eating grin stays plastered on my face as I free fall through the sky at 120 miles per hour. I take in the pristine beauty of New Zealand, awed by the natural landscape free of man's touch. The twenty-thousand feet give me eighty-five seconds to view it all.

I pull on my cords and float safely to the ground under my parachute. Years of experience allow me to land on my feet at a run.

Damn! That was spectacular!

The ground team hustles over to help me with the open parachute. They relieve me of my harness as I remove my helmet and goggles.

Once my heartbeat slows, I thank them for their help.

A screech draws my attention to the petite blonde running at top speed towards me. Instinctively, I catch her in my arms as she leaps into the air and clings to me like a baby monkey. She peppers my face with kisses as she squeals in delight.

"Sir! Are you all right? I was so scared! I hate when you do these crazy stunts!" Vicky exclaims holding my cheeks between her palms.

Her cornflower blue eyes search my face for any sign of distress. A scowl mars her pretty features as her eyebrows pull together and the corners of her mouth droop.

The rush of the jump has more than my blood pumping in my veins. My cock throbs, hard as steel. Nothing gets me more amped than a dangerous encounter. A dance with death. A fight to the end. Bring it.

Instead of answering her question or assuaging her fears, I slam my mouth against her pouty lips and kiss the breath out of her.

Vicky moans and melts into the onslaught of my demanding kiss.

Her soft sounds make my cock twitch and beg me to fuck her raw.

She must sense my need as she squeezes her inner thighs against my hips and rides my growing erection through my jumpsuit.

I allow her to have at me a bit longer before I take back

the control. A swift slap to her ass has Vicky squealing for a reason other than my safety. Hers.

"Be still, Pet. Or need I remind you who is in charge?" I ask in my most dominant tone of voice.

Her shudder and the way she drops her widened eyes show Vicky understands her place in our D/s relationship.

"No, Sir," she whispers as her movements grind to an immediate halt.

On the one hand, I hate the loss of the friction against my aching dick. But on the other, she has to realize I'm in control.

Recently Vicky shifted into the realm of clingy and demanding. Asking where I've been if I don't respond to her text messages or phone calls… or emails. She gets surly when I tell her I'm not available to scene with her at LEVELS New York or at my penthouses in New York City or in West Hollywood. Going to her penthouses on Wilshire Boulevard or in TriBeCa are off limits. Too close to partner status.

She has my commitment as her Dom. Even longer than my usual three months now that it's been six.

For one, the bicoastal aspect makes our time together less consistent, so not boring. Then she's busy with her filming schedule and me with my work at STEELE. It's been conducive. But these last couple of months have been taxing.

Her requests for more time with me coupled with her ring innuendos make me want to run.

I may have an enormous member, but I'm not a dick. I

can't just dump her because she's heading down the path we both said we didn't want at the onset of our contract.

Yeah. Contract.

I don't get involved with subs without one, plus a nondisclosure agreement. I need them to understand before we start the relationship is temporary—three months typically—and will not lead to marriage. It's to satisfy our sexual needs and proclivities mutually. Nothing more. And never to discuss it with anyone.

The sense that Vicky wants more haunts me, which is why I was hesitant for her to join the crew for our latest outing. I agreed reluctantly when she went on and on about not having gone to New Zealand before.

The sucker that I can be caved to her request. So here we are with Vicky in my arms and my dick eager to fuck her.

Go figure. I'm a virile male, so how can I say no?

"Good, Pet," I respond. "Go to the helicopter and wait for me."

Vicky slides to her feet, and I swat her ass in the tight ski pants that cling to her butt cheeks beneath her parka. She giggles and skips ahead.

"Okay then. Looks like your girl is overjoyed you landed safely."

A glance to my right reveals Lucien smirking at me as he runs his hands through cropped, dark brown hair. His emerald green eyes shine as his dimples pop onto his annoying face.

Not my *girl*.

I swipe at him with my foot, but he jumps and lands his

own roundhouse kick. Not enough to harm me, merely to get me away from him.

We laugh good-naturedly then follow Vicky to the Sikorsky S-92 Executive Helicopter where Anton and Borya wait with the pilot.

Still hyped from the exhilarating jump, I sit in the back two seats with my hand between Vicky's thighs. I slip my fingers between her wet and puffy folds to stroke her clit. The tips brush just inside of her pussy, enough to get her juices to flow without an orgasm.

As she moans softly with her teeth in her plump lower lip, I keep her on the edge for the duration of the thirty-minute flight. Vicky thrives on exhibitionism. The risk of being caught proves her adrenaline rush.

The crew and I rented a house nearby as a base for our five-day trip. The less time between the two locations, the better for our plan to sky dive, ice climb, and to hike the glacier. It's only day one, and I can't wait for the rest.

Vicky chokes on a sob when I withdraw my soaked fingers for her pulsating pussy one last time before we disembark.

I smirk at her. Then lick my fingers clean off her sweet juices.

She wanted to interlope on my Guys' Trip.

Well, let's play.

Vicky rushes—beside herself—to the awaiting Mercedes-Benz G-Wagens. Her eagerness makes her hips and ass sway enticingly. They're like a Siren's Song to grip them and bury my thick girth balls deep inside her willing body.

My dick jumps in appreciation. I run my fingers under my nose to inhale the remnants of her sweet essence. Yeah, we'll have some fun as soon as I get her in the bedroom and tied to the makeshift St. Andrew's Cross with a blindfold.

And a crop.

"—I know… Yes, not much longer… Mmm hmmm… Mother! I know how much he's worth! I said I'll get the ring, didn't I… No, Malcolm can't hear me. He's in the shower… Hell! I'm doing all the kinky shit he wants me to do! Do not dare talk to me like I'm not doing my part… Well… His giant cock up my little ass for starters—"

In a rage, I snatch Vicky's mobile from her ear and jab my finger on the screen to end the call. The pressure I put on the device almost cracks the screen.

WHAT THE ABSOLUTE FUCKING FUCK?!?!?!

Through the red haze of my vision, Vicky cowers on the bed with her mouth agape. She sits as stunned by my outburst as she is in me overhearing her conversation. A conversation that never should have taken place given the ironclad nondisclosure agreement she signed.

The steam from the shower I just finished resembles a puff compared to the fire streaming from my nose. If this were a movie, I'd be a fucking dragon about to sear the maiden.

Except Vicky is no maiden. The lascivious liar.

Now it all makes sense.

When we first met at a dungeon party, she didn't come across as a sub, but she played coy when I made innuendos about her participation in the lifestyle. Not at all turned off. The second time we did a scene with her bound to a spanking bench for edge play, followed by a rough fuck with multiple toe-curling orgasms for her. All within Vicky's approved limits. She didn't balk. She went into subspace...

I took her word and trust.

Dumbass.

Vicky's recent hints towards a commitment beyond our contract I extended from the original three months then the marriage bomb of "I'm ready to settle down with you" had me on high alert.

But this? Telling her mother about our sexual activities and plotting to bamboozle me?

She's in it for the money. Of course.

Fuck this!

"Get dressed and packed"—I raise my hand to stop Vicky from speaking—"You will leave as soon as the crew prepares the Sikorsky. A ticket to LAX will be ready for you when you land at Hokitika Airport. The crew will give you the airline and your mobile before they leave you."

I stride to the nightstand to grab my mobile, then leave the bedroom without another word. A swipe of my hand over my face brings me back into control.

Down in the living room, a quick call to the pilot and to Miles Crawford—my administrative assistant—finalizes the details for Vicky's immediate departure.

Anton struts into the room laughing with the brunette he met at the bar last night. One glance at me standing in nothing but a towel and a scowl, and he tells the woman to wait for him in the kitchen.

"What happened?" Anton asks, his Russian accent creeping in as it does when he becomes agitated.

In fluent Russian I fill him in, and a string of curses fall from his mouth. His glacial blue eyes turn frostier. Anton runs his hands through his long blond hair and growls.

"Motherfucker!"

A gasp from the entryway draws our attention.

Vicky stands there in my cashmere sweater. She shifts from one bare foot to the other as her wide eyes dart between the brawny Russian and me nervously. She opens her mouth to speak, but I cut her off.

"The car will take you in ten minutes. Unless you want to travel as you appear, I suggest you go upstairs, change, and pack. My attorneys will contact you upon your return to Los Angeles."

By the end, the last word is a growl deeper than Anton's. My control thins.

He glances at me, then turns to Vicky as he points to his Rolex Cosmograph Daytona.

"Eight minutes, *dorogoy*," Anton sneers in a voice dripping with disdain.

Tears pop from Vicky's eyes as a cry escapes her lips. She scans my face for any sign of forgiveness.

I blank my expression and square my shoulders. I will not fall for her melodramatic act.

This shit is O-V-E-R.

STARR

"Leonie… Hello there… Leonie?"

I use my voice to bring her back to our meditation session gently.

She shakes her head to clear what must be distractions. Then opens her eyes to see me, Lola, Haley, Blair, and Billie peeping at her. Leonie's golden-caramel cheeks redden as she laughs in embarrassment.

The biracial Parisian megamodel stuns in person with her lustrous mane of mahogany wavy hair pulled into a topknot. Feline amber eyes, angular cheekbones, and a sleek body ending in long, toned legs to die for prove she's *The Lion* of the catwalk.

Lola told me she was coming to Beverly Hills for business but was taking some time to hang out with her girlfriends. It's the first time I met her BFF Leonie Beaulieu, Haley Lola's boyfriend and Malcolm Steele's sister, and Blair Thomas and Billie Chandler Lola's administrative assistants.

Their first stop to jumpstart their girls' time was to Starr Light Fitness & Wellness Beverly Hills for yoga and meditation classes. Since Lola and I met at my Fijian Laucala Island retreat, she's raved about her experience and how cool of an instructor I am to her friends and associates. Many who live here and those who are in town come to the center for classes or private sessions with me. So it's a straightforward decision for Lola and friends to come while we're here.

Since they wanted to leave the stresses of life behind, I structured a vinyasa that requires concentration. To focus on the breath synched with the movement of the asanas creates the best means to prevent one's mind from wandering.

Naturally, they tuned into their breath and the sequence of challenging asanas I used in the flow. The vigorous physical and mental workout was just what they needed as opposed to the slower pace of a Hatha class. My dynamic teaching style made it fun.

Lola mentioned her best friend was going through some guy problems, so I won't push Leonie too far. I can understand completely.

Quinn calls and sends text messages to me. He even stopped by here unannounced. Adrienne dealt with him while I hid in the staff room.

I doubt he wants to get back together for us, rather to soothe his ego. He's all, "Come on, Starr, call me back. We can make this work."

Seriously? *Make this work*? Like we're some case he has to win. Give me a break already.

He's really pushing my balance off kilter. Ugh!

Then Vicky has been glum the past couple of months. Her Dom broke up with her unexpectedly. What a jerk! She didn't reveal her usual details, just that their time ended. She seemed so pitiful.

My heart broke for her.

The world of men has gone crazy…

I return my focus to Leonie and offer her a warm smile.

"No judgement…!" I say as I join in her laughter.

What else can women do but take their antics in stride? We sure as hell can't murder them! The ludicrous thought makes me giggle as we leave my studio.

After a few minutes in the steam room and a quick shower, we head to lunch at nearby Crustacean Beverly Hills. The modern Vietnamese fare specialties include delicious seafood that's the perfect light meal after yoga.

We settle on the gray suede seats at a banquette near the Walk on Water. The path runs from the front door through the restaurant between tables. Interspersed with wood and weight-bearing glass, the water below appears to offer a glimpse of the ocean's depths. Aside from the cuisine, the path is the eatery's highlight.

When the server arrives, we order An Sum—Crustacean's version of dim sum—to share and salads for our meals.

"Have you spoken to Malcolm Steele, yet?" Lola asks me.

"No, we keep playing phone tag. Right now he's it!" She laughs. "I was unreachable in India, then traveled a few more weeks. He was away on business, followed by a holiday in Italy."

Lola grins like the Cheshire Cat, and her hazel eyes dance with delight.

I giggle in response. She's so silly! Then I get it.

"Oh, well, you see..."

Exaggeratedly, Lola brushes her left hand against her cheek. She must have removed her ring for the class and locked it in the safe at the center.

Now, it's my turn for my eyes to bug out of my head as the light bounces off of the gigantic diamond nearly blinds me.

"Holy shit! Are you serious with me right now? That's humongous!"

My quiet calm, namaste, om, center your mind blows clear out of the water.

Lola and the girls giggle at my reaction. The server places our drinks on the table with a smile, enjoying our mirth.

Well, all righty then!

"Here's to the woman who got her man!" I raise my sparking water in a toast.

Lola smiles graciously at us as we raise our glasses to her happiness.

The grin on my face spreads just as wide. I'm thankful for her benevolence and for including me in her circle of friends. It's nice to have a group of women who get along, support one another, and have each others' best interests in mind. I raise my glass even higher and offer my cheers.

Once we clamor over her proposal and details of her upcoming nuptials end, Lola explains how I want to expand my business. She tells everyone my plan to include regular fitness retreats at five-diamond resorts around the world, preferably in unique locales. Fiji was just the start.

Then she tells them about Malcolm as head of STEELE's Entertainment Properties Division oversees their hotels and resorts. He could help me with a partnership.

"So at some point, I'd love to get on his calendar. Ha! Or on my mat! Give him a taste of what he's missing."

Suddenly Leonie laughs so hard she snorts.

Surprised at her reaction, I gaze at her, befuddled. And turn to Lola, who also looks confused.

Leonie clears her throat and smiles.

"What you said about getting him on your mat and showing him what he's missing sounds like a double entendre. Especially when the Steele men are involved!"

Lola cracks up and can't stop.

Even I laugh, now clear on the cause of Leonie's hysteria.

She's in a bit of a way with Roger and a guy she dates off and on named Giovanni Mattei. Now there's a story!

"Yes," Haley starts. "My brothers can be a bit much, I must admit. Trust me, growing up with them and observing the hordes of women falling all over them was sickening!"

We laugh some more until the server swaps our appetizers for our main dishes. Silence descends on the table as we replenish our stores after our workout.

"D'accord, where do we go for our Girls' Not Out?" Leonie asks.

"The latest hot club to open is the Remy West Hollywood," Billie, who knows all the West Coast happenings responds. "Their It thing is dancers bound by ropes Shibari style suspended from the ceiling. It has a BDSM vibe, if you know what I mean."

She giggles and wiggles her eyebrows up and down.

Lola and Leonie glance at each other, then snort.

I have to hold back on my laughter. Do they take part in such activities? And if so, do Sebastian and Roger? Because being Malcolm's brothers… Does he?

Leonie laughs uncontrollably, and the sound pulls me from my wistful thinking.

"What did I say?" Billie asks, confused.

"Oh, Billie, nothing! It's aah… How do you say… graphic!" Leonie giggles. "Let's meet at eleven in the lobby. *Oui?*"

Billie nods, accepting my save.

"What are you wearing?" Haley asks. "I have a black mini dress or a light blue sequin romper."

Fortunately, the conversation switches to a safer topic. Blair chimes in on how well the light blue would contrast with Haley's gray eyes and ebony hair. Meanwhile, Lola's eyes still twinkle with glee.

My girls and I sit in the VIP area of the Remy West Hollywood. Billie was right. This is a hot spot. The Shibari tied dancers hover inches above the crowd. The colorful silken cords artfully swathe their long, toned limbs. They blindfolded some. While others stare boldly at the revelers. The dungeon-like atmosphere adds to the BDSM theme. It's first time at any place that resembles a sex club.

As I glance around the room, my body tingles as it wonders what it would feel like to have the silks binding me. No movement or escape from the erotic acts inflicted upon me. My nipples tighten and my pussy clenches just from the thought. Damn…

"Time to get our groove on one more time, Ladies!" Blair announces as she pulls Billie to her feet. "Let's go. No time to decorate the banquette!"

My reverie fades, and the Remy replaces my fantasy. I shake my head to push the vestiges away.

She's right. We've been dancing and drinking for the past three and a half hours. Girls' Night Out is fun. We enjoy each other's company and our drinks. I finish the last of my cocktail and join my friends on the dance floor. I'm going to make the most out of our GNO, too.

I slam back the last of my mojito cocktail, then follow the girls to the dance floor.

The DJ's music and callouts have everyone bouncing to the beat. I throw my hands up and shake my hips in my silver chain-mail micro mini dress. It's front drapes to my cleavage and the back scoops to the top of my ass. Only a tiny g-string covers my bare mound. Silver Swarovski crystal five-inch sandals adorn my feet, making my shapely legs go on forever. I work hard on my body and have no qualms about showing it off.

"The DJ plays the best music!" Blair says as she bumps her hip against Leonie's side.

Blair flips her chestnut brown hair over her shoulder as she twirls on the dance floor. Her cerulean blue eyes like her ice-blue sequin mini dress sparkle in the lights. She catches the attention of a few guys who make their way over to us.

"Hello there, beautiful," one of them says as he bends down to my ear. His warm breath brushes the delicate shell. I shiver in response.

He's taller than me, so I lift my gaze to take him in. He's an attractive model type—strawberry blond hair, jade-colored eyes, lean build. Why hello there…

I smirk and turn my back to him while I continue to dance. No need to appear eager.

Undeterred, he places his hands on my hips and pulls up behind me. His body melds to mine—hard against soft.

"Where do you think you're going, Beauty?" he rasps in my ear. "No getting away from me."

We move to the sensuous pulse of the music. His hands don't wander, only tighten their grip as he bends his knees to align his groin to my ass.

Mmmmmm.

I just want to dance and have a good time. So I let the handsome stranger move us to the beat. After a while, he twirls me around and with bent knees; he grinds his pelvis into mine. The sensation of his hard dick against my ass makes my pussy clench on air and ache for him to fill it.

Already keyed up from my earlier fantasy, I squeeze my thighs together. The need overwhelms me.

We move as one, glued together for a few songs. His lips nuzzle my neck, and I angle my head to allow him more access. My hands rest on top of his broad shoulders, fingers entwined in his shoulder-length hair. His hands flex to grip me possessively. As the next tune begins, he murmurs in my ear.

"Come on, Beauty, time for us to head out."

I glance around to find the other girls. No way will I leave without checking in with them. I notice Lola wrapped in a tight embrace with a dark-haired, sinfully sexy man. It can only be her fiancé Sebastian grinding with her. I hadn't seen him arrive. They look so good together, like they belong with no one else. Lost in their own world.

That's what I want. Not some guy I meet at the club and go home with for a one-night stand. I've only had three lovers, and all in committed relationships. As much as I want to explore my erotic sexual needs, I'm not willing to go the wham-bam-thank-you-ma'am route.

If you believe, it will happen.

So with a deep, cleansing breath, I shake my head and slip from the hottie's embrace.

"Don't leave me like this, Beauty," he groans.

I step away and give him an apologetic smile.

He nods disappointedly and strides away.

I turn and make my way through the crowd to Billie, Blair, and Haley. They're dancing not too far from Lola and Sebastian. The girls cheer when I reach them.

Moments later, Sebastian strides away from Lola. He leaves her standing with her mouth hanging open. She glances from him to us, apparently torn between her man and her friends. She hesitates.

"Go! Be with your boo!" Billie laughs in her Southern Belle accent and shoos her hands at Lola.

With her wavy, medium-blonde balayage hair and pecan-colored skin, Billie reminds me of Tyra Banks' doppelgänger. Billie is curvy like the megamodel, but a petite version at five feet, four inches.

Haley, Blair, and I nod, giving Lola the thumbs up as we continue to dance.

She only hesitates a moment. Blows kisses to us. Then rushes after her man, pushing her way through the pulsating crowd.

Hell, I don't blame her. I'd do the very same thing. In fact, all of us would opt for our sexy fiancé if given the chance. Girls' Night Out is fun. Being with your friends is fun. But it doesn't compare to a night in with your more than fun lover!

"What's so funny?" Haley asks over the bass of the music.

"Girls' Night Out or Lover Night In?" Leonie asks, raising and lowering her hands like a scale.

Haley giggles as her gray eyes shine like liquid platinum behind her glasses. She looks like a female version of her brothers—gorgeous.

"That's a straightforward decision… Girl's Night Out!" She responds.

Leonie's eyes widen in surprise as she stares at her.

Haley giggles some more and claps her hands.

"Gotcha! Lover takes all every time!"

Billie and Blair ask what's the joke, and Haley fills them in. They laugh and high five with us in agreement. Then we dance some more, getting lost in the beat and a fun night with friends—old and new.

MALCOLM

Talk about a crazy week... Roger *The Responsible* loses his stoic cool in a fight with his ex-girlfriend Leonie's Italian boyfriend—fucking prick—at a Lola's Coterie grand-opening party in a STEELE property. Sebastian the self-proclaimed *Never Gonna Marry Playboy Alpha Dom* surprises Lola with their wedding. What the hell else can happen?!

"Oh, oh my! Excuse me!"

The melodious, sultry AF voice slides into my musings as I'm jostled from behind and a pair of delicate hands grab a hold of me.

STEELE Dubai I teems with four hundred guests for Baz and Lola's nuptials. We closed the entire hotel and resort for the extravagant four-day affair. Baz worked his magic with the help of our mother Shelley and two wedding planners to pull it off without a hitch.

I half swivel my body to face the clumsy guest—sexy

tone and all—who bumped into me. Hopefully she's not drunk off her ass, or using an excuse to get my attention. I damn sure don't need another Vicky-style deception. Three months free of the conniving broad, and I don't need a setback, thank you very much.

STARR

Damn these marble floors! Who's bright idea was it to gloss them into a giant ice skating rink? Especially when I'm wearing five-inch Manolo Blahnik satin and Swarovski crystal sandals.

To avoid a face plant before I reach the ballroom for Lola and Sebastian's wedding, I grab the closest person in the crowd. One hand wraps around his waist while the other clutches his elbow.

Awkward much?!

Fortunately, he's a tall, solid mass of muscle and doesn't waver as I collide with him. Not yet stable on my wobbly feet—I feel like a newborn foal—I tighten my grip on his waist as I glance up at him.

My mouth falls open, and I freeze.

Holy God and every deity in every religion's pantheon!!! It's Malcolm Steele. And he's even more gorgeous in person, even if his expression is one of annoyance.

Eek!!!

. . .

MALCOLM

The face of an angel stares up at me. Her sorrel brown eyes widen in surprise as her lush mouth forms a perfect O.

My cock twitches for the first time outside of the LEVELS clubs I've visited to sate my sexual and Dom needs.

As my eyes scan her, bent at the waist and still holding onto me, a flush of heat races through every one of my cells. From the hairs raised on my scalp to the tips of my curling toes. My heartbeat speeds up faster than my Bugatti Chiron.

I reach out to steady her but jump as though shocked when our fingers touch. Tingles explode. If I 'm not mistaken, she shuddered in response to our connection. Did she feel it, too?

What the hell is wrong with me?! Get it together, Steele! Then again…

Once she stands, we're five inches apart, and I can brush my lips against her temple. More heat radiates off of her body. And what a body.

She may have the face of an angel, but that body belongs outside of the pearly gates of Heaven. I'd be happy to welcome her to my home. My cock weeps in agreement.

The coral-colored long-sleeved dress clings to her bodacious curves. Padded shoulders highlight the deep vee-neckline where her full perky tits play hide and seek with the draped opening. A mock cummerbund cinches her tiny waist. My eyes follow the light bouncing off of the minuscule crystals sewn onto the material. From the flare of her hips to the asymmetrical hemline cut high at one knee to end in a point at the middle heel of her glittery fuck-me sandals.

Well, fuck *me*...

"Excuse me!" The angel squeaks, then shakes her head to clear her throat.

Her long, curly dark brown hair moves gently along her back. I want to wrap the glossy tresses around my fist to hold her in place while I pummel her from behind into pure ecstasy.

"Hey, are you okay?"

I have to rip my eyes away from the angel to focus on the concerned voice. Another woman takes My Angel by the arm, glares at me, and leads her away from me towards the ballroom.

Frozen in place, captivated by her round ass in that sinful dress, I watch her disappear into the crowd.

The vibration of my mobile in the pocket of my trousers rouses me.

Shit! I'm late and I'm the best man!

THROUGHOUT THE CEREMONY, the picture-taking session, and the toasts at the reception, my mind wanders to My Angel. After these hours, I give up on not referring to the mystery woman as mine.

Why the potent attraction? No clue.

I can't find her amongst the sea of four hundred guests. Damn the need to invite everyone in our social circle, business associates, friends, and family.

Sure, it's a big deal since Baz is the first of the much-wanted Steele siblings to marry and remove himself from the supposed STEELE Quaternity. But the humongous gathering doesn't help me find a needle in a haystack.

As I stand to the side sipping a Jackson Special Blend Scotch with Anton, he straightens suddenly.

"Fuck me! There's the *khlopushka!*" He exclaims.

I frown at him, wondering who the hell could be the firecracker that has him excited. Anton is not one to show such blatant interest in a woman.

My gaze follows his to the dance floor.

Not only is his *khlopushka* shaking her thing, but My Angel shimmies to Beyoncé performing "Single Ladies"—another of Baz's surprises for his new bride.

Once again I find myself stuck in place, unable to move. Damn, she's stunning.

"Hi, handsome."

A figure appears before me, blocking my Angel from my sight. In the time to extricate myself from this female guest's clutches, my Angel disappears. Funny enough, so has Anton and My Angel's friend.

I weave through the crowd, giving brief acknowledgements as business associates want to offer congratulations and women want to snag me next.

Finally, I spy Baz whisk Lola from the dance floor and see Leonie and Roger talking. My Angel stands beside her.

Leonie raises her finger to gesture for a moment. Then turns back to My Angel to whispers in her ear. She nods and smiles at Leonie. A smile that lights the room brighter than her crystal-embellished coral gown.

She must be a friend of Lola and Leonie. Now I can capture My Angel.

STARR

I cannot believe I made such a fool out of myself in front of Malcolm Steele. The man I want to partner with for my business. I damn near rumpled his custom-tailored classic tuxedo—looking fine AF in it, mind you—and he was the best man in my friend's wedding!

All night I avoid him to think of a way to amend the fiasco of our initial meeting. Cue the eye roll…

Then to top it off, a giant sexy Russian makes off with Adrienne. It was okay until Sebastian snagged Lola from the dance floor as expected of the lovebirds. Then Roger swept Leonie away.

Now I surreptitiously exit the ballroom, praying I don't bump into Malcolm Steele again, no pun intended. Thankfully, I make it to my room and pack. After the brunch tomorrow, I'll make my escape to Rishikesh. Since I'm on this side of the world, I might as well stop by the ashram to see Ganika for a week. By then, a plan will emerge.

* * *

FINALLY! Thank fuck!

I spot My Angel from a distance. She's with Sebastian and Lola, chatting with them during brunch. Anton was of no use since I couldn't get a hold of him, or Roger for that matter. Undoubtedly, they booed up with the firecracker and Leonie, respectively...

At last I can catch My Angel, and I make my way over to her with the newlyweds. But a redheaded wedding guest waylays me. A look of annoyance crosses my face when she steps right in front of my clear path. As quickly as I can, I get away from her and rush across the room.

Not fucking again!

"Where did she go?" I ask Baz and Lola agitatedly.

They turn to see me peering over their shoulders in the direction My Angel walked away. They glance at each other and laugh.

"What's so damned funny?!" I demand of Baz.

He chuckles, but Lola answers.

"So you finally met Starr! Did you schedule your meeting?" She asks.

I glance down at her, perplexed. Starr? Meeting?

Holy shit!

My Angel is Starr Knight?!?!

A TROUGH MUST FORM beneath my feet as I pace back and forth in front of my desk.

Where the hell is Anton?! He's never late for our weekly status meeting.

I don't care if it's ten minutes before the start time. *To be early is to be on time; to be on time is to be late; to be late is unthinkable.* We live by that adage.

Another irritated glance at my Patek Philippe Grandmaster Chime. My life is more complicated than the most complicated wristwatch ever crafted. It's 1,366 pieces may work in perfect harmony, but my one quest to get a hold of My Angel is complete discord.

It's been over a week since I first laid eyes on the beauty. And I'm no closer to seeing her again.

Forget trying to reach Lola during her and Sebastian's no-contact-allowed honeymoon. Leonie could only offer My Angel's mobile number after I explained my need for it. Sure, I said it was to schedule the expansion partnership meeting. I'm not laying my cards out before I get a chance to speak to My Angel directly.

Unfortunately, her mobile goes to voicemail every. Single. Time. A fruitless call to her center in Beverly Hills resulted in the front desk staff not disclosing her whereabouts to a stranger.

A stranger?! Not for long, if I can help it.

Then there's Anton… After he disappeared from the reception, more than likely with My Angel's friend, I couldn't reach him either. Sure, he had scheduled a holiday prior to the wedding and stated he would not be accessible since he was off to Nepal for ten days. I left voice messages and sent texts anyway, beyond desperate.

At first I tried to convince myself the reaction was a fluke. Nothing more than the sight of a gorgeous… voluptuous… mesmerizing… woman. Then I tried to clump her with the other gold diggers I've encountered, including Vicky…

But My Angel is close friends with Lola and Leonie

apparently. And they're not at all with Sebastian and Roger for their billions. So, by deduction, neither would My Angel want mine. Plus she owns a thriving fitness and wellness center—has her millions—graduated from Stanford undergrad and B-School—highly intelligent—and her parents are high-powered attorneys even if they have weird names—excellent family background. What more do I need to know?

I freeze mid-stride when Miles announces Anton's arrival over the telephone intercom.

Finally!

Anton strides in with a shit-eating grin on his face as he continues to speak Russian into his mobile. He raises his hand before harsh words tumble from my mouth.

"I've got you covered, *moy drug*!" He chuckles as he lowers his mobile and gestures for me to sit at the conference table.

My molars grind to bite back words of annoyance. But I sit because he must be up to something worthwhile. At least he better be…

"Okay *khlopushka*, we're ready," Anton says in Russian into the mobile as he brings the videoconference up on the wall-mounted television across from the table.

The image of My Angel's friend appears onscreen. She's sitting in an office in what must be the fitness center. Apparently she's fluent in Russian. She scowls at Anton's use of the word firecracker to describe her. Then shifts her bright green eyes to me.

Another beauty who reminds me more of a tigress with her feline features and predatory stare.

"Hello, Mr. Steele. I'm Adrienne Anthony, the CMO and general manager of Starr Light Fitness & Wellness Beverly Hills"—she glances at Anton with a look, then back at me as my heart pounds—"Your veep reached out to schedule the expansion partnership exploration meeting again. Ms. Knight has returned to the United States and is available next Tuesday at ten in the morning or at one in the afternoon Pacific time. Which do you prefer?"

"Thank you for scheduling the meeting. However, I have a suggestion"—I lean forward in my chair and pin Adrienne with my most panty-melting smile—"Ms. Knight wants to open a location in the Caribbean and host international fitness retreats. Let us—Ms. Knight, you, Anton, me—meet at STEELE St. Barth's on Tuesday for five days. During which Ms. Knight will hold a sample two-day retreat with a few of your clients as a demonstration where Anton and I will take part. Then the four of us will meet to discuss the partnership. My administrative assistant will arrange a STEELE private jet for your and your clients' transportation. Kindly ask Ms. Knight if she agrees to my terms. Anton and I will await her answer by the end of day today."

Adrienne sits back, surprised. Her buttery pecan-colored cheeks flush crimson. I can tell she's a firecracker who prefers control, but I'm a dominant who doesn't give up control. At all.

Anton caught how I checked his firecracker and smirks knowing my exact intentions. He can put together my frantic communications to him regarding My Angel easily.

His frosty eyes glitter with devilry since he'll have the added benefit of seeing his current interest again.

Pleased with Adrienne's reaction, I lean back and chuckle to myself.

I always get what I want. And I want the brown-eyed beauty.

STARR

Inhale

Om Gum Ganipati-ya Namaha

Exhale

Inhale

Om Gum Ganipati-ya Namaha

Exhale

Inhale

Om Gum Ganipati-ya Namaha

Exhale

With my eyes closed and my aventurine mala in my fingers, I repeat the Sanskrit mantra to remove obstacles and bring success for my japa practice. It's normal for me as a part of my daily meditation. However, today holds special meaning because I meet with Malcolm Steele in two days, at last.

I need all the strength I can get to make it through the next seven days. Well, five since I won't see Malcolm until Adrienne, another teacher, and six VIP clients we selected for the sample fitness retreat arrive the day after tomorrow.

Although I expect a STEELE property to satisfy our needs, I opted to come ahead of time to make sure all is ready and to get a feel for the property. The classes agenda will feature yoga sessions for meditation, pranayama, and asanas with Pilates and Barre for strength training. We'll gather for group breakfasts both days and for dinner the first night. An excursion around St. Barth's on the STEELE resort's power catamaran will make the dinner exciting. Clients will depart the afternoon of the second day.

Leaving me alone with Malcolm Steele…

How the hell will I survive???

I still don't have a plan to make up for the fiasco of our initial collision, even Ganika couldn't help me. My brain went haywire when I gazed into his soulful gray eyes. At first his expression was annoyance, then a spark ignited followed by a flicker of… lust?

Shivers race through me and my pussy throbs from memories of BOB—Battery Operated Boyfriend—alleviating my ache as fantasies of Dom Malcolm Steele ravished me with a flogger, then fucked me bowlegged.

I sigh and open my eyes to paradise.

The breeze off of the Caribbean Sea wraps around me as I straighten my legs from lotus position on my oversized Hermès beach towel. Salty air fills my lungs, and the warm sun soaks into my skin. It's early morning so no one's out except for a kitesurfer in the distance and two resort staff members watching him by the shoreline.

With ease, the kitesurfer harnesses control of the wind

to master the waves beneath his board and to complete front and back rolls in midair. The colorful kite dances above him. I noticed his aerial acrobatics when I stepped onto the sand. He's been at it for almost an hour. This guy must be a hell of strong.

I'm totally impressed by his command of nature and of himself.

As he makes it to the shore and gathers his equipment with the help of a resort staffer, I continue to watch him, mesmerized by his incredible body. He must sense my stare because he turns in my direction, then does a double take.

I glance behind me, not sure if he sees someone else. When he waves, I wave back and clap as he approaches me. Not wanting to appear rude or a gawker, I walk towards him smiling as I continue to clap.

The sun glistens on his olive skin, further kissed by the warm rays. A sexy as sin intricate tattoo wraps around his well-defined pecs. He slicks his longish ebony hair back from his sculpted face where a touch of a five o'clock shadow covers his firm jaw. His broad shoulders taper to eight-pack abs that flex as he rubs a towel over his torso. Biceps bulge with each pass.

My mouth waters when I follow his happy trail past his Adonis belt. Then my gaze takes in his muscular thighs beneath his board shorts... Hold up! There's no extra muscle along the inner thigh...

My mind reels when I realize it's his dick. His incredibly massive, hard dick. Unconsciously, I bite my lower lip and shift from one foot to the other for a bit of friction at my core. This guy is hung and ready!

A deep chuckle draws my eyes back to his face. His knowing smirk makes my cheeks redden in embarrassment.

Great, Starr! Good going…

"Wow! That was phenomenal! I wish I could—"

The words die on my lips when he removes his goggles. Soulful gray eyes twinkle at me.

Holy God and every deity in every religion's pantheon!!! It's Malcolm Steele. AGAIN!

At once I freeze, my limbs stiffen like the goats that faint when startled. However, the rest of my body responds in the opposite. My tongue slips out to moisten my lower lip. Nipples bead to poke against my triangle bikini top. Lower abs tighten as my pussy contracts and its juices pool in the string-bikini bottom.

"Ms. Knight… How lovely to see you again."

Malcolm

WELL GOOD GOT DAMN!!!

My Angel fails to even reach the first rung of Jacob's Ladder. Her beyond banging bodyody makes my mouth water and my cock thicken and lengthen along my thigh. It's a damn good thing I have on board shorts or my junk would be on full display.

Once again her sorrel brown eyes widen in surprise. But this time her little pink tongue pokes out to lick her plump lower lip.

My nostrils flare and my eyes narrow as I home in on her lush mouth. I want her tongue and lips on my cock. Now!

However, I refuse to speak another word. This time no one is around to take her away from me. The sound of the waves slapping against the shore makes me wonder what it'll sound like when I spank that ass.

"Mr. Sttt—eele, ah!" My Angel starts as her voice stutters on my name and her body shudders back to life.

Yeah, no question. She feels it too.

STARR

No! I will not make a fool of myself again! I simply refuse to lose it.

I take a deep, cleansing breath and feel it course through my body, reactivating my limbs. Then I speak, "Mr. Sttt—eele, ah!"

Just saying his name caused my body to shudder and my voice to stutter. Got damn!

"Pardon, me. Mr. Steele, lovely to see you again, too. Thank you for the opportunity to discuss a partnership," I respond, proud my sentence came out coherently this time.

A flash of lust sparks in his hooded eyes.

I replay my words in my mind and catch the—as Leonie says—double entendre. I must be careful around the Steele men like she told us!

So, it wasn't my imagination after all. The flare of heat that shoots through me at the knowledge he's as taken with me as I am with him makes me feel powerful.

Well, not as powerful as Malcolm kitesurfing…

"I look forward to a conducive and long partnership with you, Ms. Knight. Your eagerness to come early pleases me immensely," Malcolm quips.

More color floods my face even as more juices flood my soaked bikini bottom at his purposeful play on words.

He continues in his baritone voice that captivates me. "Have you eaten, Ms. Knight? I am starving. The breakfast offers a selection of delectable dishes."

I bleat what I hope is a positive response.

Malcolm chuckles and places his hand on the small of my back to guide me towards the sea-front terrace for one of the resort's restaurants. As we pass my towel, he scoops it up and shakes out the sand before folding it under his arm.

I risk a peek up at him since he towers over me by what must be ten inches. An uncontrollable giggle falls from my mouth when I wonder if his dick is the same length!

Malcolm grins down at me, then spreads his fingers further across my back, sending a jolt to my clit. The tip of one finger brushes against the curve of my ass. I shiver and bite back a moan.

When we arrive at the restaurant, the staff trip over themselves to accommodate Malcolm, particularly the female hostess. She makes a show of guiding us to a table and placing the menu in his hands as she skims her fingers on his.

Mine!

I shock myself at the visceral reaction to another

woman touching Malcolm. To hide it, I put my menu in front of my face to study the "delectable dishes."

A finger appears at the top of my menu and lowers it slowly.

"Ms. Knight—"

"Starr," I interject.

The most seductive smile spreads across his face before he starts again, "Starr."

The way my name rolls off of his tongue as though he tastes every letter makes me shift in my seat. If I don't change my bathing suit, it will remain forever destroyed. Sort of how I hope he destroys my pussy…

"I know you're a yogi, but do you have an aversion to meat?" He asks with a straight face.

Again I bite back a giggle. This guy.

"No, Mr. St—"

"Malcolm."

"No, Malcolm," I reply.

"I do not enjoy the word 'no' coming from your mouth when you speak to me. How about, 'meat is definitely on the menu,' instead?" He smirks.

This time, I can't hold back the snort that escapes my mouth. Even when the server arrives to take our order, I can't control myself.

Malcolm grins and offers to order for me. I wave my hand and nod my agreement, still laughing as tears fill my eyes.

Once the server leaves, Malcolm's gaze lands on me. He studies my face for a moment before he speaks.

"It pleases me we meet officially. I did not know who

you were in the lobby of STEELE Dubai I. Lola told me she is a huge fan of yours and your plans for expansion"—he raises his hand to stop me from interrupting—"Since the retreat and our business don't occur for two days, I propose we spend the time exploring our sexual attraction."

My mouth falls open at his bluntness. But my mind screams, HELL YEAH! as it recalls my nightly erotic fantasies of Dom Malcolm controlling me and extracting absolute bliss from my body one spine-tingling orgasm at a time.

He reaches over to run the tip of his index finger around my O-shaped mouth with an expression of such longing, I moan.

"You do not know how many times I fantasized about your luscious mouth wrapped around the girth of my cock with you naked on your knees before me. That first sight of you bent at the waist gripping me will forever remain imprinted on my mind," Malcolm murmurs in a voice thick with lust.

I blink and swallow. Hard.

"You feel the same, do you not, Angel?" He asks softly.

More blinks follow a slow nod.

"Let us explore one another. This will have no impact on our business. I am a man who knows a sure thing and will not hesitate to follow through," Malcolm finishes with a simmering smile full of promise.

I know I should stop him and demand an apology for his audacity. But something holds back my indignation.

Why not see where this goes?

It's not as though he's unknown to me. Lola recommended him. He's her husband's brother. She wouldn't marry into a family of crazies!

Sure Malcolm is a playboy. But why shouldn't I have some fun with my fantasy Dom? I have to think he's no different from his Alpha male siblings. Lola and Leonie wouldn't be with them if they were questionable.

"As long as it won't impact our chance at a partnership negatively," I state. "Or else this… interaction ends now."

Malcolm's expression turns staid, "I swear to uphold my promise to you. Our business will proceed no matter the result of our 'interaction.' Agreed?"

I hold my hand out to shake on it.

Without hesitation, Malcolm envelopes my small hand in his larger one. Deal made, we stare at one another, unsure what to say next until the server places our entrées in front of us.

I take a bite of the sausage link and moan around the fork, "Delectable, Malcolm."

It's his turn to shift in need as his eyes darken to a stormy gray.

"We shall see very soon, Angel," he says mysteriously. "But leave room in your belly. I have something even tastier to fill it."

Damn… Every time I think I have the one up on Malcolm, he gets me back in line. I love it!

"Yes… Sir," I whisper more to myself than to him as I absorb his nickname for me.

But when his fork clatters to his plate, my eyes snap to him immediately.

Forget the storm, all sorts of emotions churn in his eyes and across his face.

"After you finish your breakfast, you will return to your villa and wait for me in the bedroom naked, lying supine, legs spread, arms above your head on the bed. Clear?"

I choke on my iced green tea, but recover quickly with a nod.

"Words, Angel. I will have your words," Malcolm demands.

"Yes, Sir," I reply confidently, eagerly even.

He watches me for a moment, then as though satisfied nods to himself as he retrieves his fork.

We finish our breakfast as we chat casually about his extreme sports and my interest in trying some less than heart-stopping kinds. I'm intrigued by his fearlessness and his willingness to take me under his wing. No pun intended.

Faster than expected, the time comes for me to obey his first command.

My heartbeat increases as I rush to the spectacular four-bedroom beachfront villa, the largest of three available to guests. I wondered why Miles reserved such spacious accommodations for me only. No doubt at his boss' request.

Now, I'm thankful for its size and its separation from the primary hotel. How awful would it be for a staff member or other guest to see the company's president entering or exiting my room? Or worse, to hear my cries of ecstasy...

No way do I want anyone to assume the partnership

between Starr Light Fitness & Wellness, Beverly Hills and STEELE International, Inc. has anything to do with me banging a Steele. I pride myself on making my own way. Connections formed, great. But no favors, thank you.

All negative thoughts evaporate from my mind when I strip out of my bikini, take a quick shower—no need for sand in my huckus-tuckus—then spread out on the bed. Only five minutes pass—five minutes of my brain envisioning the powerful Dom Malcolm ravishing me—when the man himself appears in the doorway.

Fuuuuck…

"*E*xcellent, Angel."

Malcolm's growl makes goosebumps raise on my heated skin. His gray eyes darken to obsidian as they roam over my naked flesh. A pause at the juncture of my thighs elicits another growl as he licks his lips hungrily; the full bottom one beckons for me to bite it.

"Already wet for me, Little One?" Malcolm asks with an arched eyebrow pointedly.

A shudder runs through me, ending with a low moan.

"Yes, Sir," I respond, knowing the title pleases him.

When he flares his nostrils and a carnal smirk appears on his face, I know for certain Malcolm is a Dom. The question: am I a sub, or better yet, can I be *his* sub?

"Once I finish a shower, we will talk"—he drops his board shorts and his dick springs free—"Until then, do not move. Understood, Little One?"

My jaw drops. What the hell?!

I raise up on my elbows to get a better look. Besides his

colossal cock, the glint of silver at its mushroom head shocks me speechless.

The movement of his hand to stroke his turgid member languidly draws my attention to his face where a seductive smirk greets me. His eyes dance in delight at my surprise; whether from my reaction to his size or to the jewelry, I cannot discern.

Malcolm rubs his thumb across his tip from the silver ball above to the silver ball below, then asks, "Any questions, Little One?"

"N-n-no, Sir," I say in awe.

He nods and gives his dick a last tug before he pivots and strides into the en suite bathroom.

When the water gushes from the rain shower, I collapse onto the bed, my mind already spent from trying to make sense of what I just beheld.

Is Malcolm a freaky Dom, too? Why does my body tremble in erotic anticipation of accepting his gigantic dick into my pussy with the added sensation of the jewelry? Am I a freaky sub???

No sooner do I realize the thoughts turn me on to the point my pussy juices drip down the crevice between my thighs and ass to pool beneath me on the bed does Malcolm return. He stands before me with damp skin and hair, his cock still erect.

"Tell me, Little One, what is your experience as a sub?" He asks as he pins me with his unblinking stare.

"I… Uh…" My gaze shifts away from him as I struggle to convey my lack of experience.

After a deep cleansing breath, I face him again. Encouraged by the no sign of judgment in his eyes, I continue.

"None. I.. I've only heard about a D/s relationship from a… a friend who has a Dom or rather had one. I've researched the lifestyle a bit, but I never did anything…"

My ramblings carry on for a bit more. But Malcolm remains expressionless, as he patiently waits for me to finish. I lower my gaze and twiddle my thumbs as I stop babbling, awaiting my fate.

"Are you interested in learning more about a D/s relationship and the BDSM lifestyle, Little One?" Malcolm asks.

"Yes, Sir," I answer softly.

Instantly, I feel the bed dip as Malcolm sits beside me, then lifts my chin with his forefinger. Once our eyes connect, he slants his mouth over mine and kisses me breathlessly. The possessive, passionate kiss makes me reel as his tongue dominates mine.

Malcolm clasps my face between his sizable palms and holds my gaze again.

"Communication and trust serve as the foundation for Doms and subs. Your safewords are green to continue, yellow for a moment, and red to stop all play at once. We will push your limits, so be sure to choose the appropriate safeword. I will respect your wishes. You learn a sub holds all the power, not the Dom. Do you understand, Little One?"

He finishes his first lesson, and I nod enthusiastically.

A rumble comes from his massive chest to reverberate

through me, peaking my nipples and making my pussy clench with need.

"Forearms and knees. Ass up towards me," Malcolm commands as he rises to tower over me.

Now his steely gray eyes glint more than the penis piercing.

I scramble into position.

"So beautiful," he murmurs, a single fingertip whispers down my spine. "Your pussy lips glisten. Just as enticing, your bottom hole winks at me. Which shall we play with today, Little One?"

A moan pours from my mouth as I drop my forehead to the sumptuous Egyptian cotton bedding. The sensation of his fingertip stroking my wet pussy lips then rimming my puckered hole, draws a staggered inhalation from me.

"We have time to explore your dirty little hole. Let us enjoy your succulent pussy, shall we?" Malcolm asks with a wicked chuckle when I groan.

"Y-y-yes, Sir," I sputter.

My back bows when his wet, velvety tongue swipes in one motion across the seam of my slick pussy lips. His fingers splay over my pelvis and his thumbs press into my butt cheeks as he grips my hips. Held in place, I can only accept the onslaught of his carnal torturous licks, nips, and pokes as Malcolm feasts on my core.

When my thighs quiver from my impending orgasm, Malcolm pulls back and smacks my ass three times. I gasp as the pleasure recedes, replaced by the sting of his palm.

"Do not cum, Little One" he commands, then returns to his meal with the addition of his thick fingers.

Each time I near bliss, Malcolm withdraws and spanks me, alternating between the pleasure and the pain. The last smack catches my clit, and I yowl as I jerk away from the sting. Immediately, he buries his face between my thighs and sucks on my poor clit.

My body convulses, and fists slam into the bedding as I attempt to stave off the orgasm.

"Yellow! Yellow!" I cry out in anguish. "Malcolm, please! I can't take anymore! I need to cum! Fuck me… Please!"

His only response is to plunge his middle and index fingers deep inside my aching pussy as he leans over me. His chest presses against my sweaty back in dominance while his lips brush my ear.

"Cum for me, Little One! Cum for your Dom! Now!" He roars.

My head explodes as the most epic climax rips through me. Stars shoot behind my closed eyelids. My greedy pussy squeezes his thick digits, pulling them further inside.

"Aaaaahhhh…" I keen as wave after wave of erotic bliss takes me over the edge to oblivion.

The cool touch of metal to my fevered pussy entrance brings me back from Malcolm's sexual thrall. Oh, my God! The twin balls scrape my G-spot and tunnel through my channel to bring erotic frisson to my very soul.

My core stretches to accommodate Malcolm's mighty girth and the twin balls. He takes no time for me to adjust. Brutal thrusts slam into my pussy as his groin and heavy ball sac slap against my reddened butt cheeks.

More pleasure and pain erupt.

Immediately, I cry out in wild abandon.

"So fucking tight and wet, Little One! Fuuuck!" Malcolm groans between his grunts and slaps of my ass.

"Uh. Uh. Uh. Uh." I respond after each thrust.

Malcolm widens his stance and bends his knees to shift the penetration angle as his grip tightens on my hips. He continues to saw inside of me as orgasm after orgasm overtakes me.

By the time he slams against me one last time with the twin balls bumping against my cervix, I'm a blubbering mass of jelly. Malcolm's passionate growl precedes a torrent of his seed deep in my pussy. He slumps his sweat-soaked torso against my back and drops us to our sides, still connected intimately.

Exhaustion—mental and physical—consumes me. As I drift off, I hear a gasp from Malcolm, and he withdraws his still-erect cock from me. Our combined juices drip from my core as I mewl and give in to the slumber.

MALCOLM

Oh, fuck!!!

So enraptured by My Angel submitting to me and welcoming a D/s relationship, I forgot a condom... I chance a peek at her, but she sleeps peacefully. A satisfied smile graces her gorgeous face.

Fuck it.

I spoon behind her and hope she doesn't lay me out when she awakes. Communication and trust include protection, dumb ass. Since I've never gone bare in my life and take regular tests, I don't pose a risk to her. It's doubtful my health-conscious Angel would not take precautions with her body.

The only concern is whether she's on birth control. The caveman in me is pleased my seed fills his mate's womb, but I have to be realistic.

A contented sigh from My Angel draws me from my musings.

Again, fuck it. We'll deal with it later.

I cuddle—what the hell???—behind her with my face in her soft curls and drift off.

* * *

As Anton and I wait for the other retreat guests to arrive at the beach for our first class, a Cheshire Cat smile covers my face. My Angel wasn't pissed with me—thank fuck! And she takes a birth control shot every few months. Not sure how my caveman feels about that news…

Female laughter floats through the air from behind us. We turn in their direction. Like a magnet, my eyes find My Angel. She's splendid in a white tank top and matching leggings with sheer mesh panels strategically placed on both pieces. Her long curly hair in a high ponytail—perfect for tugging her head in place. A shy smile flickers across her face as she sees me.

After our two incredible days of delving into our fledging D/s relationship, it's time for work. I reassured her we'll be all right with no one the wiser. Well, as long as no one notices the instant hard-on beneath my athletic shorts.

A flash of golden blonde hair juxtaposed against My Angel's chestnut-colored skin creeps into my periphery.

"*O chert voz'mi, net.*"

Anton's curse comes just as the blonde shifts her blue eyes to my gray ones. She gasps and covers her mouth in shock.

Oh, hell no, does not even cut it.

Vicky Reynolds… You've gotta be fucking kidding me!

Quickly I glance at My Angel. Fortunately, she's distracted by the other participants and Adrienne. Then my gaze moves back to Vicky.

She's recovered and moves forward with the crowd. They take their places at ballet barres set up in the sand opposite each other with some space between them for My Angel to walk.

Anton stands beside Adrienne with a smirk on his face. She ignores him and chats with the woman on her other side.

I hold off until Vicky settles at one barre, and I stand at the other. The women on either side gravitate toward me, like moths to a flame. No thanks.

"Ready to step up to the Beach Barre, ladies and gentlemen?"

So this is how My Angel gets that round fuckable ass…

* * *

TWO DAYS LATER, I've successfully dodged Vicky and gotten my ass kicked by barre, Pilates, and yoga. Go figure. I promised My Angel I wouldn't interrupt her last moments with her retreat guests, so I head to my villa ready for a well-deserved shower and soak in the hot tub.

I'm looking forward to binding her with silk ties to my bed tonight. Her body ripe for the taking, begging for release as she writhes beneath—

"Hello, Sir."

The softly spoken words stop me in my tracks like a sledgehammer to the head. I curse inwardly, but put a stoic expression on my face before I turn.

Vicky.

"I am not your Dom, Vicky. Kindly refrain from addressing me as such. In fact, do not address me in any way. Excuse me," I respond, then pivot to continue on my way.

A small hand grips the back of my arm.

"Please forgive me! I've been so lost without you! What can I do to make it up to you?" Vicky asks with tear-filled eyes.

Drama Queen… I extricate my arm from her hand and shake my head.

"Vicky. It is best for you to move on," I answer, then raise my hand when she speaks. "No. Enou—"

She flings herself onto me, wrapping her arms and legs around my body. Automatically, I cup her ass. Vicky slams her mouth on mine.

STARR

One thing I answered: I am a sub, but unfortunately I cannot be Malcolm Steele's sub.

He's Vicky's Dom. Former Dom or not, he's off limits for me.

When I witnessed their exchange as I headed to his villa since the retreat guests boarded the private jet early, I couldn't believe my eyes or my ears. No wonder Vicky wanted to stay longer. I thought she wanted time away from LA to clear her mind of her failed relationship.

It may be failed on Malcolm's end, but not on Vicky's. She still wants him. And it's too messy for me to get caught in the middle.

Besides, I reminded myself of the Google search results that showed Malcolm as a rebel playboy and of Vicky's description of him. I don't need the heartache she suffers. After Quinn, I swore off men for now, anyway. I must remain true to myself.

The two days of sheer bliss Malcolm and I shared will have to suffice. As much as it pains me—not at all pleasurable—I must let it go.

During the days of our partnership discussions, I kept my distance from Malcolm, only focusing on business. He tried making contact with me or plans to hook up, but I made excuses to avoid being alone with him. When he caught me around the corner from the conference room asking why I was so aloof, I cried red.

Immediately, he jumped back from me.

I told him I changed my mind and hoped he would stand by his word of not allowing the sex to interfere with the business. He reaffirmed his pledge. We came to an agreement and ended the meetings with Malcolm's legal team drafting a contract for my team to review. They'll send it via email next week.

Malcolm remained professional and did not make me feel uncomfortable in any way.

However, I couldn't stay another minute and chose to fly back to LA a day early. While he and Anton were in a meeting, Adrienne and I headed to the airport for a commercial flight.

Wistfully, I walk across the tarmac to board the plane home.

MALCOLM

"*Brat*, this woman has you hung up. I've never seen you so out of sorts over a hookup. You need to just fuck someone else and move on already. *Da?*"

I finish hammering the speed bag with a four-punch sequence of fist-circle and fist-straight punches. Then turn and glare at Anton, who's warming up with Borya. Along with Sebastian, we're in the full gym on the first floor of Baz's penthouse duplex at The STEELE Tower in New York.

"*Net!* And watch your mouth about Starr Knight, Anton. She's not a hookup, *brother*," I spit out at him.

Baz chuckles and Borya guffaws.

I pivot to glare at them, but Baz holds his taped hands up as he shakes his head in surrender.

"Listen, I'm the last one to poke fun at someone who's bent out of shape by a woman unexpectedly. Look at what Lola did to me. She had me all messed up in the head when we first met… Hell, she still has me going!" He says with his gray eyes twinkling.

"*Da!* And I had to beat his *zhopa* to get his *bashka* back in the game. Come on in the ring, and I'll help you, too!" Borya adds, smashing his fists together. His muscular arms flex from the impact.

"Listen, no disrespect, *da?* Why don't you go see her? She should be back from her latest trip, and the contracts need her signature…" Anton recommends with a conciliatory nod.

THE FIRST COUPLE OF WEEKS, I fought the attraction I have for her. I tried the route of considering her just a hookup like Anton mentioned. Why should I—the bad boy who has women lined up to fuck—care about one stubborn woman who disappeared on me, then denied my calls and text messages?

Later it morphed into me thinking I only want what I can't have. Malcolm Steele gets everything he wants and even more.

But when I went to LEVELS New York and couldn't focus on any of the available ravishing subs, I knew it fucked me thoroughly. I couldn't get My Angel out of my mind. Once again…

Anton's bright idea made up for his stupid-ass comment.

So as I stride into Starr Light Fitness & Wellness, Beverly Hills, my eyes scan the entry for any sign of My

Angel—and Vicky, I think with a shudder. One woman I'm desperate to see and the other not at all.

The interior is elegant, tranquil, and beautifully appointed, just like the woman who owns it. A soothing instrumental melody and the scent of rose and ylang yang fill the air. A sense of relaxation fills me.

But my heartbeat increases when I hear someone mention Starr's name as they pass me on their way out. From the sound of it, they just finished a class with her.

Great! She's here.

The front desk staff directs me to her private studio. Each step closer increases my pulse—and my cock stirs. Too many times whacking off in the weeks since I last saw My Angel. It knows she's near, like a heat-seeking missile.

The studio door stands ajar. Through the opening, I watch My Angel floating in the air. She's draped in some sort of silk hammock—reminiscent of a swing found at any of the LEVELS clubs.

My cock punches against the zipper of my trousers when My Angel flips backwards. Her long toned legs go in the air as her hands reach for the floor. The deep back bend props her open. Just for me.

With no hesitation I enter her studio then lock the door behind me. As I stand before her, she lowers her legs. A wicked chuckle falls from my lips when her calves brush against my hips and she startles.

"Oh! Excuse me! I didn't realize anyone was still—"

My Angel's words trail off when she rights herself and comes face-to-face with me. The swing sways gently.

My smirk widens when her lush mouth opens in a

perfect O. Her wide eyes skitter over my face as her cheeks flame with embarrassment. Or do I dare suspect lust?

"What are you doing here, Malcolm?" She demands while she attempts to climb out of the swing.

My hands shoot out to grip the edges of the soft fabric and pull her closer to me. The tiny, fitted shorts cover her pussy barely. Heat from her core ignites my cock.

I groan from the pressure as it hardens further to the point of pain. Tingles ripple down my spine to zap my balls. They grow heavy with the need to fill her pussy with my seed; mark her with my scent.

Mine!

"You cannot get away from me again, Little One. I respected your request for space even after you left St. Barth's without a word. I allowed Anton to handle the partnership negotiations so as not to upset you. But enough… is… enough," I growl as I grind my erection against her pussy lips.

Her eyes flutter closed from the intimate contact, and her D-cup chest heaves with her pants. Nipples strain against the material of her tank top.

I take advantage of her distraction to swipe her seam with my middle finger. Dampness meets my touch, and My Angel gasps.

"You cannot deny your attraction to me, Little One. So tell me, what made you cry red? Remember honesty, communication, trust," I command in my most dominant voice knowing her submissive nature will yield to me.

My years of being a Dom do not fail me. I read My Angel well.

She sags in the swing, and her grip on the silk lessens. Then, with her head tilted down, she peers up at me through her long eyelashes.

My cock jumps.

"We cannot be together," she breathes.

I lift my eyebrow and incline my head. Not enough.

She continues on a sigh, "She hasn't confirmed it, but I know you must be her Dom."

A cold band wraps around my lungs, sapping the air from them. Did Vicky tell her mother and Starr?!?! She's the only person we know in common to whom I'd be a Dom.

Fuck!

"—way she jumped on you says enough."

I missed the rest of Starr's answer. So I refocus.

"What do you mean?" I ask.

She recounts the scene outside of my villa. The band tightens when Starr's voice catches. Her angelic face falls, and she drops her gaze as she finishes.

"Vicky told me how upset she was after her Dom broke up with her before the retreat. That's why I invited her to get away for a while. Had I known you were her Dom, I never would have asked her. Hell, I don't know if I can do business with someone who's so heartless," Starr says with more conviction in her tone.

She glares at me, then pushes against my chest.

The swing arcs back, but returns with more force to press us closer. A frustrated growl slips from her lips, and she tries to wiggle away.

I grip her hips to still her. Then cup her chin to align our eyes.

"Starr, you cannot make a decision like that without allowing me to tell my side of the story,"—she protests, but I continue—"Vicky was my sub, but she broke the nondisclosure agreement we signed along with plotting to marry me. I will not go into details since I cannot. But know I am an honorable man who is far from heartless."

My Angel studies me intently while she considers my words.

I leave my facial expression open to allow her to find no guile. However, the first to speak loses ground. And I will not lose. My Angel is mine, even if she doesn't want to admit it. Yet.

She blinks away for a moment and nods her head. Decision made, she brings her gaze back to my unwavering one.

"You're right. I should have spoken with you about the… situation. But I really don't want any drama in my life after ending a six-month relationship recently," Starr says.

The idea of another man with My Angel makes me want to claim her even more. But I can sense her hesitation. So rather than going ballistic, I ask what she wants.

Thankfully, she wants me—us. To explore our D/s relationship. But to take it slow.

Slow?

Damn, I'm a speed king. How the hell am I going to downshift?

I'll figure it out later. For now, I agree with her terms, and my cock weeps with joy.

My Angel must sense the change in my demeanor. She

shivers and brings her plump lower lip between her teeth. Her sorrel-colored eyes sparkle with a carnal fire.

"Well, Sir. I apologize for my errant behavior. How can I make it up to you after these weeks? I must admit I missed your colossal cock greatly… BOB did not compare, Sir," she purrs.

The fuck?!?!?!

"Bob who, Naughty Girl?" I snarl.

Starr's giggle changes into a squeak when I turn the swing around and bend her at the waist. Her arms flounder as her hands reach for the floor. The angle hoists her ass in perfect alignment with the palm of my hand.

A swift smattering of spanks alternating from one butt cheek to the other has My Naughty Girl gasping and squirming to avoid her punishment. I wrap my arm around her waist and rain a sequence of left, right, sit bones, right, left smacks.

My Naughty Girl squeals and begs for forgiveness.

Undeterred and adamant she learns her lesson, I continue until she hangs limp and the thin strip covering her pussy blooms with a spot wet from her juices. The sight of it draws a groan from deep in my chest.

One hand grips her inner thigh while the fingers of my other hand peel the material away. Her clit appears, swollen with need surrounded by her soaked folds. A quick pinch to the sensitive bundle of nerves makes My Naughty Girl jolt with a strangled cry.

Both of us hiss when my thick fingers plunge inside her pussy, still rippling with aftershocks from her climax. Her inner muscles clench my digits, drenching them with her juices.

"Oh, how your pussy is soaked and ready for penetration, Naughty Girl. Do you deserve my 'colossal cock' or another spanking?" I demand.

The swing bobs with the movement of her nodding head.

THWACK! THWACK! THWACK!

I spank her clit with my fingers, then grind my palm against it.

"Words, Naughty Girl. I will have your words!" I bark.

She cries out yes and slaps her hands on the floor in emphasis.

"I have not been with anyone since you, Naughty Girl. Can I fuck you bareback, or do we need a condom?" I growl as I bend over her hanging body.

She mewls and cries, "No one since you, Sir!"

FUCK YES!!!

My fingers fly across my jeans to free my aching dick. My Prince Albert piercing balls wink in the light before I slam forward into her channel.

"Yes! Yes! Yes! Malcolm!" My Angel screams.

Her pussy clamps on my dick like a vice as I wring one orgasm after the other from her convulsing body. The swing jerks with my carnal possession of My Angel.

"Who… do… you… belong… to… Starr?" I growl as I spank that ass. "Tell me, or you will not cum for a week!"

She wails.

"Who?" I bark.

"Youuu!!!" Starr cries out on an extended moan.

"Do… not… forget…" I say between pistoning strokes. "Now, cum with me!"

Starr's body goes rigid as her pussy clamps onto my cock. When I reach around her hip and pinch her clit, she keens.

Her pussy throbs around my dick, drawing me deeper within her core.

"FUUUCK, STARR!!!" I roar as I throw my head back and unleash a torrent of cum inside her.

The grip on her hips will leave the impression of my fingers marking her as MINE.

"So, who the hell is Bob?"

We're sitting on the rooftop terrace of my penthouse in West Hollywood on the Sunset Strip. After Starr assured me her private studio is soundproof and no one could hear our raucous makeup sex, we hopped onto my Ducati Desmosedici.

She shifts on the double chaise lounge to face me. Her eyes light with mirth in the setting sun.

"Oh… BOB. He helps me when I'm in need. Never waivers and always gives me satisfaction. Particularly late at night when I can't get a certain rebel playboy Dom out of my mind," Starr says coyly.

I growl low in my throat, and she giggles.

"Down, boy! BOB is my current—"

With a warrior's whoop, I tackle Starr to her back and cover her with the full length of my body. The burgeoning erection presses into her mound.

"Bob cannot give you satisfaction like I can, Starr Knight," I cut her off in a guttural growl. "Admit it."

She laughs out loud and grabs the sides of my face.

"BOB stands for Battery Operated Boyfriend, Malcolm Steele!" Starr giggles, then gives me a mind-blowing kiss.

"Well, you do not need a battery operated one when you have the real thing, My Angel!"

Her laughter stops abruptly with a gasp.

I stare into her wide eyes as I still reel from her kiss. When she continues to stare at me, I replay my words in my head.

Holy shit!

I referred to myself as her boyfriend and called her by the nickname I gave her!!!

That kiss wasn't mind-blowing, it was mind-altering.

Baz thought he was messed up in the head…

"*I*mpressive."

My thought exactly whenever I come to the restaurants or Sky Bar at STEELE Rodeo Drive an iconic property at Wilshire Boulevard. The sleek, gray-glass, 70-story, mixed-use tower comprises a retail mall, office space, hotel with spa and restaurants, and an observation deck. The sun glints off the exterior as I crane my neck to gaze at the spire above.

Breathtaking!

But not as incredible as the weekend Malcolm and I spent together. Not only did we catch up where we ended in St. Barth's, we went beyond the edge—no pun intended.

Malcolm gave pleasure to me I never knew existed. From his attentiveness to my needs to his pushing my limits, opening me up to new carnal joys—and pain. The juxtaposition made me soar in subspace, a term I only read about and never thought I'd experience.

His insistence on caring for me afterwards made our

connection even greater. He calls it aftercare; I call it sublime.

My body still hums from his erotic ministrations.

"Hey! You're not listening to me. Where's your head, Starr?" Adrienne asks as she prods me with her shoulder.

The action brings me back to the present, and I shake off my musings with a shudder of delight.

She rolls her eyes, knowing I was with Malcolm since she taught the rest of my classes. My best friend snorts at my Cheshire Cat grin.

"Yeah, impressive indeed!" I snicker as I waggle my eyebrows suggestively.

"Come on, Whipped Girl. We have business to attend. Not stand gaga at Steele's spire..." Adrienne laughs, looping her arm through mine.

The elevator doors open on thirty for STEELE International, Inc.'s executive floor. One of the three receptionists not busy with other visitors or on the telephone greets us as we walk through the waiting area. The modern decor features shades of gray from dove to platinum and white for the color palette. Luxurious accents of silk wall treatments, crystal light fixtures, and rich ebony wood floors complement the leather furniture, Lucite tables, and steel pieces. Original artwork with spotlights on them lines the walls. The sense of STEELE's power exudes from all angles.

My gaze flits past the receptionists' station to the panoramic view beyond the floor-to-ceiling windows. From this height, one can observe the Ferris wheel on the

Santa Monica Pier to the west and the Pacific Ocean glittering in the distance.

"Ms. Knight, Ms. Anthony, welcome to STEELE Los Angeles."

I pivot to face the pretty brunette and smile.

She informs us Malcolm's assistant will be with us shortly and asks if we care for a beverage. So LA she offers coffee, tea, bottled water, or a morning smoothie.

We decline and settle on the sofas along with my legal and marketing teams.

Today, we sign the contract for Starr Light Fitness & Wellness Beverly Hills' partnership with STEELE International. My dream of expanding to luxury resorts for retreats around the world and a location in the Caribbean comes true in moments!

It's not long before Miles appears and escorts us to a conference room. He introduces us to STEELE Entertainment Properties Division's legal and marketing teams already seated at the large, oval-shaped, ebony wood table. They rise from the black leather chairs and greet us warmly.

Just as we seat ourselves, the double glass doors open, and Malcolm and Anton enter.

My pulse quickens and my pussy floods with my arousal at the sight of My Dom. He's dressed immaculately in a lightweight wool charcoal gray with a hint of a check pattern suit and darker gray shirt with a silk stripped tie and black Oxfords. His lustrous ebony hair swept back to emphasize his chiseled jawline, no longer covered by the five o'clock shadow he sported over the weekend. Simply gorgeous.

A flicker of appreciation fills his eyes when his gaze sweeps over me from head to toe.

Not one to conform, I wear a sky blue suit—with shorts. The single-breasted jacket open to reveal a white silk shirt unbuttoned to hint at the lace camisole underneath. The cuffed shorts cover my upper thighs, displaying three-quarters of my toned legs ending in gray Manolo Blahnik stilettos. My body epitomizes my skill as a fitness professional focused on health and wellness. I use it to my advantage at all times. Even to entice Malcolm.

A slight smile plays at the corner of my mouth as he nods and extends his hand in salutation.

"Ms. Knight, welcome to STEELE International. You impressed us with your retreat greatly. We expect a conducive partnership with you," he says with a smug grin. "Shall we begin?"

"Thank you, Mr. Steele, Starr Light Fitness & Wellness agrees you make an excellent partner. You have proven you will always hold our needs as your utmost priority. I could not find a more capable partner," I respond with a firm grasp of his much larger hand.

Anton chuckles, but stops when Adrienne pins him with her intense stare.

Everyone settles around the table, and the STEELE legal team presents us with the contract. Since my team reviewed it before the meeting, we sign without delay.

My heart flutters as I beam at Adrienne. We're on our way to expanding SLFW!

Next Anton's development team presents the Jackson Hole at STEELE Resorts concept as members-only, high-end beach clubs for the jet set where SLFW will host retreats. Our fitness and wellness programs will offer more amenities for Jackson Hole and increase activities for guests and provide accommodations for retreat participants.

St. Barth's will serve as the center's first global location. They recommend others in Cabo San Lucas, Monte Carlo, and Koh Samui in Thailand, initially with others as demand requires.

The additional resorts surprise us. Adrienne turns to me with raised eyebrows, and I clap with glee. Malcolm and Anton smirk.

Fantastic!

The marketing teams present their plans, including timelines and recommendations for feedback. The ninety minutes pass quickly. In the end, I'm even more impressed by STEELE and their ability to generate revenue opportunities and their teams' skills.

We drink my favorite Krug Clos d'Ambonnay Champagne to celebrate our partnership.

Over my Waterford Crystal flute, I watch Malcolm. He must sense my stare and turns to face me. His eyes smolder for a moment, and I nod in recognition.

I'm ready to jump his bones. Now.

"Ladies and gentlemen, thank you. Now if you will excuse us, I have a matter to discuss with Ms. Knight," Malcolm says as he raises his flute for a final salute.

My insides melt.

The room hums with both teams jumping to action. Ever the Dom, Malcolm has them doing his bidding eagerly.

A giggle slips past my lips at the thought, but dies when Malcolm approaches and takes my elbow to lead me from the room.

He's silent as we walk, only acknowledging those we pass with a nod or a brief word. When we reach his office, he ushers me inside, locks the glass door, and blackens the glass walls. Cocooned in his soundproof lair, my heart rate increases and my eyes lower in submission.

His wicked chuckle makes me shiver.

"Congratulations, Little One. Our business partnership begins officially. We may be equals in the boardroom… But you remain my submissive behind closed doors. Understand?" My Dom states with authority.

"Yes, Sir," I respond as I lower to my knees and lean on my haunches with my hands laced behind my head, chin tilted downward, eyes to the floor.

"Excellent, Little One," My Dom croons as he steps forward and cups the nape of my neck to lift my gaze. "So beautiful. You please me tremendously."

My chest lifts on a deep inhale, ecstasy courses through me because I please My Dom.

The move draws his attention, and his fingers ghost over my exposed skin to slip inside my shirt. He hefts the weight of my heavy breast, then tweaks its turgid bud between his thumb and forefinger. As he rolls my nipple, My Dom leans over to brush his lips over mine as he murmurs naughty words of his plans for me. Plans that do not include Pilates or meditation.

He lifts me to my feet, and I tremble under his touch when his warm breath and wet tongue meet my nipple. He latches on and sucks. Hard.

My knees buckle as he moves between my breasts to lave, suck, and nip, devoting equal time to both. But I stumble on my stilettos when he steps back abruptly.

"Strip. Now." He growls.

My Dom folds his arms over his chest and watches me with hooded, lust-filled eyes as I remove my clothing without hesitation. Each piece drops to the floor until I'm exposed fully to his heated gaze.

As I stand naked before him clothed fully in his office only a door apart from others on the floor, I can't help but yearn for My Dom. No longer the Independent Woman, I've become his sub. And I do not regret my decision.

Malcolm walks around me. His gaze burns with longing. The light touch of his large palm on the small of my back makes me jump. He soothes me with his voice thrumming into my ear as he guides me to his desk.

Once there, he places my hands on the surface and glides his fingertip along my spine before he presses down to lower my torso to the top. My ass remains high in my stilettos, positioned for him perfectly. The most private parts of me on full display.

I drop my forehead to the cool leather and sigh when his finger finds my damp slit. Then I jerk from pressure on my puckered hole.

"As I told you this weekend, I will claim each of your

holes. Soon, I will fill your tight, virgin ass with my 'colossal cock.' So no need for shock at my touch," he smirks. "In fact, I have something for you, Little One. A gift."

I hear his footsteps retreat as Malcolm walks to the other side of his office. I chance a peek over my shoulder to find him removing an item from a closet. Unable to see it, I turn forward again and await my gift.

A cool, wet sensation slides from the top of my ass crack to land on my bottom hole. I shiver when I realize it's a lubricant. Oh dear.

My Dom smooths a generous amount of the substance over my hole as my legs quiver and my breath hitches. He spanks each butt cheek when I move away from his finger as he glides it inside.

"Oh no, Little One. You will hold position," he reprimands me.

The pressure increases until his first knuckle pushes past the tight rings of muscles. I groan and slap the desk.

Slowly he pumps his finger in and out, then adds a second one to scissor with the first. More murmurs of encouragement fill my ear as My Dom leans over me, his torso flat against mine.

The pain morphs to pleasure, and I squeeze my eyes shut, embarrassed to enjoy the foreign invasion.

"Very good, Little One. You like my thick fingers inside of your tight ass. I feel your pussy clench and smell your sweet arousal," Malcolm says with a throaty growl. "Now, for your gift."

Immediately, his fingers withdraw and cool stainless

steel touches my bottom hole. He pushes it into my stretched back passage. With a pop, he seats it deep inside of me. The wide base rests between my butt cheeks.

I mewl.

Malcolm kneels behind me and covers my pussy lips with his mouth. He rims them with the tip of his tongue, then darts it in and out, picking up a steady rhythm. Soon his fingers join in. The erotic sound of my moans joins his rumbles of satisfaction.

The impending climax barrels towards me at full speed. I beg My Dom to allow me to cum as my pussy juices slide from my core to his hungry mouth.

He stands, and the sound of his zipper lowering makes me cry out in joy.

"Yeeesss!!!" I scream and slap my palms against the desk when he slams his engorged dick deep inside of me with its piercing scraping my sensitive tissue.

The added butt plug makes for a tight fit, and I squirm under the onslaught of his passionate, controlled thrusts. Malcolm pummels me. His groin pushes the plug deeper, and his seed-filled balls slap against my swollen clit.

It's all too much, and I keen as my orgasm rips through me. My back bows, and I grind against him, wanting to take him as deep inside of me as possible, and then even more.

"So fucking tight, Little One… Your greedy pussy wants more… I'll give you more!" Malcolm snarls as he slaps my ass.

His thrusts turn into a jackhammering as he pistons his hips to ramp up his domination of my body.

When wave after wave of orgasms follow, I can no longer focus and give in to the power of My Dom as he chases his release. My mind blanks and my legs go boneless.

Malcolm increases his hold on my hip and slips his other arm under me to wrap his fingers around my throat. Held in his grip, I rock with his movements and cry out in carnal bliss.

One last thrust lifts me to the balls of my feet, and he stills. His cock hardens further, then jerks as a torrent of his seed coats my womb.

We groan in unison as my pussy muscles milk every drop.

Malcolm collapses on top of me until our breath returns to normal. He nuzzles my neck, then kisses my sweat-soaked skin.

"How do you like your gift, Little One?" He asks against the shell of my ear as he slips from my core and taps the base of the butt plug with his fingertip.

I moan, then respond in a low throaty voice, "I love it, Sir. Thank you."

His dark chuckle reverberates through my body.

MALCOLM

"**O**h, my goodness! This is amazing, Malcolm!"

After the last month of working on our new partnerships—business and pleasure—I have the urge to bring Starr further into my world. I want to experience more with her than just fucking or a D/s relationship. Crazy? Yeah. But when do I dodge the crazy?

Thus our trip to the Mayan city of Tulum in Mexico for cave diving at the Cenote Angelita.

It's the top site in the world for the extreme sport and one I enjoy the most for its challenging environment. With its cloudy layer resembling a magical veil separating the clear fresh water from the salt water below and a depth of 200 feet, one must hold an advance open water scuba diver certification. A surprise underwater river adds to its risk level.

The sandy bottom with tree branches and rocks lit by the sunlight as it filters through the fish-filled water can appear eerie or tranquil depending upon the person. For me, its mysterious environment intrigues me and tests my limits.

Fortunately, My Angel also loves a challenge and doesn't find the idea of diving in an underground hole squirm-worthy. She's bouncing on her feet as we wait in the dense tropical jungle to descend into the cave. She's excited to explore the famous sinkhole and its shadowy caverns.

The muscles in her long, toned legs flex and her D-cups jiggle in her triangle bikini top as she slips into her diving swimsuit. Her sorrel-colored eyes dazzle as she winks at me.

"I cannot wait to get down there! I've been to Ben's Cave in Grand Bahama since it's ideal for beginners who want to experience the world of cave diving"—Starr raises her hand to silence my reminder and lifts it to her heart in a pledge—"I promise not to stray from your side."

We had a long discussion about her interest in extreme sports. I agreed to invite her on some trips I take with the guys. Since she's athletic and remains calm under pressure with her breathing techniques, My Angel will make for a perfect mentee.

"Right! Do not under any circumstances stray from Malcolm or any of us. Remember the hand signals we discussed on the helicopter ride here," Lucien adds.

I have to control the caveman in me from snarling at his suggestion of my mate seeking protection from any other male.

"You'll do well, *malen'kiy*," Anton says as he high fives Starr.

Then, I let a growl rip out of my mouth at his *little one* reference. Asshole!

He and Borya chuckle at my possessive behavior while My Angel gapes at me. Even the guide and his team appear startled by my outburst. Like I give a fuck.

"Let's do this!" Lucien interjects as he claps his hands to diffuse the situation.

We spend the next forty minutes exploring Cenote Angelita's incredible submerged world. As promised, Starr stays at my side then only an arm's distance away when we swim along the misty underground river near the bottom of the water-filled pit. No need for the current to sweep her away.

The entire time Starr swivels her head left and right to take in the majesty of the sacred site. Through the face mask, her eyes flicker from one side of the limestone cavern to the other. She nods and points to the fish and formations in wide-eyed fascination.

I'm more intrigued by her than by the cenote.

Once we're topside, we pull out our mouthpieces, and Starr throws her head back to laugh.

"I want some more!" She says as her eyes twinkle gold in the sun's reflection from the water's surface.

The guys and I join in her laughter as we swim to the edge of the sinkhole. The guide and his team hoist us out, and we remove our scuba gear.

Starr leaps into my arms, wraps her limbs around me, and slants her lush mouth over mine.

I stagger back at the unexpected impact. But instinctively cup her ass and squeeze the round globes agreeably.

My cock proves more entranced when it hardens against the tight scuba suit.

"Thank you, baby!" My Angel enthuses when we come up for air—literally.

I press my forehead against hers and tell her how happy I am she enjoyed the dive.

She slides down my body and kisses my lips before she shimmies out of her suit. Disappointment fills me when she pulls a long-sleeved t-shirt and track pants over her bikini. Then drops to the ground to put socks and hiking boots back on.

Soon we're changed and line up to head out. Starr slips her hand in mine and smiles up at me.

My Angel is a trooper who could not care less we have to trek through the humid, lush overgrowth to the clearing where the STEELE Tulum Hotel and Resort's Sikorsky S-92 Executive Helicopter awaits our return. She may be from a wealthy family, but her parents raised her down-to-earth as my mother insisted for my siblings and me. Plus being hippies, it accustoms the Knights to roughing it at outdoor festivals with rain, mud, and other uncomfortable situations.

"We take it you had a solid dive, *da*?" Borya asks when we're on board the helicopter.

Starr grins and nods, "Absolutely! It was an incredible experience. I'm ready for my next one!"

I beam at her reaction, then point out some sights, including the Mayan ruins as we soar overhead. The glittering water of the Caribbean Sea and the islands of

Cozumel, Cuba, Caymans, and Jamaica appear on the horizon before us.

After the hike through the jungle, we're ready to hit the beach at the resort. Time for a dip, ceviche, and a pitcher of mojitos—My Angel's favorite cocktail.

When we land on the helipad, we race to the beach as we strip, then dive into the warm, sparkling water. Starr's melodic laughter fills the air along with a splash as I toss her into the waves. She resurfaces and pays me back with the sweep of her arm to arc water in my direction.

I wrestle her into my embrace, and she moans when she feels my erection against her belly. One swift move allows me to slide her bikini bottom to the side and impale her on my cock.

We groan as my girth stretches her tight pussy to bring our bodies as close as a man and woman can get. With the water up to my shoulders, I use my grip on her curvaceous hips to ride my rock-hard length. So aroused from my pent-up desire, I bring us over the edge to an epic climax.

The shudders from our sated lovemaking make ripples in the surrounding water.

Starr buries her face in my neck and cries out her pleasure against my heated skin. I press my mouth against her wet hair and groan in total carnal euphoria.

Fuck, she feels so good. This feels so good. I don't think I can ever get enough of my woman.

How crazy is that???

* * *

STARR TWIRLS in my arms as we dance at the resort's beachside club. Each night a local deejay or a live band performs for an authentic experience beneath the starry sky. The deep bass of the sultry music combined with the gathering of writhing bodies in the tropical heat makes erotic energy swirl around us.

My hands roam over her voluptuous body as the red slip of a dress skims the tops of her thighs. Her plump, brown nipples stand out in bas-relief, still swollen from my earlier suckling. The only thing she wears beneath the silky material is her butt plug gift.

Tonight I will claim her virgin puckered hole.

In the meantime, we join the other dancers as the rhythm pulsates through us—a prelude to the evening's hedonism.

"Sir, I don't know if I can continue to hold the plug inside of me. The sweat makes it slippery," Starr whispers in my ear.

Her warm breath—minty from the mojitos we drank before we stepped onto the outdoor dance floor—tickles my skin.

I spank her butt cheek and appreciate the jiggle of her firm flesh.

"You will keep your gift deep inside until I remove it to fill your ass with an even better present… My cock. Understand, Naughty Girl?" I respond.

Starr closes her eyes and her lower lip trembles before she nods in the affirmative.

Another quick smack jars the butt plug, and she whimpers a verbal answer against my neck. Her arms tighten around me as she lifts to the balls of her feet in strappy fuck-me sandals.

I keep her on the dance floor for another twenty minutes before I take her hand and lead her to the path for our villa. We pass Borya grinding with a Mexican beauty, then Lucien with a blonde from Sweden. I scan the crowd to find Anton. He's at our VIP table whispering in the ear of the Cuban heiress to a tobacco company.

Knowing they set my boys for the night, I can enjoy My Angel. Time for my cave exploration…

STARR

"Hi, Starr. Long time no see. Hmmm… You're all tan. Where have you been, sweetie?"

I turn to the syrupy voice behind me to find Vicky in the doorway of my private studio.

The smile on her face doesn't reach her frosty blue eyes. She may be an actress, but she's having a tough time reigning in her emotions. With her tense posture and fingers fiddling the corner of her yoga mat, I sense her displeasure despite the forced smile.

"Oh, hi, Vicky. Good to see you, too, honey," I respond, returning her unnecessary term of endearment and ignoring her question.

I re-focus on the room's sound system to prepare for my next class. My class roster didn't include Vicky's name, so I guess she's a last-minute addition…

For the past month, I could avoid her since she was filming a movie in Toronto. Being on the other side of the continent proved the perfect barrier. Her scenes must have wrapped. So here she stands.

Hopefully Vicky doesn't have an inkling about my relationship with Malcolm. That would be a major disaster. I'm really not interested in her histrionics.

Not that I'd mention it. For one, Malcolm and I signed a nondisclosure agreement—in both our best interests. Another reason, it's none of her affair—no pun intended.

Once Malcolm explained the cause for their demise, I didn't harbor bad feelings for him, and I inclined no longer to feel sorry for Vicky.

I mean, who goes against an NDA and even worse plots to marry a multibillionaire. A giggle slips past my pursed lips when I remember the classic romantic comedy *How to Marry a Millionaire*. The screen sirens Marilyn Monroe, Betty Grable, and Lauren Bacall set up shop in a penthouse with the aim to snag wealthy men. The end cracks me up each time!

So, yeah, it's not farfetched for someone to plan on a big ole diamond ring from Malcolm Steele.

Except that's not my goal.

I'm thrilled with our time together thus far. But don't have the end goal of a walk down the aisle. He's still a playboy, no matter how many toe-curling orgasms he gives to me. I guess he wouldn't be able to give them to me if he didn't have the experience of being a playboy.

"So, where did you get your tan?"

Vicky's repeat question brings me back to the studio. She spreads her yoga mat in the front row opposite mine. Then turns her questioning gaze back to me.

Great. Talk about a dog with a bone.

"I visited some locations for more international retreats and an additional location for SLFW," I respond with enough truth I hope satisfies her curiosity.

I hate to lie. But will if necessary to protect what's mine. Plus, I don't trust Vicky exactly.

The marketing teams will release a joint statement to the press next week now that we've had plenty of meetings to iron out all details and to complete the timeline. So it's no big deal to give Vicky a heads-up.

She eyes me for a moment, then grins.

"Congratulations, sweetie! You deserve it," Vicky says as she pulls me into a hug.

I pat her back, then sigh with relief inwardly when more voices sound behind us. One more squeeze, and I turn to the students arriving.

"Namaste, ladies and gentlemen," I say as I press my palms together at my breastbone and bow to the light in my students.

And thank God and every deity in every religion's pantheon for intervening Vicky's inquisition!

"HI, BABE. HOW WAS YOUR DAY?"

I'm seated on my cushion after meditation in the side garden of my home. Now's the time to tell Malcolm about Vicky while I have a clear head amongst the relaxing fragrance of the flower blossoms.

The class went smoothly. Some students stayed after for some hands-on adjustments and tips. Fortunately,

Vicky left when I focused on the students and not her lingering on her mat. With a huff, she left my studio.

Crisis averted for now…

"You handled her well. She can be a gossip in general. But if she knows about us, I'm not sure how she'll react. However, I will protect you from any harm she may try to inflict on your or SLFW," Malcolm *The Enforcer* Steele declares vehemently.

A smile threatens to split my face. My body heats with warmth, not from lust. But from happiness he cares so much for me. His reaction makes me wonder how serious he is about us beyond our D/s relationship.

I've noticed Malcolm calls me babe or angel if we're not in a scene where I'm Little One or Naughty Girl.

Do I mind? No, not at all. It's a change from Quinn, and his concern for himself only. From Malcolm's focus on my sexual needs to my business goals to my protection, perhaps I could get used to being with him on a regular basis.

The thought warms me further.

"What did you conquer today, Mr. Steele?" I ask him.

His dove gray eyes glitter with mischief as I stare at my iPhone's screen. Malcolm is so damned sexy.

It's been a week since we last saw each other in person. FaceTime makes up for it. Well… Along with the explicit videos we share each night.

Fuck! I'm horny just thinking about them. That man's body, I swear!

Malcolm tells me about his latest acquisition of a floundering beach resort in Uruguay and his plans for a LEVELS Beverly Hills.

That perks my ears. The New York, Paris, and London locations appeared in my Google research on BDSM. I would love to become a member of the luxury clubs to live out my fantasies. Even better, as Malcolm's sub.

Lucien spotted an optimal location, and Malcolm plans a site visit in the coming weeks. Plus, we'll have a status update from our teams with Lucien for the first Jackson Hole retreat.

My alarm chimes.

"Oh, I have to get ready. I'll talk to you tomorrow," I tell Malcolm as I rise from my pillow.

He frowns and asks, "Get ready for what?"

Taken aback by his tone of voice, I bring the iPhone up again to gauge his facial expression. His frown deepens when I scowl at him. Really???

"Girls' Night Out," I answer vaguely.

Malcolm narrows his eyes and tilts his head to the side.

"What does that mean?" He demands.

I put my hand on my hip and deepen my scowl.

"What do you mean by 'what does that mean?' I'm sure you've heard of the term?" I respond indignantly.

Is he seriously trying to control me outside of the bedroom??? I don't think so!

Malcolm takes a breath and wipes his hand over his face. Then pins me with his Dom stare.

Oh hell, no!

Before he can utter a word, I hold up my hand.

"Do not use your Dom-mind-control voice on me, Malcolm Steele! We are not in a scene, and this is my life to do as I choose. And I choose to enjoy a night out with my friends. Understand?" I retort, using his word for emphasis.

Malcolm stares at me for a solid fifteen seconds.

I refuse to give in. He will not control me. I am not into a total power exchange relationship. Not at all.

"Fine, Starr. As I said when we began our D/s relationship, the sub holds all the power, not the Dom. Enjoy your Girls' Night Out. I'll talk to you tomorrow," Malcolm responds with a stoic expression.

We end the call.

Somehow, I feel unsettled, as though I let him down. Hell, my stomach even hurts. As I walk inside the house to my bedroom, my mind replays the end of our conversation.

Maybe I was too harsh on Malcolm. He wasn't rude or anything.

Just as I consider begging off of my plans, my mobile rings.

"Hey, girl! I need your advice. Should I wear the black sequin romper or the fuchsia backless top and matching mini skirt? Claudia votes for the romper."

Adrienne's FaceTime call helps me to make up my mind.

Girls' Night Out it is!!!

MALCOLM

"Lucien, you did it again, cuzz. This is the optimal location for LEVELS Beverly Hills. The view of the Hollywood Sign seals the deal for me. In the heart of luxury combined with an iconic landmark, we couldn't find a better spot for our hedonistic playground!"

I clap my partner in the pursuit of carnal pleasure on the back as we stand on the roof of the six-story former atelier. It once served as the workshop and later storefront for a famous costume designer to movie studios during the height of Hollywood glamour from the thirties through fifties.

The property remained in the family's possession, but they've since lost their fortune and failed to preserve the treasure. Lucien heard about it from a friend of theirs. We'll be able to purchase the building, its land, and its air rights for a fair price.

Just eyeballing the structure—interior and exterior— the renovation will require at least three months of construction and two weeks for the decor. Staffing will start immediately so we can vet the potential employees, have them sign the contract and NDA, and complete their training a month before the opening party.

Once we close on the property, we'll inform the current members for their referrals and we'll open the application to those we have on the wait list. Over the years, we learned it's best to boost the majority of our numbers from within with a smattering of those who come through the dance club or restaurant. Members and interests voice interest in a West Coast LEVELS, and now we can deliver.

"Like totally rad, dude!" Harris says in his surfer impersonation. "But seriously, this is spot on. Still within Beverly Hills with the added benefit of being on a street with less foot traffic. It will blend in amongst the surroundings and not call attention to its purpose—a hidden exclusive jewel."

We inform the real estate agent and the family's representative of our decision to move forward with the deal. Another glance at the Hollywood Sign lit up in the distance, then we leave.

"Smart idea to tour the property at night for a sense of its full impact. But even better, since it's time to hit the lounge, gentlemen!" Lucien says when we settle in my Black Badge Rolls-Royce Cullinan.

When we arrive, the valet parks the SUV while the three of us stride inside past the line of hopefuls. It pays to know the owner.

Lucien shakes hands with the door security and hostesses on our way to the VIP section, where we settle at his banquet in the center. The decadent lounge features plush leather and velvet seating, two bars, a spacious outdoor patio, and an opulent benitoite fireplace—the rare crystal known as the official gem of California discovered by James Couch. Hence the lounge's name: Jackson's Couch.

Immediately, the server sets a selection of bottles from Jackson Corporation's labels on the low table and pours our selections. Another server places platters of finger foods including wild mushroom crostini, salmon caviar sushi bites, and skewered shrimp with ham. All derived from Lucien's creative mind to tantalize one's palette with the dishes' rich flavors and just salty enough to increase one's thirst for the expensive libations.

The hungry eyes that followed us as we crossed the sofas and oversized chairs hone in on us as we sit back and survey the room. Two members of the STEELE Quaternity and one of the three Jackson brothers draw attention.

The preening and fluffing precede their stroll over. Low-cut tops reveal all sizes of tits; sparkly mini dresses cover asses barely; mile-long legs end in fuck-me sandals. Brunettes, blondes, redheads; long or short; curly or straight; a veritable rainbow or stunning women flock to us.

Everyone wants to score a young, hot, multibillionaire...

My mind turns to My Angel.

So unlike any of these females. She's more stunning. But that's where the similarities end. My wealth didn't draw Starr to me. Her interest lies with the success of her company and how STEELE can help her achieve it.

Not to mention she fell into me from behind with no

clue as to my identity. Her speechless reaction wasn't from recognition of me from the *Forbes* World's Billionaires List or gossip pages. It was an instantaneous attraction on the carnal level. We called to one another through our pheromones. And I must say my cock sprang to life when I dazzled My Angel.

Since then, not one other female has done it for me. So the women strutting in my direction are about to waste their time.

Harris on the other hand leans back with his arms on top of the banquet and his legs spread in invitation. A cocky grin plays on his face.

And right on cue, a buxom beauty with smooth caramel skin and a mane of curly hair saunters over to stand between his legs.

Harris' smoky gray eyes travel over her curves in the white silk, drape-necked mini dress. She leans over and whispers in his ear. His smirk widens, and he tilts his head to suggest the space next to him.

The woman's topaz-colored eyes glitter in triumph as she sits beside my youngest brother, crosses her shapely legs, and places a small hand on his muscular thigh. She offers Lucien and me a brilliant smile, then turns her attention to Harris.

Just as Lucien and I glance at one another and chuckle, a voice calls out.

"Lucien, honey! We didn't know you were in LA!"

We shift our gazes in the woman's direction to find two statuesque brunettes beaming at *The Sexy Chef*. The gold bangles on their arms clink as they run their fingers through their silky tresses. Dressed similarly in miniskirts and midriff-baring halter tops. The nipples of their enhanced tits strain against the thin fabric.

Their gazes dart between Lucien and me.

I turn my head and sip my Jackson Special Blend Scotch. Hopefully, they'll get the hint…

Not deterred, one of them squeezes between Lucien and me while her friend sits on his other side. The one with the green eyes asks if she can have something to drink, then takes my snifter. Her gaze locks on me as she flicks her little pink tongue out to lick the rim before she takes a taste.

"It fills my mouth with a burst, then goes down so smoothly… Delicious," she purrs. "I'm Missy. You look familiar. Are you an actor?"

Her hand not cradling my snifter slides up my thigh as she cocks her head to the side in concentration.

Just as I clamp my hand on top of hers to stop her from reaching my crotch, she grins and squeezes my leg.

"Sebastian Steele! Oh wow! So—"

I stand disgusted by her and how she just proved my point. The world knows Baz married Lola since it's all over the Internet. The monikers *Couple of the Century* and *SeLo* trend on Twitter and Instagram since they announced their engagement.

Again, these thirsty broads don't give a damn. And I don't have the inclination to correct the mistaken identity.

Instead, I stride to the outdoor patio to collect a fresh drink from the bar in that section. The cooler night air has fewer people buzzing around. A few couples snuggle around the fire pits and some singles linger at the bar.

A woman gives me the eye while I wait for the bartender to fix my drink. But I pretend to receive a text message and lean against the bar facing the opposite direction. I turn at the clink of the glass on the surface and stride away with my Scotch.

I take a moment for a taste before I head back in. My thoughts drift to My Angel. She had dinner with her parents so couldn't meet me for the walk-through. Nor did she invite me to meet them. It's been four months and neither of us has introduced the other to our parents.

The realization shouldn't bother me. I'm not the heads-over-heels type, but I also realize I wouldn't mind the connection Sebastian has with Lola and Roger has with Leonie. Of course, neither of my brothers had their women sign a D/s contact and an NDA…

Then again, I can't understand the visceral reaction I had to Starr going on her "Girls' Night Out" last month. When she didn't back down, I attributed my irritation to the Dom in me wanting control of his sub. Later it occurred to me what I really didn't want was some fucker flirting with My Angel or worse.

Mine!

"Hi, do you mind if I joined you?"

I glance down to see the redhead from the bar smiling at me as she inclines her head towards a chair for two beside one of the fire pits.

"Thank you—"

"Yes! He would mind as would I!"

My head swivels to my left.

Vicky! Fuck. Me.

She glares at the other woman. Icy daggers shoot from Vicky's eyes as she stares the redhead down. She closes her mouth agape in surprise, then silently pivots on her heels.

I watch as she retreats to the bar without a backwards glance.

The pressure of a hand on my forearm brings my focus back to Vicky. I shoot my dominant glare at her until she releases me from her hold.

I step around her. But Vicky reaches out to clutch my upper arm with both hands. Not wanting to make a scene since a few of the patrons on the patio watch out every move, I take Vicky by the elbow and lead her to a corner.

She leans into me and reaches up to put her arms around my neck.

"Sir! Please! I miss you so much!" Vicky whines.

I put my hands on either side of her waist and push her away. She clings to me like a little monkey and squirms in my grasp, wiggling her hips.

"Enough, Vicky!" I command through clenched teeth. "Remove your hands and stop with the 'Sir' bullshit. You only acted submissive to get a ring. And… you… failed. Let it go already."

She steps back and stares at the ground as she twists her hands in front of her. A faint sob comes from her down-turned mouth. Peeking at me from beneath her thick eyelashes, Vicky gives me a beseeching look.

"Malcolm, I am truly sorry. It's not that I don't derive pleasure from your… ways. You're the best lover I've ever had. I promise I won't tell a soul. Above all, I truly miss you… Miss us! Please forgive me and give us another chance," Vicky begs pitifully.

I scan her face for any sign of guile. The last thing I want is for her to become vindictive and talk shit despite the NDA.

But again, not even a spasm from my cock. And certainly nothing from my heart. No, My Angel has me whipped.

I shake my head and raise my hand when Vicky opens her mouth to protest. The memory that she questioned Starr in her studio about her tan gives me pause. We don't think Vicky knows about us, but we can't be too careful.

So instead of leaving Vicky with tears in her eyes, I try to assuage her.

"Vicky, I forgive you, and I want you to understand my goal is not to hurt you. But our time is over. It is best for you to move on. Good night."

I move past her, but stop at her words. A chill races down my spine.

"Like you have, Sir?!?!" She shouts.

Instead of reacting, I continue to walk inside. Without breaking stride, I send a text message to my attorney to handle this situation. Apparently Vicky has not learned the meaning of a nondisclosure agreement, and he will have to remind her. Again.

Next I send a text to Harris and Lucien to tell them I'm out. They'll get Lucien's driver to pick them up whenever they're ready.

See, this is the shit that can happen on a night out…

I ignore other attempts from women as I weave through patrons gathered on the furniture and past those at the interior bar. I acknowledge a few acquaintances with a nod or a raised hand. But my goal is to get out posthaste.

Once outside, I ask for my keys from one valet. They left my Cullinan to the side for easy access. In a matter of moments, I settle behind the wheel.

A glance at the dashboard clock shows it's nine-thirty. Starr's dinner started at eight o'clock. Not wanting to waste time before I can see My Angel, I decide to wait outside of the gates to her mansion. It's been long enough since we last saw each other in person. One can do so many FaceTime fucks.

Not long after I park, headlights flash across my windshield. Their light fills me with a brightness at the thought I'll have My Angel in my arms, then beneath me shortly.

I flip my high beams and wave.

Starr's eyes widen behind her window before she recognizes me. I drive behind her silver Tesla and follow her car to park in front of the garage. She marches towards me.

My gaze glides from her eyes to her curls piled atop her head to the cream, long-sleeved knit dress to her gold metallic pumps. It's not until she smacks me in the chest with her handbag do I realize My Angel is not at all happy to see me.

I grasp her wrists and hold her still.

"It's me, angel. What? What's the matter?" I ask when she yanks away from me and swats my reaching hands away.

Starr folds her arms over her chest and scowls.

"The better question, what are you doing here, Malcolm?" She snaps.

Baffled, I stare back at her with my mouth open.

She shakes her head and folds her arms tighter around her body as though she's protecting herself from me. Or worse, blocking me out.

"Well?" Starr asks as she cocks her head to the side and raises an elegantly arched eyebrow.

"I honestly do not know what happened. We agreed to meet after your dinner. So, you tell me why you pushed me away," I respond with my hands palms up in surrender.

Starr narrows her sorrel brown eyes as they glint in the light from the wrought-iron sconces on the garage. Again she shakes her head, then reaches inside of her handbag. Her fingers fly across the screen. She advances with her mobile held aloft.

I peer at the screen and see several photos of me.

Me with Vicky in my arms. Caught in a compromising embrace: my hands planted on her waist; her arms around my neck with her fingers tangled in my hair; connected at our groins as she wriggles against me.

FUCK!

My eyes dart to Starr's, and I swear they glint not with light but with tears.

Fucking Vicky Pain in my ass!

Someone took photos of us at Jackson's Couch and posted them to Instagram. Then the bloggers picked it up, followed by the gossip rags. Headlines scream: Another Steele Down the Aisle? Billionaire Daredevil Malcolm

Steele's Latest Feat. In a matter of thirty minutes, we were trending.

The world never sees me with a woman other than one-offs with a model or socialite at an event. I prefer to keep my dalliances private. Hence the contracts and NDAs...

Now I'm blowing up the Internet with Vicky, of all people.

I shift my gaze to Starr, who stares back at me with a flushed face.

"Angel, baby, I wasn't holding Vicky. She approached me at the lounge unexpectedly. Then she tried to hug me after she begged for my forgiveness. I was pushing her away," I say.

When Starr's expression changes to skepticism, I add, "Trust me, Angel. I will never lie to you."

She continues to gaze into my soul, then glances away as though a battle rages inside her mind.

I wait for My Angel to speak. I won't push her now, but I won't give up either. After what seems like a decade, she faces me.

"I trust you, Malcolm. But you have to understand how it appears to me. Hell, to anyone who sees the photos," she responds as she throws her hands in the air and blows a breath. "Fine, let's go inside, it's chilly."

My breath rushes from my constricted lungs—I didn't even realize I was holding it. I say a silent prayer of thanks, then catch up to My Angel. Satisfied, I clasp her hand in mine and bring it to my lips before I pull her into my arms and carry her inside.

"I'll warm you up real quick, My Angel," I croon against her neck.

She shivers against me, then squeals when I latch on her neck and suck. Hard.

The caveman in me wants to leave a bright red mark on her chestnut-colored skin. If I could make it indelible, I would. A permanent tattoo to prove she's mine all mine.

My Angel directs me to her bedroom where I make it my sole purpose to pump her inner fire and make her mine.

"Oh, this is just what I needed... Sun, sand, cocktails, and my girls."

Lola says as she sighs and leans back against the chaise lounge. She sips her Tipo Tinto R&R rum and raspberry with a sigh. Her mouth stained red from the iconic Mozambican specialty drink.

Leonie, Blair, Haley, Billie, and I laugh at her drama.

"Hold on! You just returned from your two-month long honeymoon full of sun, sand, cocktails, and a sexy as hell husband," Leonie starts. "How could you need more two months later?"

Lola swats the pillow away that Leonie tosses at her and sits up.

"Right!" Chorus Blair and Billie.

I shake my head. My curly, dark brown hair sways along my back as my dimples deepen with my smile.

"Lola, you crack me up! Even I, a staunch believer in self-care, can't imagine why you need a break this soon!"

With that, I throw my pillow and ding Lola on the stomach. She laughs and hugs the pillow to her chest.

"I agree! Give us a break already, Lola!" Haley adds as she rolls her sharp gray eyes behind her glasses.

"Well, so that you know, I've been extremely busy catching up on work I missed while on my honeymoon with my sexy as fuck husband. Now, I need you, Ms. Knight, to work your magic to clear my head and relax me. And boy do you have your work cut out for you, again!"

Lola throws the pillow back at me, and I catch it.

"Fine. Challenge accepted, Mrs. Steele!" I reply with a giggle.

Lola swoons clutching her ginormous engagement ring to her bosom. She's right, it's definitely like her idol Elizabeth Taylor's ice skating rink ring. The nearly 30 carats glimmer in the torchlight.

The ring is a Steele family heirloom Shelley most recently wore. Since Sebastian is the eldest son, he inherited it and will pass it to his eldest son in time.

Lucky girl!

My thoughts turn to her brother-in-law and My Dom. We've been in our relationship for five months, and it's fantastic. Well, aside from the Vicky Internet Scandal... Sometimes when he sleeps curled around me, I think if our D/s situation can be more. Now listening to Lola, I wonder if Malcolm and I will go further like Lola and Sebastian. Hell, even Roger seems to have won Leonie back.

"Leonie... Hello there... Leonie?"

"Girl! Snap out of it!"

"Oh, don't tease her..."

"See, I knew it! He's blown her mind and her back—"

"Okay, okay! I hear you already!" She cuts into the girls' chatter with a laugh.

All eyes are on her, varying from expressions of concern to smirks.

When I called to invite everyone to my second international fitness retreat, we agreed to make it a Girls' Getaway, too. Time for us to reconnect with our minds, bodies, and friends. Over the seven days, we plan to do just that.

The retreat is at a luxury beachfront resort on Buenguerra Island off the coast of Mozambique in the channel between the country and the Indian Ocean. The island is a haven known for its pristine, white-sand beaches, peaceful vibe, and five-star resorts.

The property we're staying at is the most exclusive with only three cabanas, ten casinhas, and one large villa scattered across eleven acres of beachfront and lush tropical vegetation. The retreat participants and my staff along with the girls secured the entire resort. It's our private oasis.

Lola, Billie, Haley, Blair, and Leonie claimed the villa since it features five large bedrooms with sitting areas, living room, dining room, and kitchenette. The outdoor areas include a pool, deck area with thatched-roof cabana and chaise lounges, plus chaise lounges down by the ocean. It's stunning and tranquil.

I chose a casinhas since I'm working more so than relaxing. Plus, I need more space to meet with my team and for one-on-one sessions with guests. It's just through the palm trees on one of the sandy paths that crisscross the property.

"Spill. You've been mighty quiet about Roger and you…" Billie says as her green eyes flash.

"Right! I know I've been away and busy. But even so," Lola starts. "You can always call me. I am your BFF!"

"Oh, don't pressure her!" Blair says concerned.

"No pressure, but… Do tell!" I join in the laughter.

Leonie smiles at her closest friends. Then takes a sip of her Tipo Tinto R&R. When she sets it down on the side table, we stare at her expectantly.

"I'm in love with the man of my dreams!" She throws her head back and roar. "He's mine, all mine! And I'm all his!"

We holler and stomp our feet.

"Another brother taken so he can get off my back about my love life! Thank you, Leonie! Hooray!" Shouts Haley, pumping her fists into the air as she falls back onto her chaise lounge.

Lola jumps up and grabs Leonie's hands to pull her to stand. They do their happy shimmy dance around the chaises.

"Yeah, Girl! Strut your stuff!" I call out as I fan herself.

Billie jumps up and joins their parade. Soon we form a conga line and weave in and out of the furniture. Then we head out to the beach where we form a circle under the brilliant moonlight and star-filled sky. My girls and I continue to dance around as our laughter carries out over the silent, inky black water.

* * *

"Let us end our practice with three oms together. Inhale through your nose gently, hold it for a heartbeat. Then slowly release your breath back through your nose. Let us begin."

The next morning, I set aside my thoughts on Malcolm and focus on my yoga session.

My entrancing voice guides the students through the last part of the class. We started with breathwork for five minutes to prep us for a vigorous, forty-five-minute flow sequence. As I moved through the poses to demonstrate, my muscles craved the fast-paced tempo. It allowed my body to focus on the asanas and not wander. The ten-minute meditation grounded the students as much as me.

"Namaste. The light in me honors the light in you," I intone when we finish.

We bow to each other with palms pressed together at our heart centers. We remind ourselves of the good energy and intention we set forth in our practice. As we sit up and open our eyes, I beam with happiness. My love of helping others reach their best mental and physical potential shines from my sorrel brown eyes.

Students murmur words of gratitude, then wipe down their mats before they hang them on the wooden racks inside the beachside, open-air pavilion. Some students gather around to glean more advice. Two of my assistants offer adjustments for those who want more instruction.

I glance up and wave at my friends. They wave back before they walk down the steps to the sandy shore. Two other assistants wait to offer frothy shot glasses filled with refreshing juice made from local fruits. The delicious concoctions cool the students down and fill them with energy.

The tasty refreshments have ashwagandha in them. An Ayurvedic herb that many studies show increases energy and reduces stress and anxiety.

I can take my time with the students who remain since the next session for Pilates isn't for another two hours. Once I answer their questions, I stroll along the beach to my villa. The sun glistens on the water between the island and the Mozambique coast. The waves splashing on the sand call to me.

I decide to change into my bikini and go for a swim. It's a good idea and a great way to wash away the sweat from my yoga class. Mind made up,. I jog the rest of the way and yank my sports bra over my head as I rush into my bedroom. I ditch the skimpy yoga shorts and stride to the wardrobe. Snatching the first bathing suit I can reach, I step into the bottoms as I head to the door. Then slide them up over my hips. I don't worry about a top since we're on the secluded side of the island—no paparazzi to snap unwanted photos for Malcolm to go berserk about. I zip out the door, down to the beach, and dive into the first wave of the warm tropical Indian Ocean.

"HOW DID YOU LIKE THE RETREAT?" I ask as the girls and I sit at the outdoor dining table surrounded by fragrant torches.

The other participants left yesterday morning. We stayed two extra days to spend some quality time together off of the mats. Yesterday we took a long hike through the verdant patchwork of forests on the island. Then had a rejuvenating swim in one of the crystal-clear freshwater lakes.

Now, we're eating a delectable dinner of flavorful local favorites prepared by a chef on the outdoor grill and cooktop. The aroma is mouthwatering. I sip my Tipo Tinto R&R and nibble on a flaky chamussa. The appetizer is just enough to keep us sated until he presents the main dishes.

"You did such a superb job, Starr! I can't wait for the next one," Billie answers as she clinks glasses with me.

"Indeed! I thought nothing could top your first one on Fijian Laucala Island last year. That private paradise is surreal," Lola chimes in.

"It was the best I've ever been on! Fantastic!" Haley says as she rises to give Starr a standing ovation.

"Sign me up for all of them! I feel incredible, thank you very much!" Leonie exclaims.

"Me, too!" Blair says as she raises her glass. "A toast… Here's to good friends, good loves, and good times!"

Everyone cheers and clinks glasses. Lola pauses and peers at me.

"What's the latest on your conversations with Malcolm?"

I choke on my Tipo Tinto.

Damn! Is Lola a mind reader or what?!

I wonder if she's prying because she knows something I don't or at least I haven't admitted to the girls yet. Unsure, I avoid Lola's probing gaze. I shift in my chair and pretend to straighten the napkin on my lap.

Lola is relentless.

"Well?" She demands.

I think back to the conversation Malcolm and I had the morning after they photographed him with Vicky. Although he was apologetic and made my body vibrate with climax after climax, he had to ruin the afterglow.

He told me snarkily, "That's what can happen during a night out, even a Girls' Night Out."

He couldn't let it go how it irritated him I went out with my girls the month before despite him not wanting me to go. I snapped back how I didn't end up in bed with any of the guys who flirted with me. Of course he blew his Alpha male top. We argued, and I called him an arrogant control freak.

That was a couple of weeks ago…

I clear my throat and return Lola's gaze.

Defiantly I lift my chin as I respond, "Malcolm Steele is an arrogant, self-focused cretin!"

Blair, Billie, and Leonie gape at my heated reaction. Haley covers her ears, not wanting to hear such things about her older brother.

They're astonished since I'm no longer the normally quiet calm, namaste, om, center your mind friend. Now I'm flustered completely. Their gazes dart between Lola and me in shock. The question, what the hell did Malcolm do to Starr files their faces.

Lola bursts out laughing. Her last sip of Tipo Tinto comes out on a snort. She pulls back from the table, doubling over in glee. The sight is too comical. They can't help but join in—even me.

Once Lola gathers herself, wiping tears from the corners of her eyes, she straightens. She lifts her left hand and waggles her fingers. The ice skating rink on full blast.

"That's the same thing I said about his doppelgänger brother, Captain Caveman… Now look at me, my friend!"

My mouth falls open. I look just as stunned as the rest of the girls. But Lola just keeps giggling. She definitely knows something I'm clueless about. When they question her, Lola shakes her head and sips her drink, laughing to herself.

"So, who's next of my boys to walk down the aisle? My guess is Roger. But after him, who do you think, darling?"

Sebastian chuckles. Harris and I gape at each other. Our mother Shelley smirks wickedly.

The Steele Matriarch—the true boss of our family—is a striking woman in her mid-fifties with shoulder-length, wavy black hair and expressive brown eyes. At only five feet, six inches, we tower over our mother. But her feisty New Yorker personality doesn't allow us or anyone to bully her.

Hence Harris and I know we have to give Shelley some kind of answer. We use telepathy to spar over who speaks first. But they don't call me *The Enforcer* for nothing.

"Mom... I'm only twenty-nine years old. I have my entire life ahead of me," Harris says in defeat, having caved to my unspoken command.

Her smirk deepens as she leans forward across the dining room table.

"'Only twenty-nine?' You say. I married your father when I was twenty, and I had you and your sister—the youngest of my five children—at twenty-seven. So, who do you think, darling?" She finishes as she swings her gaze towards our father again.

Morgan smiles at her lovingly. He may be an Alpha Dom, but he melts for his wife and sub.

With his strong genes, all of his children resemble him with varying shades of gray eyes, wavy ebony hair, and height. His sons are splitting images of him standing well over six feet. While his daughter is a stunning female version at five feet, eight inches tall. Although at sixty-six years old and still fit, his thick ebony hair is more salt and pepper.

"Sweetheart, when I met you nothing and no one could prevent me from claiming you as mine. Sebastian felt the same with Lola. I agree Roger recognizes Leonie as his finally. When Malcolm and Harris meet their true loves, we can be certain age will not matter," our father responds as he holds her dainty, manicured hand between both of his sizable palms.

Well, damn.

I sit back in my chair and stare at our parents. We know it was love at first sight. But every time they express their enduring love for one another, it's the most beautiful thing I've ever seen.

Aside from My Angel…

My Angel who I pissed off after being a bit of a jerk

about going out and what can happen. She was none too pleased with my comment. She told me so without holding back her disdain. Then proceeded to tell me she's busy with her upcoming fitness retreat and wouldn't have time to see me.

I returned to New York after a few more days in LA and a stopover in Las Vegas for business. That was almost two weeks ago.

True to her word, Starr couldn't spare me but a few minutes a day before she flew off to Mozambique. She's there with her clients and her girls, including my brothers' true loves. They're extending their stay after the retreat participants leave for a Girls' Getaway.

My only consolation is them being on the small island of Buenguerra off the coast with few people aside from the hotel guests. It's doubtful My Angel will meet the man of her dreams with limited options available. At least I hope she doesn't, or I'll be fucked.

The hair on the back of my neck tingles. I glance up to find my mother watching me intently—Roger inherited her reach-into-your-soul stare. I swallow.

"Malcolm?" She asks with a raised eyebrow.

My eyes skitter to Sebastian for some help.

He sits back in his chair and steeples his fingers beneath his chin. His shoulders shake with held-back laughter, dove gray eyes sparkle.

I shift my gaze to Harris, and he offers a devious grin.

Fuckers.

My last hope to run interference, I glance at my father. His expression of answer your mother doesn't help me in any way. I sigh inwardly and drag my eyes to face my mother's inquisition.

She raises her eyebrow higher and cocks her head.

"Mom, you know how busy I am with STEELE and my sports. How can I have time for a serious relationship?" I ask.

Then my stomach churns.

How the hell can I deny my attraction for My Angel? And to my mother?

But I'm just not ready to admit out loud it's more than satisfying my Dom and my sexual needs. Especially since we ended our last time together angrily.

Honestly, I've never been in a relationship where emotion outside of a BDSM scene plays a part. I'm out of my depth.

My mother stares, unblinking.

I squirm.

Fuck. Am I thirteen years old again or what?

"Fine. When you're ready to share your newfound love…" Shelley says mysteriously, then slices into her *Steak Fromage.*

I steal a glance at Baz.

He grins behind his glass of Petrus.

Fucker.

"OKAY, fess up, Malcolm. How's it going with Ms. Knight?"

Baz asks as he raises the Baccarat crystal snifter to his mouth and sips the Rémy Martin Louis XIII Cognac.

He, Harris, and I sit around the fire pit on the terrace

off the living room of my penthouse in The STEELE Tower New York. We retired here after dinner at our parents' duplex on the top two floors. My kid brother and I needed a drink after our mother's probing.

Baz swirls the reddish-grayish-brown liquid, watching the flames from the fire brighten its color as they flicker behind the crystal glass. He lifts his gaze back to me and cocks his head questioningly.

We stare at one another. Once again holding out on who speaks first. This time I cave. I need Sebastian's advice.

"She's driving me crazy, bro," I say with a sigh.

Then lean forward and place my snifter on the ledge of the fire pit. I run my fingers through my hair. A tug snaps pain to my scalp. My senses sharpen. Focus returns. I need answers.

"You never had more than a one-night stand, maybe two nights with someone at a LEVELS before Lola. I've only had D/s contracted relationships. How the hell do you handle the emotions outside of the sex? What do you do when Lola defies you? And why the fuck do I want to tie Starr to my bed, claim her, and mark her for every male to see?!"

I finish with another yank on my hair. Then throw back the rest of my Rémy.

"Bro… You. Are. Fucked!!!" Harris chortles.

Baz snickers and leans forward to pin me with his gaze.

"As I remember, you and Harris called me a 'Lost Puppy' not too long ago… You even made goo-goo eyes and clutched your hearts. Your loud guffaws filled the jet's cabin," he says pointedly. "You know what I did? I cringed, but couldn't care less. You know why? *That's my girl*, I thought to myself. And guess what? Now Lola is. All. Mine."

He flicks his gaze to Harris and adds, "When Dad told you to cut your shit and suggested you settle down, the two of you zipped your lips. Harris, you checked your newfangled gadget. And you, my lovesick brother, preoccupied yourself with refilling your drink."

Baz gestures to my snifter and holds his empty one up.

"Now go get that expensive bottle you cherish and bring it out here. You're going to need it for the knowledge I'm about to impart to you," Baz finishes with a wicked chuckle.

Dutifully—and gratefully—I rise and do as he bid. It's going to be a long night.

LATER IN THE early hours of the morning, as the sun's rays brighten the star-filled sky, I lie in bed and replay a key point Sebastian made:

Yeah, I get where you're coming from. At first in the back of my mind a niggle reminded me I was a wimp for allowing more feelings where there should be none. I shook it off and moved forward.

It's exactly my situation. I'll just have to shake it off, too and let our relationship progress organically.

I close my eyes and take a cleansing breath before I contemplate Sebastian's lesson:

Apologize. Period. Then listen while Starr says whatever's on her mind. Apologize. Listen some more. Apologize. Again. And again. Until she has no more to say. Then let my body express my true feelings better than any words as I make love to My Angel.

With that in mind, I roll over to grab my mobile off of the nightstand. A quick check of the time shows it's 5 a.m. here and 11 a.m. in Mozambique. Starr will be teaching according to the retreat schedule. Perfect, I can leave a voicemail.

Hi, Angel. I apologize. Let's talk when you return. I miss you.

Hi, Angel. I apologize. Let's talk when you return. I miss you.

"You will wear my collar to show your status as a partnered sub—my sub—at all times. You will obey me in all sexual interactions unless you want all play to end with the use of your safeword, *tantric*. For a Dominant to place a collar on a submissive equals the pair's commitment to their D/s relationship. On some levels as important as a wedding ring to a marriage. Do you understand, Little One?"

A giggle would bubble out of my mouth at Malcolm's 180-degree change from his gentle voicemail a week ago to his authoritative statement now if it wasn't hanging open.

The sight of the beautiful, intricate platinum lacework covered in tiny sparkly diamonds leaves me speechless. So delicate it looks as though it could break in his sizable hands as he lifts it in front of me and puts it around my neck. The soft click of the closure makes me blink and lift my gaze from the collar to his intense gray eyes in the mirror's reflection.

I trace my fingertips lightly over the exquisite craftsmanship, then place them atop his hands resting on my shoulders. My heart slams against my rib cage at the enormity of the situation. Am I ready for such a commitment? With Malcolm Steele, no less?

"Yes, Sir," I whisper.

"I custom ordered this piece for you. I want to capture your beauty, elegance, fragility, and strength. Never have I given my collar to any sub, Little One. Do you understand the significance?" My Dom says as we continue to stare at one another in the mirror.

"Yes, Sir," I respond.

My Dom turns me to face him and lifts my chin with his forefinger. His eyes pierce mine as he seeks confirmation.

"Do you have any other words for me, Little One?" He asks after a moment.

I bite my lower lip and shift my gaze. My mind runs through different scenarios: what happens if we break up; how will people react to my collar, particularly Vicky; how will this commitment change me, us. Hell, it's been six months, but is it too much too soon?

The silence looms between us as my thoughts run amok.

Malcolm waits patiently without a word or reactions. In fact, he appears to hold his breath.

Is he as nervous as me?

My gaze returns to his, and it's my turn to study him.

His gorgeous face has a hint of concern despite his attempt to remain neutral. It's in the pinch around his eyes and the tension in his jaw.

I go so far as to guess he's nervous I'll turn him down, even though he closed the collar securely around my neck. The part about the marriage comparison has me anxious. I've read in my Google searches the importance of a collar, so I don't take Malcolm's gesture lightly. Add in he's given none of his many subs a collar makes it an even bigger deal.

My insides warm. Malcolm Steele wants me enough to collar me, and with one designed specifically for me? Well, hot damn!

He opens his mouth to speak.

But I place my fingertips against them and shake my head. I slip my arms around his neck and meld our bodies together. I need the connection with him, to feel his heat and to gain his strength.

On an exhale, I let go of the negativity and inhale the positive direction we're taking as a couple. With my lips pressed to his, I murmur words of consent and understanding. With confidence, I agree to being Malcolm Steele's submissive to his dominant.

WE REACH a set of heavy wooden double doors with two large, iron circular pulls opened by a man and a woman scantily clad in black leather strips and collars. They incline their heads at My Dom as he leads me by the delicate platinum chain clipped to my collar's ring past them. My jaw drops again.

The Cellar—LEVELS New York's BDSM dungeon—looms ahead of us.

My eyes scan the expansive, grand hall, austere in design. A multi-beamed high ceiling; cobblestone floors; brick walls; lighting that resembles flickering torches in brackets on the walls and in metal stands scattered around the room; an assortment of what looks like Medieval torture devices placed in clusters. My gaze skitters from one area to another. An older man cuffed to one of the several St. Andrew's Crosses, his head thrown back in pure ecstasy. His engorged dick eagerly sucked by a younger man on his knees. A woman in a swing, her thighs glistening with her pussy juices and stretched wide to accommodate the large man standing between them, aligning her core to his massive cock. Several men and women attached to hooks hanging from the ceiling in varied positions being whipped by Doms and Dommes with canes, floggers, and paddles extending from their hands. Still others lead naked subs by leashes while they crawl on their hands and knees to one of the partitioned rooms for a bit of privacy. Here and there voyeurs stand watching, mesmerized by the decadent sexual activities.

The sight has my throbbing pussy so wet I can feel my juices slipping down to coat my trembling inner thighs. The aroma of my arousal wafts around me to fill my nose and to join with all the other sex-induced scents. I shift on my feet, embarrassed by my immediate reaction to the scenes before me. My first time at a LEVELS club does not disappoint.

A gentle tug to my collar alerts me to My Dom's

forward movement. I trail behind him, taking in our surroundings discreetly.

Several pairs of eyes peer at me from head to toe.

I push my shoulders back and lift my ample chest as I strut behind My Dom in my Lola's Coterie playsuit. Yes, darlings. Stare at my banging body as triple strands of black strips with tiny rose gold studs cross over cone-shaped pasties to caress my bountiful breasts. Two additional sets of strips wind from my back and up from my sheer-thong-covered crotch to connect at two rose gold rings on either side of my narrow waist. My long legs end in black suede, sky-high stilettos. I'm bound.

Many of those eyes stay riveted on my diamond collar as it flashes its brilliance in the golden torchlight, bared by my upswept curls. Numerous women gape openly as their eyes bounce from my neck to My Dom's face. Surprise colors their cheeks red. Jealousy darkens their eyes to green.

I smirk at the realization they must be prior acquaintances…

"Well Steele, looks like you met your match… finally?"

I peek around My Dom to encounter a devastatingly handsome man with sapphire blue eyes, jet-black hair, and a cleft chin. He smirks at My Dom, then flicks his gaze to me with a devilish grin.

Heat spreads over my exposed skin.

"Keep your eyes in their sockets, Reilly," My Dom snarls.

The stunning man raises his hands, palms outward in surrender. The smile vanishes from his face.

"Whoa, Steele. No disrespect. You and I have shared before…" He responds no longer undressing me further with his jewel eyes.

"True. But note my collar adorns my submissive's neck, Reilly. She is a dazzling beauty. But you cannot miss my obvious claim," My Dom responds, then nods his head as he leads me away.

I dare not glance back even though my skin prickles with goosebumps. Without a doubt, Reilly still watches me. Instead, I add an extra sway to my hips and strut along, pleased by My Dom's possessive behavior.

He circulates in the room, proud to show me off to those present. Occasionally, we stop and he introduces me to other members, many well-known in business or celebrity circles. No one appears uncomfortable at being seen in a BDSM dungeon. Many have partners or subs. Others voyeurs, satisfied to observe and not partake in the bacchanalia.

The hedonistic atmosphere with the melodic thrum of sensual music and satisfied cries as the backdrop to intense sexual play attracts people with kinks who want to indulge in a safe, VIP environment. The air heavy with the scent of perfume, cologne, and sex entices everyone.

By the time My Dom holds back the blood-red velvet curtain to reveal an intimate alcove, I'm impressed suitably with my observations of LEVELS and cannot wait to partake.

"This way, Little One," My Dom's deep baritone voice glides over my skin like a caress as he scans my body while I pass him. He licks his lips appreciatively.

Those on my face press together as my lower lips ripple with need. I. Want. Him. Now.

"Ah, ah, ah," he chastises as he drapes my collar's chain over my shoulders, then places his hands on top of them from behind with downward pressure. "On your hands and knees, ass high, head low. Crawl to the spanking bench over there."

Without a second thought, I lower to position gracefully. The cold cobblestones bite at my knees, but I maintain my form, eager to please My Dom. A growl from behind encourages me to add an extra oomph to my movements. A pat to my bouncing ass rewards my efforts.

"Good girl, Little One. You please me with your natural poise," he croons. "A true submissive."

An ease from years of experience allows him to position then strap me to the blood-red leather padded bench quickly. Once he secures my ankles in the suede-lined leather restraints, My Dom strides to my head and squats to encase my wrists. As he rises to his full height, the massive bulge in his custom-tailored trousers align with my vision.

Yes, please!

He chuckles wickedly in response to my tongue darting out to lick my lips hungrily.

"Would you like a taste, Naughty Girl?" He asks as he strokes the tented front of his pants.

His dick twitches, and I moan.

In a blur of movement, he unbuckles his belt, pops open the button, and drags the zipper down. His pants and black silk boxer briefs drop from his narrow hips to pool at his Oxfords-shod feet. Goliath springs free.

Did I say, yes? I mean, hell to the yes, yes, yes!!!

Greedily, I stick my tongue out like a snake to savor the air full of his musky, masculine odor. I whine at the sight of his thick fingers wrapping around his length. He covers his dick and strokes it from root to mushroom tip. His Prince Albert piercing's balls jewelry glint in the low light.

"Do you deserve to suck my cock, Naughty Girl?" He asks as he tugs his turgid staff. Veins run along its surface. Velvet covered steel.

"Yes, Sir… I promise to be good," I purr.

My Dom taps his bulbous cock head against my lips. One thrust, and he's at the back of my throat, heading south.

Gag reflex kicks in, but I fight it off with a deep breath through my nose. I offer a silent prayer of thanks for my many hours of pranayama practice.

"Ah, yes, Naughty Girl, your promise holds true," My Dom grunts as he falls into a rhythm.

His hips snap back and forth—in deep and fast; out slow to the tip. The girth stretches my mouth as he glides over my willing tongue. Soon my jaw aches and drool spills from the corners onto the bench.

"You will suck me, Naughty Girl. Every. Single. Inch," he hisses. "Suck. Me. Well."

His hands grip the back of my head to hold me still as he plunders my throat. One last thrust, and his dick hardens further as it swells with his semen. Copious amounts spill down my throat in spurts as My Dom fills my belly.

I moan around his girth. My pussy creams.

His grunts and groans end as his body shudders from his toe-curling release. My Dom strokes my scalp to soothe the pain from his tugs on my hair.

So fucking worth it!

He reaches down to pull his briefs and trousers back in place. Then strides around to my rear.

I tremble in anticipation.

Pressure to the soaked gusset of my thong makes me yelp.

"All of this wetness from you blowing me, Little One?" He asks as he rubs his nose against the silk. On an inhale he continues, "Mmm mmm such a delectable aroma. Shall I have a taste, too?"

My whimpered response makes him chuckle. Then I yelp again from the pressure of my thong being ripped from my pussy. A glance over my shoulder reveals the tattered material on the floor and My Dom's face between my butt cheeks.

I buck against his mouth as he laps at my seam.

THWACK. THWACK. THWACK.

Oh. Oh. FUCK!!!

My mind takes a moment to catch up to the pain that replaces the pleasure. My globes jiggle under a flogger as its blood-red suede fringes smack my exposed ass. I grip the legs of the spanking bench as I jerk from the unexpected spanking.

"What was your first lesson in BDSM play, Naughty Girl," My Dom thunders between strikes.

I gulp and wrack my brain for the answer. My delayed response results in another volley of well-aimed smacks to the most sensitive areas on my butt and thighs.

FUCK!!!

"Hold my position no matter what unless I want to safeword," I cry out in anguish as I still my body despite the flogger's fury.

My Dom is mad at me…

Immediately he drops the offensive implement, drops to his knees, and laps at my inner thighs where my juices pour from my throbbing pussy. Grunts and growls fill the alcove as he feasts on my essence.

When my legs tremble from holding back my orgasm, My Dom returns to my punishment. His renewed efforts force me back from the edge even as they bring me closer to the orgasm of life.

I clench my eyes shut and my fists around the legs of the bench as I try to rein in my impending release.

"Aaaahhh…. Sssir… I… I… PLEASE!!!" I beg when the sensation gets to be too much.

The flogger hits the floor with a clatter again. My Dom grips my hips and slams home. He's so deep I can feel the balls of his piercing brush my cervix.

We groan in unison.

"Yeeesss, Sir!!!" I scream. My cries join those of the other members in the throes of erotic ecstasy.

"Who do you belong to, My Angel?!?!?!"

So caught up in the waves of my orgasm, I miss

Malcolm calling me by my name. But I respond in kind unconsciously, already too far gone to analyze his slip in name choice.

"You, Malcolm… Only… You!!!" I wail as I lose myself to the bliss of subspace.

"You look beautiful, Angel. A breath of fresh air on this spring evening. But I have one more thing to add."

I spin around to face Malcolm.

The voluminous, ruffled midi skirt of my silk-organza midi dress floats around my bare calves. Its pattern features painterly camellias that symbolize eternal love and beauty, perfect for the season. The dress stresses my curves with a ruched sash to nip in at the waist and boning on the sides of the gathered bodice to support the strapless neckline. A pair of flesh-tone mules and a Bottega Veneta clutch with my curls in a loose topknot and natural makeup finish my look.

Tonight we have dinner with Malcolm's parents for the first time since we started our D/s relationship. Tomorrow morning we fly with them to France for Leonie's graduation from the Paris American Academy.

I adore Morgan and Shelley, having spent time with

them for Lola and Sebastian's wedding. But that was as Lola's close friend, not their son's submissive... My armpits tingle at the thought. I pray they don't realize my collar is a *collar*. Perhaps they'll assume it's a choker necklace as others who have complimented me on it.

Well, all except for Vicky.

Her jaw hit the ground when she saw my day wear collar—platinum mesh with a diamond-pavé letter S in the center. Another student bumped into her from behind when Vicky stopped dead in her tracks upon entering my private studio. Her eyes widened in surprise, then narrowed into angry slits in seconds. She stormed from the room knocking past the other students leaving a wake of shocked faces and gasps.

Vicky's reaction confirmed my suspicions of her being aware of my relationship with Malcolm. Hell, the S could represent my initial, but not to Vicky. She'd dropped hints over the last couple of months. Prodding for my whereabouts when I took time off to go with Malcolm and the guys for a few of their extreme sports trips. Vicky never said it outright, and I never validated her assumption.

Fortunately, she's off filming in London for the next few weeks.

Good riddance to bad rubbish!

I smile at Malcolm.

He's so striking in his bespoke single-breasted three-button linen suit and chocolate brown suede, tasseled loafers. His tousled ebony hair hangs longer to curl around his ears—the perfect length to tug as he eats me out.

Freshly shaved skin replaces the five o'clock shadow from earlier.

I reach up and caress the softness along his jaw, and Malcolm smiles then turns his head to kiss my palm. His dove gray eyes shine as he takes my left wrist in his fingers.

Cool metal wraps around it.

"Oh!" I declare.

A bracelet that matches my collar coils around my wrist. The diamond-covered platinum lace sparkles. I touch it gently, then bring my fingertips to my collar as I glance up from beneath my eyelashes at My Dom.

"Thank you, Sir," I whisper. "It's spectacular."

He nuzzles my neck above his collar and kisses the sensitive area.

"You are more than welcome, Little One," My Dom murmurs. "It is our one-month anniversary, and you have been an exceptionally good girl."

I tilt my head to give him more access to my neck and whimper when he nips it as he smacks my ass.

"Temptress, I know what you are up to pressing your lush body against me. We must go now," My Dom says with one more swat.

I pout, but follow him to his penthouse's elevator with a grin. There's always later…

"Starr! What a surprise! Malcolm didn't tell us you were coming."

I smile at Shelley's excitement as she pulls me into her warm embrace. Not concerned with the other patrons at the bar for Daniel, she claps her hands after she hugs Malcolm, too. Her eyes dance with glee as she gazes at us.

"Good to see you with Malcolm, Starr. However, now I owe my wife a spa trip," Morgan says genially as he kisses my cheeks.

"Yes! You see, my husband didn't believe me when I told him I saw sparks between the two of you at Sebastian and Lola's wedding. Mother's intuition. Mmm hmmm..." Shelley adds with a chuckle as she taps her neck.

I blush and risk a glance at Malcolm, wondering if he noticed her reference to my diamond-covered evening collar. But he beams at his parents, completely unaffected.

He places his hand on the small of my back and guides me after his parents to our table. After Malcolm helps me into my chair, he sits and pulls my hand into his, resting on his muscular thigh. His thumb brushes over my bracelet as he chats with his parents.

We enjoy a lovely dinner with lively discussions on our travels, wellness, and STEELE Foundation. Shelley runs their family's philanthropic foundation that builds and manages attractive, affordable housing for urban, lower-income families. The name is a play on the house foundation, being strong and supportive like steel. She asks me to offer a custom fitness retreat for the annual gala's silent auction.

By the time the evening ends, I no longer feel anxious about their thoughts on me being their son's sub. During the meal, I notice the exchanges between Morgan and Shelley and surmise he's an Alpha Dom, and she's his sub.

Their love and ability to have a marriage that incorporates D/s makes me wonder about Malcolm and me. Perhaps I shouldn't fear how much I love BDSM and falling for my Dom lover.

Later in bed, Malcolm takes all of my fears away when he makes love to me until the sun rises and then in the shower. After we head to Manhattan's West 30th Street Heliport before boarding Morgan's Gulfstream G650 private jet at Meridian Teterboro, the deluxe FBO in New Jersey.

Sebastian and Harris grin like the Cheshire Cat when I follow Shelley aboard the jet.

No sooner than the pilot clears us to move about the cabins, Lola and Haley pull me to the rear to question me about Malcolm and of course my day wear collar. Although Lola is Baz's sub, she doesn't wear one of her collars at all times as Malcolm requires of me. Always the Rebel!

"So I see… I told you in Mozambique. Didn't I? Never doubt me, my friend!" Lola laughs as she claps her hands.

"Feel better now?" Haley asks with concern since I was none too pleased with her brother two months ago.

I grin wider than Baz and Harris combined as I nod vigorously.

We giggle like schoolgirls as I fill them in on the details —during some Haley covers her ears and hums. Shelley joins us, and we spend the rest of the flight talking.

When we land at Le Bourget Airport outside of Paris, we separate into chauffeured Mercedes-Benz G-Wagens. Lola, Sebastian, Shelley, and Morgan head to The STEELE Tower Paris for their respective penthouses. Malcolm,

Haley, Harris, and I go to STEELE Place Vendôme where we'll stay in their three largest suites.

Malcolm and I spend the afternoon being tourists. The driver takes us to our favorite spots from the top of the Eiffel Tower to the Mona Lisa at the Louvre to Notre-Dame. By the time we return to our suite, we collapse from all the walking and stomachs full of pastries and *glace* from Berthillon, the famous ice cream shop near the Cathedral.

"WAKE UP, Little One. We must go now."

I raise my arms above my head and arch my back as I stretch languorously. The silk sheet slips from my naked breasts.

My Dom lowers his head and laps at my right nipple. Then brings his lips to lick at my mouth voraciously. He nips my lower lip and tugs it as he rises. It pops from his teeth, and I whimper.

"Up. Dress in the lingerie hanging in the walk-in closet. Then met me in the salon," he commands before he strides fully clothed from the bedroom.

My heart races as I jump from the bed.

A black silk corset with voluminous, long past-the-fingertips, flared sleeves that feature French lace cut-outs at the mid arms and cuffs displayed on a satin padded hanger greets me. Next to it hangs a black sheer tulle and leavers lace panels balconette bra with matching briefs. Black suede fuck-me pumps sit below the gorgeous Lola's Coterie set.

"Sir, kindly bind me in," I purr as I sashay seductively towards My Dom.

His eyes darken to obsidian as they rake over my sexily clad body.

I pivot in front of him.

Calloused pads of his fingers ghost over my skin as he collects the strings and tightens the corset. Then he smacks my ass, covered by sheer tulle.

I gasp and spin around.

He chuckles wickedly and drapes a floor-length, hooded black silk cape over my shoulders. He bows the ties at my throat, mid-section, and mid-thigh. My Dom takes my hand in his and leads me from the salon.

"Bienvenue à LEVELS Paris."

The buxom blonde says throatily as My Dom and I approach the greeter station.

This LEVELS in the 7th Arrondissement Palais-Bourbon Le Faubourg inhabits the former Parisian home of a pampered courtesan to a French king. The magnificent *maison* on a tree-lined street sits behind duplicates of the original double carriage doors and features a spacious interior courtyard. They host grand soirees during the warm-weather months under the stars and strings of fairy lights.

The layout—the same as the other two locations—spreads across seven levels. As with each club, the Sky Lounge offers a view of a nearby landmark. With Paris, it's the grand Eiffel Tower resplendent in lights at night. The beauty and history of the property takes my breath away.

I feel like a pampered courtesan in my corset and lingerie. Of course, My Dom made the best selection for tonight's scene. How apropos. Not to mention the jewelry and the trousseau of Lola's Coterie lingerie and loungewear he's purchased for me over the last seven months.

Spoiled much? Abso-fucking-lutely!!! And I love it!

My Dom unfastens my cape and passes it to the greeter who gives him a claim ticket he pockets in his trousers. Then he dons the gold enamel bracelet to signal he's a part-nered Dom, clips the platinum chain to my collar's ring, and leads me the doors for Peepshow.

We pass the seating alcoves, primary stage, mini-stages, and performance rooms. He stops at the bar and requests a mocktail. Once the bartender serves My Dom his drink—the faux Scotch shimmers like amber in the low lighting—he tugs my chain and strides to an alcove across from the primary stage.

He sits and tosses a pillow on the floor, then beckons for me to kneel facing away from him between his spread legs. The clink of ice against crystal sounds behind me as he sips his drink. Idly, he toys with my chain.

The lights dim, and a spotlight appears on the stage. A hush descends on those gathered. A tall, lean Dom steps into the center of the light. He bows to the crowd and his sandy blond hair brushes across his face. When he stands, he holds his hand out. A beautiful Chinese woman glides across the stage. Her silky curtain of waist-length hair shines like lacquer.

She places her dainty hand in his sizable one, and he draws her to him with her back pressed to his front. Completely naked except for the colorful dragon tattoo that winds from her ankle around her calf, thigh, and hip to end with its mouth open at her bare mound. The erotic exotic imagery is a work of art.

Her Dom whispers in her ear, and she trembles. Her pert breasts judder and her porcelain décolletage flushes crimson.

So entranced by the sight of the pair, I startle when My Dom brushes his icy wet lips against the heated flesh where my neck meets my shoulder. He trails open-mouthed kisses along my shoulder as he cups my breasts. His fingers rub my peaked nipples through the filmy material.

I sigh and lean back against him, tilting my head to the side.

The Dom onstage cuffs his sub to the wooden St Andrew's Cross. He checks her comfort, then moves to the table laden with BDSM implements. He chooses a peacock feather and a studded glove before he returns to his wide-eyed sub.

"Ah, a sensory demonstration. Perfect," My Dom croons devilishly against the delicate shell of my ear.

He unclasps the front closure of my bra and tweaks my nipples until they're fully aroused. A rustling precipitates a sharp bite, then another.

"Oh! Fuck!" I hiss. Then gasp when I peek down to find diamonds pavé in platinum clamps dangling from my heavy breasts.

A tug to the connecting chain, and I realize My Dom attached the nipple clamps to my collar.

Fuck!!!

"Excellent, Little One. Do you enjoy your new jewelry?"

He murmurs as he tugs again with one hand and places the other over my throat to tip my head back to his shoulder.

Before I can respond, he covers my gaping mouth with his and kisses me until my toes curl in my stilettos.

A strangled cry of pleasure from the stage draws My Dom's attention. He turns my head back in the demonstration's direction.

The sub writhes on the Cross, flexing her fists with her mouth open as she begs her Dom to allow her climax. He's on his knees before her, pinching her clit with the studded glove while he licks her swollen pussy.

Her wails rise above those of the members who like My Dom seek their pleasure induced by hers.

My Dom rends my briefs from my body. I cry out from the pinch of the silk against my skin before it gives way. His hand slides between my thighs to pinch my clit.

I'm soaked. His fingers slip in my wetness as they dart in and out of my pussy while his thumb pad rubs my clit in a circular motion.

A strangled cry falls from my lips when another bite grips my body. I glance down to find another clamp. This time on my clit with a chain connecting it to the others at a circle below my breasts. Another tug and another wail, followed by a wicked chuckle at my ear.

"Stand, Little One. Show your jewelry to me," My Dom commands with a tug.

I rise—not as poised as usual—and turn to face him.

Shadows play over his fine face, but his eyes glow with carnal lust.

"Beautiful," he breathes.

He leans forward and cups my ass. His full lips wrap around my distended clit. He suckles it while he squeezes my fleshy globes.

My legs quiver. But I try to hold position even though my knees jiggle like jelly, not firm enough to keep me upright. I want to melt into an orgasmic puddle at his feet.

"Aaahhh… Mmmmmm… Sir, please!" I beg just as the sub onstage screams from her long-awaited climax.

Spurred on by her wails, My Dom doubles his ministrations. He adds a finger to my pussy and moves it around until he rubs my G-spot.

My legs bow.

Quickly he removes the digit and presses it to my puckered hole.

My legs give way like the muscles in my rear passage.

He puts one of my thighs over his shoulder and braces me with a hand on my opposite hip. He preoccupies his other hand with thrusting in my bottom hole.

Fingers from the hand on my hip tug my chain, and I wail. The finger in my ass slides out and reaches up to free my nipples, then down to release my clit.

Stars dance before my eyes as the blood rushes to the sensitive areas just as My Dom impales me on his turgid length. The thick invasion pushes me over the edge, and I cum, screaming his name over and over.

His grunts and groans fill the surrounding air along with the scent of our sex. He holds my hips still and thrusts up into my tight pussy faster and faster. A final brutal stroke, and Malcolm roars his thick, hot release deep inside of my pussy. My name like a prayer of gratitude on his lips.

He pulls my torso against his powerful chest, binding us together tighter than the stays of my corset while we drift in a state of sheer rhapsody.

"I want you. I crave you."

Malcolm's hoarse whisper—barely audible—floats to my ears, still ringing from the pleasure we shared.

I bury my face in the side of his neck and sigh, too consumed by him to respond with words. My body speaks for me.

And it says, *"I love you, Malcolm Steele."*

It's been two weeks since Leonie's graduation dinner scare. The situation shocked everyone, and we closed ranks as the Steele clan does to protect its family members. I remained in Paris with my parents and siblings to offer support to Roger and Leonie. However, Starr returned to Beverly Hills after a week. It disappointed her to leave, but she had business to attend to in person. Whereas I worked from STEELE Paris.

Now, I can't wait to see My Angel. And to show her off at the opening gala for LEVELS Beverly Hills.

Our nights at the Paris club brought us closer, along with my collar around her neck. She trusts me and commits herself to me as I do with her—for us.

I never thought I would find someone I want to be with longer than a contract stated. Before My Angel left, we discussed how we no longer need a contract since we're officially a couple. I'm not ready to put a ring on it like my brothers. But with My Angel, I want more.

The STEELE Rodeo Drive's Sikorsky helicopter dropped Sebastian, Lola, Harris, Haley, and me atop the roof of The STEELE Tower Los Angeles. They're staying at the hotel's Penthouse Suites while they're in LA for the club's opening.

I had one of the hotel's drivers take me to my Sunset Strip penthouse where My Angel waits for me. The gleam in her sorrel brown eyes let me know I made the right decision to give the entry codes to her. Another step in our official status.

In return, My Angel told me she'll have a set of keys and a gate opener ready for me. Although I already told Harris to up the security on her mansion while he's here. Who uses keys anymore? I'll let her know, then soothe her protests if necessary with a spanking...

"Lucy? I'm home!" I call out à la Desi Arnaz when I step into the foyer of my penthouse.

No answer. Not a sound.

With a frown, I check my mobile to reread the text message My Angel sent to me earlier.

See you soon, Sir...

Okay. So where is she?

I shoot off the question. Immediately the three dots appear as she types her response.

Meet me on the rooftop...

A grin spreads across my face at her reference to the Sophie B. Hawkins song. I race to the stairs and take them three at a time. A week is way too long!

I skid to a stop.

Fuck. Me.

My Angel sits on her haunches kneeling on a white pillow with her palms up on her thighs spread to present her shiny wet pussy to me. The swollen nubbin of her clit protrudes from her folds. Her chestnut-colored skin shimmers gold in the warm sun from the rich chocolate oil coating her body. I sniff the air and scent tiare blossom, white frangipani, ylang-ylang, and vanilla. My beauty transports me to the islands of Tahiti.

What a treat…

As I stalk towards My Angel, her D-cup chest rises and falls with her excited breaths. My pulse quickens. Erotic energy crackles between us.

I place the tip of my index finger beneath her chin. When our eyes meet, her pupils dilate and her mouth parts on a sigh. I want to ravish her.

Upward pressure from my finger brings her to her feet. Gracefully, My Angel rises to stand in all her naked glory before me. Only my collar touches her skin.

My cock punches against my tracksuit pants.

"Hello, Sir—"

I move my fingers to her lips and shake my head. No D/s now. I plan to make love to My Angel. My mouth slants over hers as I devour her with the fervor of a starved man lost on a tropical island—hungry for her taste and company.

My Angel moans into my mouth and melts her body against mine as she grips my tracksuit jacket in her fists. Just as needy as me.

One hand goes to the back of her neck to hold her in place while the other plunders her pussy. Her wet sheath welcomes me and clenches on my fingers as she undulates her hips. I finger fuck her until she cums with a strangled moan I capture in my mouth. I want her ready for me.

A tug to the drawstring of my pants, and they drop to the floor. I cup My Angel's ass, hoist her up, and impale her with my diamond-hard cock, just as long-lasting as the gems in her collar.

We groan—connected as one, finally.

I give her a moment to acclimate to my girth while I continue to claim her mouth voraciously. The temptress' tongue mates with mine. So fucking good.

My grip on her lush globes tightens as I bend my knees. With a grunt, I snap my hips upward, driving my cock to the end of her channel. Fully seated to my cum-laden balls, I piston in and out of her tight pussy.

My Angel arches her back as she pulls from my mouth to scream my name to the open sky above. Her ample tits press under my chin, and I lower my mouth to suckle her beaded, brown nipples.

"MALCOLM!!! Oh… My… GOD!!!" She cries.

Her pussy quivers around my pounding dick. The orgasm takes her breath away as she gulps for air.

No mercy.

I shift my hands to wrap my long fingers around her hips and ass to still her writhing body.

"Fuck, Starr!!! So tight… So wet… So gooood!!!"

My shout joins hers as I lose myself in her wet heat. Sweat drips down my spine along with the tingle of my impending release. Once again, I latch onto her pebbled nipple, sucking greedily.

Starr keens and shudders with another orgasm. Her nails dig into my shoulders as she seeks purchase before she spirals into carnal bliss. Pleas for me to cum fall from her full lips.

"I'm not ready, yet. One more orgasm. Give it to me!!!" I demand.

She bucks and grinds on my cock. Another scream rips from her mouth as her pussy clamps down.

The vise-like grip pulls my orgasm from the top of my head and the tips of my toes to meet at my balls. I blow my load deep inside of my mate as a primal roar streams from my mouth.

My legs give out, and I lower us to the floor. The after-shocks of our lovemaking buzz through us.

I close my eyes and bury my face in her fragrant neck, damp from her sweat. A vision of a tropical, white sand beach and an over-the-water bungalow in the distance with the sound of My Angel's laughter as I chase her appears.

The sense of complete satisfaction overwhelms me. The words—*I love you, My Angel*—beg to be said aloud.

Soon I quiet my heart and soul as I tighten our embrace. *Soon.*

* * *

MY ANGEL SHINES like a brilliant star in a universe of lesser celestial bodies.

Glittery Swarovski crystals form various star shapes on her sheer, floor-length gown with train. Material drapes over one shoulder while another swath falls off her other shoulder from the sweetheart neckline. The corset top amplifies her bountiful breasts and cinches her tiny waist. A slit up to her hip exposes her long, toned leg and one of the strappy sky-high sandals. Filmy high-cut briefs cover her mound and grace the curves of her ass cheeks. Simply stunning.

To further dazzle the members gathered for LEVELS Beverly Hills' opening gala, I gave her pear-shaped diamond earrings, a stone at her ear and one dangling below. The giant gems sparkle along with her evening collar and matching bracelet.

My Angel must sense my stare as she swings her gaze to me and smiles radiantly, taking my breath away. She's chatting with Lola, Adrienne, her sister Claudia, and Lydie, who flew in with her brothers Lucien, Lachlan, and Laurent for the party.

I return My Angel's smile with a wink.

Earlier she told me I reminded her of a dashing movie star from the 1950s in my bespoke white-tie tuxedo and patent leather Oxfords with grosgrain shoelaces. It was her idea to theme the gala after Old Hollywood Legends with women in elegant gowns and men in the highest formal wear. The members love it and decked themselves all out in their finest attire and jewels.

I scan the clusters of members and guests—potential members—on the rooftop Sky Lounge. Baz and the head of a studio talk next to the plexiglass covered pool turned dance floor. Anton and Borya stand by the bar appearing to eye Adrienne and Claudia. Harris dances with a

Brazilian supermodel while Laurent cozies up with a socialite from Palm Beach. We don't allow our baby sister anywhere near the clubs. She went to dinner with friends.

"What the fuck?!"

Lucien's furious declaration draws me back from my musings. He's no longer sipping the signature drink for the gala crafted from Jackson labels. Instead, he's glaring over my shoulder.

I pivot to follow his gaze.

Fuck me!!!

How the hell did Vicky get in?!?! I made sure she wasn't on the guest list. We even accounted for the plus ones by their names and background checks.

She teeters towards Starr, who has her back to the offensive gatecrasher. Judging by Vicky's faltering steps and the sloshing cocktail glass in her hand, she's drunk. But she's on an obvious mission to fuck with my woman.

As I move in their direction, I hear Lucien on his mobile with the head of security. They'll handle the vixen, but not before I get to her.

"—think you are? You steal my Dom—"

Vicky's accusation cuts off when I grab her elbow and pull her away from a shocked Starr. The stink of liquor assaults my nostrils as Vicky leans into me and breaths against my ear.

"There you are, Sir… I miss you so much," she slurs as she drops her glass.

Two members of the security team and the head approach me. I pass her off to them. But she doubles back and attempts to throw her arms around my neck. I duck her unwanted advances and glare at her.

In my most dominant voice, I command her to stop making a spectacle of herself since several members watch her antics and to leave quietly.

Vicky sputters as she gears up for a tirade.

The security members flank her and take her by the arms. They lift her from the floor and carry her from the rooftop. She kicks and yells obscenities, but they ignore her. Ever the professionals, they complete the task efficiently. Less than five minutes, and she's outta here!

I smooth my waistcoat and tug my French cuffs, then turn to face the audience.

Baz, Harris, Lucien, Lachlan, Laurent, Anton, and Borya stand before me placating the onlookers. Waitstaff brings forth more trays of cocktails and hors d'oeuvres. The band jumps into a lively jazz tune. With no more to see and plenty of distractions, the members and guests return to the evening's festivities unfazed.

My eyes scan the crowd for my only concern—My Angel.

She still stands with her girls, protected by their positions around her. Starr's stoic expression sends chills down my spine.

This is not how I planned our night.

Damn Vicky Reynolds… My attorneys will deal with her and request a restraining order for Starr and me. I don't give a damn if she's a client of the fitness center and retreats. Vicky Reynolds done, and out of our lives for good.

Lola gives me the once-over, and Lydie purses her lips. Adrienne and Claudia glance at Starr for her reaction. As do I…

When I tower over her, prepared to apologize, she reaches up to cup my cheek and beams with glittering eyes.

"Mr. Steele, dance with me… Sir."

And with My Angel's request, our world spins on its axis, properly aligned once again.

MALCOLM

"Thanks, bro, we appreciate it. Get home safe."

I give Harris a pound and put my arm around his shoulder for a hug. Then step back for Starr to tell him goodbye or, as she says, *see you again.* As he hops into the G-Wagen, I put my hand on her hip and draw her into my side.

Since the LEVELS Beverly Hills opening gala, the world's gone crazy.

Gossip rags and social media trolls blew up the Vicky situation into the *Fiasco of the Century.* They ran stories and posts—even created fucking hashtags—to depict My Angel as a pain slut who frequents seedy BDSM dungeons and uses Starr Light Fitness & Wellness Beverly Hills as a cover. Of course, all details provided by a credible source close to My Angel. Even worse, they left me out of the narrative, and instead had her with a different dominant every night. Nor was LEVELS mentioned.

All fingers point to Vicky.

She had it in for Starr since she guessed Starr as my new sub, then saw her collar. The sight of Starr at the gala proved Vicky's assumption. Add in my dismal of her as my sub and thwarting her advances—not to mention ignoring the many text messages, voicemails, visits to my penthouses and to STEELE—made her flip.

Undoubtedly, Vicky is the "credible source." My legal team took over. This is shit show is my fault, and I will handle it. I take My Angel as my responsibility very seriously. She is mine to pleasure and to protect.

Therefore, Harris and the Technology team worked on Starr's new security system for her mansion and SLFW. I assigned four of STEELE International's security team members to work in pairs with her at all times, including driving her in one of the corporate G-Wagens. She didn't take kindly to the idea at first.

Then the hang-up or heavy-breathing calls started, along with salacious DMs to her social media accounts. Haley stepped in with the Cyber Security side to investigate. That is, after she reamed me for allowing Vicky to get out of control and threaten Starr.

Now, she agrees with the added security.

The news traveled down the grapevine…

My mobile blew up with calls from Sebastian, with Lola in the background on a rant. I calmed both of them down after I laid out the steps taken to protect Starr and to put an end to Vicky's shenanigans.

Roger called to suggest Starr travels with Leonie while she's doing a whirlwind marketing and photoshoot tour for Lola's Coterie before her pregnancy shows. The trip will get Starr out of LA and away from the fiasco. Starr as her yoga instructor and doula can continue Leonie and Roger's sessions in person instead of virtually. By the time the global three-week trip ends, the shit will have blown over and Vicky handled.

My Angel was hesitant at first because she didn't want to run away from the situation, rather to face it. She said she owes it to her clients, even though the fiasco caused ripples with some more narrow-minded ones. But after she spoke with Adrienne, My Angel realized it's best.

My parents called when the news reached their branch of the vine. We explained the situation, and they offered their full support. Later, my father called me separately to confirm I know how to handle a D/s relationship…

Which brings us to tonight. My Angel and I have cocktails and dinner with her parents at Spire 70, the open-air bar on the roof of STEELE Rodeo Drive with dinner at Restaurant 69 below. Not the optimal circumstances, I want to meet my girlfriend's family for the first time. But they need to see for themselves I'm serious about their daughter, not Starr assuaging them.

A squeeze to my waist wakes me from my train wreck of thoughts.

I glance down to a quizzical expression on My Angel's beautiful heart-shaped face. Not wanting to worry her any further, I lean over and kiss the tip of her nose then buss her neck. Her warm giggles unwind the cold, negative coil from around my heart.

"You were so far away, you didn't hear me speaking to you," she says as she strokes my cheek.

I kiss her palm and respond, "I'll never be far from you, My Angel."

Her face softens and unshed tears shine in her eyes. She bows her head, and I feel her chest expand on an inhale. She's reigning in her emotions with a calming breath. But I want her emotions.

My index finger lifts her chin.

We stare at one another, and I convey my love for her without words. The corners of her mouth curl up with a hint of a smile. I arch my eyebrow in a demand for more. My Angel unleashes a megawatt grin as she wraps her arms around my waist and buries her face in my chest.

"Never hide from me, My Angel," I murmur against her silky curls.

She nods and squeezes me tighter.

"Every time I come here, the panoramic view takes my breath away. So expansive!"

My Angel says as she gazes past the glass surround that separates patrons at the Spire 70 rooftop bar from the pavement seventy stories below.

The setting sun glints off her halter neck, crochet jumpsuit embellished with light-catching gold sequins layered over silk-georgette. Its artfully twisted bodice features cutouts at the waist and the back and suspends from a braided rope at the neck encrusted with Swarovski crystals. The wide, floor-length legs move with the breeze as we walk towards the table reserved for us.

Of course, the diamonds in her evening collar sparkle even in the sunset.

I want to make a good impression on her parents. So I chose the best bar and restaurant in Beverly Hills: STEELE Rodeo Drive's Spire 70 and the 3 Michelin star Restaurant 69. Peace and Sun may be hippies, but they're wealthy free spirits who enjoy the finer things in life.

Along with the best table, I had the mixologist craft cocktails with organic ingredients and liquors ethically and sustainably sourced. For dinner I asked the chef to create a twenty-course tasting menu to not only showcase her culinary artistry elaborately, but to take advantage of fresh seasonal ingredients. It'll also give us three hours to spend together without being obvious.

My Angel stops short in front of me, and her body stiffens under my hand on the small of her back. She stares at a couple near our table. The man raises his head and does a double take. The woman with him shifts in her seat to follow his surprised gaze.

With a sigh, My Angel moves forward. The man stands as we approach; his eyes dart between her and me.

"Starr. How are you?" He asks, his chocolate browns narrow on me.

What the fuck?! Who is this guy?!

Then I get it. He must think I'm one of her dominants, so colorfully depicted by the gossips. A protective growl rumbles in my chest.

MINE!!!

"Hello, Quinn. Well, thank you," My Angel responds

and turns to me. "Malcolm, this is Quinn Peters. Quinn, this is Malcolm Steele—"

"Her boyfriend," I interject as I place a possessive hand on My Angel's hip.

Quinn's eyes dart to my hold. His chest puffs out, and he glares at me.

"I'm Courtney Rhodes. Quinn's fiancée."

The petite-Starr lookalike extends her hand to me.

I glance down, then shake her dainty hand.

"Malcolm Steele, and this is Starr Knight," I respond.

The women exchange greetings while Quinn and I size up the other.

"Starr, sweetheart?"

"Quinn, you're joining our dinner?"

The four of us turn.

A couple who can only be My Angel's parents stand behind us. The distinguished older man stands an inch taller and analyzes me with his obsidian eyes. Starr obviously inherited her father's height and her mother's stunning beauty. Three inches shorter than My Angel and a mirror image.

I won't have to wonder what Starr will look like twenty-five years from now. My eyes widen at the long-term thought.

"Mom, Dad, hi," My Angel responds as she embraces her parents. "No, Quinn happens to be here with his fiancée, Courtney Rhodes. This is Malcolm Steele, my boyfriend."

My Angel holds her hand out to draw me from the

Quinn face-off into her family's circle. I smile and grasp her outstretched palm.

"Mrs. Knight, Mr. Knight, it's a pleasure to meet you at last," I tell them as I extend my other hand.

They smile and return my greeting and tell me to call them Peace and Sun. I gesture to our table—fortunately two away from Quinn. Her father turns to him and nods before he joins us as we walk away.

"So, Malcolm, our daughter tells us you handled this mess. How so?" Her father asks, not very peacefully.

I appreciate and respect his concern as I would ask the exact thing for my daughter. His attorney's mind absorbs what I recount and questions me ruthlessly. No wonder Starr says he's known as a great white shark in the court-room. Sun watches and cross-examines me.

Fifteen minutes later, after My Angel intervenes. I'm grateful for the environmentally friendly drink in my hand...

Even more so when Peters stops by the table to bid good-night to my woman and to her parents. He gives me a cursory nod, and I give him a chin lift. The thought of another man inside of my woman makes me grind my back molars. Mine!

Shortly thereafter, we move downstairs to the restau-rant. As expected, the chef impresses My Angel's parents by presenting each of the courses personally and by offering insights. The sommelier matches the wine pair-ings perfectly. They make up for the blip with Peters.

"Malcolm, this is extraordinary!" Sun exclaims as she swirls her wine glass of Château Lafite Rothschild Pauillac.

Peace nods and adds, "Indeed. Excellent choice of dishes and wines, Malcolm."

My Angel tilts her head to grin at me and squeezes my hand beneath the table. I lean over and press my lips against her full mouth. She sighs softly.

The rest of dinner continues with engaging conversation about their causes, Starr's upcoming trip, and vacations. We even have a lively discussion on the impact of real estate development on the environment. I gain major cool points when I point out STEELE has been eco-friendly for the last decade with improvements each year. We have an entire department devoted to staying abreast of the latest technology and laws. They're pleased, and we move on to other topics.

By the time dessert and the after-dinner drinks arrive, everyone is enjoying each other's company.

"THAT WENT WELL! Thank you for a lovely evening, baby."

My Angel wraps her arms around my neck once we're settled in the back of my Black Badge Rolls-Royce Cullinan.

Her parents just pulled off from the valet stand in their BMW i8 convertible. Again, the hippie in them calls for their careers as environmental law attorneys while their love of luxury calls for a two-hundred-thousand-dollar electric car.

"You think so, Angel?" I ask as I scoop her onto my lap to bask in her elated glow.

She nods her head and kisses me.

When we come up for air, she nuzzles her head under my neck and sighs.

"And Peters?" I ask.

She stiffens, then inhales and relaxes with an exhale.

"My ex-boyfriend. Funny, he was there tonight. If I didn't know better, I'd think he arranged it on purpose since I haven't answered his calls after the Vicky thing—"

"What do you mean 'his calls?!' What the fuck is he calling you for anyway?!" I snarl.

The caveman in me wants to hunt down Peters and beat his ass with my club. Contacting my mate?! Fuck no! MINE!!!

Starr sits up to pin me with an annoyed look, then rolls her eyes as she purses her lips.

"Calm down, Mr. Steele… He was just concerned about me and the bad press since he knows how important my image is to me," she says, then continues. "That's all, obviously, since he has a fiancée."

I snort.

"Let him 'concern' himself with his fiancée. It is for me to have concern for you, Little One," I respond in my most commanding Dom voice.

My submissive lover shivers in my arms and bows her head.

I pat her ass and add darkly, "I will remind you of my responsibilities to you all night long, Little One."

Hours later, My Angel slumbers as I spoon my larger body around her exhausted form. Suffice it to say she learned her lesson threefold and then some more…

"*Oh, Chérie! I sooo love being with you for our sessions! I mean, virtual is great and all. But I miss your live energy and hands-on adjustments. How perfect we met every morning at your studio. What a treat!*"

Leonie says as she stretches on her yoga mat like the lion she's named after.

"Yes, Starr, fantastic as usual!" Roger grins as he rises to his feet in one fluid motion. He reaches down to help his fiancée up, then hugs her close.

Leonie melts against him and sighs contentedly.

It's been a week since they flew in for the start of her whirlwind Pre-The Twins Modeling and Marketing Push for Lola's Coterie. No pun, I giggle to myself as I think of Leonie. As her doula I shouldn't tease her, but she thinks it's funny, too.

Tonight we'll have dinner at STEELE Rodeo Drive's steak restaurant to satisfy Leonie's craving, then fly to Las

Vegas for the second leg of the trip. Malcolm, Lola, Sebastian, Billie, Blair, and Luc Montaigne will join us. Luc flew in from Paris to take part in the trip since he's Lola's mentor and the multibillionaire investor in Lola's Coterie. Blair's happy he's here because the two can spend time together as she's in New York more often than in Paris where he's based.

As I move about my private studio at SLFW to put away the props from Leonie's and Roger's session, I thank her for insisting we meet here. Originally, I planned for them to come to my home studio—just as well-appointed—to avoid any traces of the Vicky fiasco at the center.

By now the members who were "offended by such behavior" canceled their memberships and private standing appointments. But murmurs from those who stayed—whether positive or negative—still echo off the locker room walls.

Leonie's fierce and now maternal behavior stood firm. She would not allow *"idiotes"* to ruin her close friend or her yoga sessions with me. Roger agreed and came ready to handle any wayward comments or stares. Some days Malcolm came, too. He stayed in LA to go with us to Las Vegas, then New York City, where he'll stay for meetings.

I turn to let Leonie and Roger know I'm ready to head out and see him holding her with one arm and his other hand on her still flat belly. They gaze lovingly at each other. Lost to the outside world. I duck my head and preoccupy myself with folding a stack of blankets until Leonie calls to me.

We leave my studio and walk past members as they

bustle about the center for class, the boutique, or the café. They nod in greeting, and I smile assuredly.

"Starr, chérie, you are the absolute best! We adore you!" Leonie exclaims loud enough for those near and far to hear.

"Most definitely! We prefer no other!" Roger adds with even more gusto.

My smile widens, and I loop my arms through theirs as we head to the spa.

"Honey, you are lit up like the Christmas tree at Rockefeller Center!"

Billie teases Leonie since she wears her new suite of rich, pure yellow and white diamonds set in a necklace, bracelets, ring, and hair comb.

"Ho, ho, ho! Well call me Santa!" Roger chuckles as he kisses Leonie's radiant hand.

"Thank you, Santa Baby," she purrs.

"See… That's what got you preggie in the first place!" Lola exclaims.

"Oh, don't tease them. They're so cute!" I chime in, smiling so wide my dimples flash.

We're gathered at the steak restaurant in STEELE Rodeo Drive for dinner on our last night. Billie flew in from Las Vegas for the week. Blair sits leaning into Luc, who's been super attentive the whole night.

"They're my rockstar yoga couple!" I add with a wink.

Since Leonie misses hands-on sessions, I promised them I'd fly with them to Paris after Dubai next month and stay for a week. Anita Green—a yoga instructor with a flourishing practice I know from our fitness world—can help. She's also the wife of Roger's luxury gym business partner, the former world heavyweight champion Norman Green. While we catch up, I'm going to ask Anita to partner with me on Leonie's sessions. Since her pregnancy is progressing, I want a teacher in the room with her. Roger and Leonie think it's a great idea.

"Okay. Besides, it'll help with the authenticity of the new maternity lingerie collection… Surprise!"

Lola's announcement appears to catch Leonie off guard, just as Lola hoped based on her gleeful expression.

"What do you mean?" Leonie asks excitedly.

Lola claps her hands and shimmies in her seat. Her hazel eyes shine.

"I want you to collaborate with me on a sexy maternity lingerie and loungewear collection! We can design the pieces together as you go through the stages. Plus shoot campaigns with you and Roger all along!"

She pauses and gazes at Leonie steadily. Suddenly serious.

"As long as Dr. Berger gives his approval. We will not overtax you," Lola adds.

It's Leonie's turn to clap and shimmy in her seat.

"How exciting! I already have some ideas! Like a bra with removable cups to allow The Twins to feed—"

"Hey! That's enough!" Roger cuts her off, growling at the mention of her breasts in front of other men.

"Cue the scene—Caveman Roger drags Leonie by the ponytail back to his den…" Lola jokes.

"And you are next, Lola," Dom Sebastian interjects.

Malcolm cocks his eyebrow at me, and I squirm in my seat, my face flushed with arousal.

Luc turns to Blair and asks, "Do you have anything to add, Blair?"

She blushes bright red from her hairline to her ample bosom.

"No, Sir!"

Billie chokes on her glass of Marcassin Estate Chardonnay. Then stares gobsmacked at Blair.

Lola's shocked eyes snap to Leonie and me, and we burst out laughing.

Dom Luc! Who would have thought? I guess their relationship is definitely doing well after all. To hell with long distance…

* * *

"THE BRIGHT LIGHTS of Las Vegas always give me a thrill! I love the partying, dining, and the cheers when people hit it big… The baccarat table is calling my name, baby!"

I exclaim as I lean closer to the window, my excitement palpable.

"It never gets old for me. Even after years of living here. I love Vegas!" Billie adds as she peers out of her window. Her Savannah, Georgia accent still prevalent. Forever a Southern Belle.

We finished the last business in Beverly Hills and now jet to Sin City for Lola's Coterie Las Vegas. The campaign for the latest collection exclusive to the boutique needs to get done earlier than expected. Thanks to The Twins—Leonie and Roger's future bundles of joy!

Billie, Malcolm and I flew with the parents-to-be aboard Roger's G650 private jet. Luc opted to fly with Blair on Sebastian's plane.

Leonie glances out of her window to take in the view of the world-famous Las Vegas Strip.

"You're so right, Starr! It's just so flashy with the neon lights in stark relief to the darkness of the night desert beyond," she says.

As the jet flies into McCarran International Airport, the lights are like beacons luring travelers to the revelry of the "What Happens in Vegas, Stays in Vegas" city.

Having grown up on the West Coast, Las Vegas is my go-to city for decadence. Leonie always speaks of Monte Carlo and Macau as her choices for gambling. Yet, as much as I enjoy those cities, I'm still drawn to Vegas.

"Really, Little One? Las Vegas gives you *thrills?*" Malcolm murmurs in my ear, his breath warm on the sensitive shell.

I shudder and turn away from the sparkling vision. My hooded gaze takes in the much more tempting visage of My Dom. My lips curl into a seductive smile as I scan his handsome face.

He hasn't shaved. So the five o'clock shadow adds to his sex appeal. The longer length of his hair softens his sharp cheekbones as the tips brush against his strong jawline. Gorgeous.

"Your *thrill* with Las Vegas lets me know I am not fulfilling your desires adequately. As your Dom, my duty is to heighten your desires. So you will appreciate the pleasures of release, no orgasms for the rest of tonight, Little One…" he murmurs in my ear with a wicked chuckle.

I shiver from his warm breath tickling my skin and the subsequent jolt of electricity that zings my pussy. Uh oh.

Soon we're headed to STEELE Las Vegas in Malcolm's Black Badge Rolls-Royce Cullinan, driven by a hotel chauffeur. The two five-diamond resort and casino properties in the middle of the action on the Strip are magnificent. Each soaring tower features the signature STEELE gray glass. They shimmer from the neon lights' reflection on their surfaces.

The valet opens the doors on the passenger side while the driver opens the other for us. Malcolm takes my hand just as Leonie and Roger hop out of their SUV. We stride through the ornate, but tasteful main lobby towards the private reception foyer for the twelve Bridge Penthouses.

They're designed to attract high rollers and the über-wealthy clientele. The penthouses act as a bridge to connect the two properties with the mall between them from the ground level to the third floor. Malcolm and I will stay in his penthouse that's on one of the top six floors. While Billie stays in another; Roger and Leonie in his; Sebastian and Lola in theirs, and Luc and Blair in a fifth.

As we pass through the lobby, various staff members greet Malcolm by name. A few of the woman watch the girls and me.

I smirk and peek up at him through my eyelashes. He brushes his lips against my forehead. Yeah, sweeties… He's very much mine.

Cameras flash to our left, and we turn to the source. What appears to be a soon-to-be-bride and her gaggle of girlfriends recognize Leonie. No doubt the images will show up on Instagram and Twitter shortly.

Used to the commotion her presence causes, she smiles and winks. Roger keeps his typical intense stare straight ahead, even increasing his speed.

I shudder and not in ecstasy, rather relieved the pseudo-paparazzi aren't targeting me. Malcolm was right, I need to get out of LA and away from probing eyes. Let things cool off and restore my peace of mind.

We reach the etched-glass, double doors for the doorman to allow us entry to the separate foyer of the Bridge Penthouses. Beyond are three reception and two concierge desks, four sitting areas, and a bank of three private elevators, each accesses two of the Bridge Penthouses in this tower.

"Hey, we just arrived. I can't wait to hit the casino floor!" Lola says as she shimmies, her hazel eyes lighting up like the Strip.

"Where are Luc and Blair?" Leonie asks, glancing around the expansive room.

"Their penthouse is in the other tower. Billie and Malcolm and Starr are in two here," Sebastian responds.

Hmmmmm, more privacy for him and Blair, not in sight of the rest of our party…

Lola must think the same, because she titters as she shakes her head.

The receptionist brings a card key to Billie. Malcolm,

Roger, and Sebastian's penthouses have entry plates coded to their palm prints. So we have no need for keys.

The porters take our bags via the service elevator as we ride up in the guest ones for each of our penthouses. We agree to meet in the foyer in an hour.

"Now what was it you said about *thrills*, Little One?"

Malcolm's deep Dom baritone makes me shiver as he pulls my back to his front. He bends his knees so his thick length nestles against my ass.

"Does my ten-inch long, thick-as-steel, velvet-covered cock not make you squeal in delight?" He rasps in my ear.

"Yes… Yes, Sir!" I mewl as I grind against him. "More than anything in the world…"

My Dom pulls the hem of my linen halter neck midi dress up to slip his hand underneath it.

"The bouquet of your arousal mimics the colorful patchwork of delicate roses printed on your dress," My Dom says as his fingers slide along the damp gusset of my silk thong.

The delicate material poses no barrier to his wandering fingers. His other hand slips the bow out of the slim ties at the neckline to cup one of my full breasts. The v-neck bodice exposes my bosom to provide ample room for him to explore.

"Ooohhh, Sir…" I moan as he flicks my pebbled nipple with his fingertip.

When two of his thick digits press past my slippery pussy folds, I moan and increase my grinding on his impressive erection with my ass.

My Dom's arousal mimics mine for some erotic foreplay.

Oh, fuck…

"So tight… So wet… So sweet…" My Dom says as he slips his fingers out of my channel to suck them clean of my juices in his mouth.

The sound of his slurps intensifies my desire for him. I want more!

"Sir," I plead, arching my back to bring my breasts closer to his mouth.

He plucks my nipple as my breast fills his hand even more. Then returns to his fingers fucking my dripping core.

The juices slide down to coat my inner thighs, and I beg for release. The pressure builds as I ride his fingers, humping my bare mons against his palm to start my orgasm.

WHAP… WHAP… WHAP

"Aaarghhh!" I screech as My Dom spanks my aching pussy lips. The last strike hits my swollen clit, and I jolt, half ready to cum and half ready to flee. "Owww!"

"What did I tell you only an hour ago, Little One?" He growls.

"No… orgasms… for… the… rest… of… tonight, Naught Girl," he repeats in my ear huskily.

Each word marked by a smack to emphasize his jaw-dropping reminder.

Aaaah fuuuck!

The doors ping as they open onto the foyer of the penthouse. Disappointed and aroused painfully, I lean on My Dom as he leads us through the doors.

"Sir, please!" I beg woefully. "My reference wasn't to the way you make my body sing! What I meant was the gambling and decadence of Vegas!"

He grins wickedly and strides to one wall of windows without a backwards glance.

I want to drop to my knees and plead my case as I envelop his cock in my mouth with hopes he puts it in my empty pussy. Instead, I walk behind him, rubbing my thighs together for a frisson of relief.

When he senses my staggered stride, he tugs me along by the hand to keep up. He tsks at me disappointedly.

"Do you want to make it three days, Naughty Girl? Or have you forgotten I provide your pleasure?" My Dom throws over his shoulder.

Vigorously, I shake my head. Heavens, no!

At the windows, once again, he stands behind me and holds me in his powerful embrace. I sigh at the feel of being in my man's arms and at the sight of the Strip shining brightly all around us.

We stand in silence for a moment, absorbed in our separate thoughts. Malcolm brushes his lips across the top of my head and reminds me it's time to get ready for dinner and fun at the casino.

"Well, Mr. Steele, if I cannot cum, neither can you!" I quip as I sashay ahead of him to the bedroom. Then squeal when he slaps my ass.

"We shall see, Naughty Girl. We shall see," he smirks again.

* * *

THE FOUR DAYS in Las Vegas lead to our New York City leg of the whirlwind three-week trip.

We'll spend the next five days in the city. Then go out to the Steele Southampton Village waterfront family compound for the remaining four.

Billie stayed in Vegas while we flew a red-eye flight plan to arrive this morning. Today, after Leonie's session, I'm going to visit some friends at their studio and teach a couple of classes while Malcolm has meetings. At fifteen weeks, Leonie needs to rest as I notice her stamina decreasing because of the activity. So it's the best time for me to go.

"Remember to breathe with intention, Leonie. Inhale to reach; exhale to return. Your breath will guide you through the postures," I intone as I lead her through our session.

Roger surprised her with a custom yoga studio in at their penthouse in The STEELE Tower. He asked me to help him outfit it with every yoga-related item imaginable. Mats thick enough to protect her knees; straps to extend her reach as her belly grows; wool blankets to keep her warm during Savasana. Not to mention the candles, meditation pillows, and a *Puja* space.

I love it! She declared when we walked in.

We finish the opening sequence and move on to the standing asanas. As we flow through each pose, I instruct Leonie to allow her mind to focus on the movement and her breathing. The breath sets the way.

"Hi, ready for me?" Roger asks as he joins us for yoga

nidra.

I smile and nod to the mat, bolsters, and blanket I set up for him next to Leonie's space.

"*Bien* sûr, *Mon Cœur,*" she replies, holding her hand out to him.

Roger smiles at us and takes Leonie's hand as he lowers himself to a cross-legged position with ease. Once seated, he kisses her cheek. Then turns to me expectantly.

"Namaste, Enlightened One," he says, placing his palms together at his heart center and bowing his head to me.

"Namaste, Sassy Student," I say as I return the gesture.

We laugh good-naturedly.

I help the future parents to get into comfortable positions as they lie supine on the mats. I place the bolsters under their knees and necks. Then, like babies, I swaddle them in the blankets, ensuring they're covered fully. Before I step away, I place lavender-scented pillows over their eyes. I dim the lights and allow the candles to glow around the studio.

My soothing voice guides Leonie and Roger through the session from consciousness to a state of semi-consciousness. The mental countdowns and memories I ask them to invoke keep them from falling into a slumber. Not like Leonie's first few sessions where her snores woke her up!

The forty-five minutes pass peacefully. I use the sound of chimes to bring the pair back to full awareness. I ask them to recall how far they could count and the recollections from the past. It's amazing how their practice has improved.

Fully rested with the equivalent of three hours' sleep, Leonie tells me she feels rejuvenated. She and Roger head to their bedroom while I take the family's private elevator up one flight to Malcolm's penthouse on the fifty-third floor.

Situated high above the Manhattan streets, it's on the fifty-second floor of The Steele Tower skyscraper. Through the gray-tinted, floor-to-ceiling windows, the city stretches out with unobstructed views. The prime location at the southwest corner of Fifty-seventh Street and Fifth Avenue is in the heart of Billionaires' Row.

Central Park to the north, the Hudson River to the west, the East River opposite, and the rest of Manhattan to the south from Midtown to Battery Park. On a beautiful, cloudless day like this morning, the vista draws you to gaze out of the windows for hours.

But not this morning. I have an hour to get to my friends' yoga studio in the Flat Iron District. It's *the* neighborhood for fitness lovers with its many high-end gyms, sportswear stores, juice bars, and luxurious spas. I'll stop by my favorite athletic clothing boutique, Sweaty Betty, for some new leggings and tank tops before I head back uptown.

After a quick shower, I change into a pair of white biker short shorts and matching scoop-neck, midriff-bearing tank top. It's my go-to outfit for a hot yoga class. The sweat-wicking and quick-drying material works wonders!

I slip a pair of comfy joggers over the shorts and pull on a matching hoodie. Perfect to change into after I shower again. A quick head flip and I pile my long curls atop in a messy bun. Then slide my feet into a pair of sneakers and grab my gym tote.

Just as I put my mobile in the front pocket, it vibrates and dings with a text message in Malcolm's ringtone. Without breaking stride, I check the screen.

Hey, Angel, I have a last-minute business dinner tonight. Are you free to join me? I booked your favorite restaurant, Momofuku Ko...

My heart skips a beat, and my mouth waters. I hope the chef has Black Bass Dashi, Cherry Blossom and Mushroom Salad on the tasting menu tonight. I lick my lips and grin. How can I say no to his enticement?

Absolutely! What time should I be ready?

Right away the three dots appear, a sign of his forthcoming response.

Great, thanks Angel! 7:30 dinner is at 8

I reply with a kiss emoji and step into the elevator. Well, this requires a trip to SoHo for a cute outfit after Sweaty Betty! How I love New York!

"THESE SHOTS ARE INCREDIBLE!" Lola says as she peers over the photographer's shoulder.

We're in Dubai, the last stop on the five-city global trip. Luc returned to Paris after New York for meetings. The rest of us spent three of the seven days allotted to the United Arab Emirates' boutiques in Abu Dhabi.

Leonie suggested they contrast the city's sea of desert with the turquoise waters of Dubai, The Empty Quarter

Desert in Abu Dhabi serves as the first backdrop. The Bedouin noblemen see the world's largest sand desert as a vast ocean to travel across on their journeys.

They paid homage to the local history with a twist. Leonie portrayed a desert princess who captivated a desert traveler, Roger. Their steamy affair took place over the course of three nights in a lavish tent.

Lola outdid herself with the collection exclusive to her Lola's Coterie Abu Dhabi boutique. The vibrant colors, sumptuous materials, and sophisticated lines make for extraordinary pieces. Of course Malcolm ordered a few sets of the lingerie and loungewear for my growing trousseau...

As a surprise, he was able to change his meetings to videoconference so he could join us. I think he just can't get enough of me!

Unlike the other days when he and I spent time together away from everyone else, today we're aboard the six-hundred-foot megayacht. They're using it for the Dubai photoshoot. It's lavish and belongs to one of the royal family members. The impressive boat parallels the view. Spread out beyond the dazzling water with glittering ripples that reach across to the shore is the city's varied skyline.

Architectural marvels grow out of the surrounding desert. The contrast of the modern glass towers—some in unusual shapes—to the nature around it is remarkable. It provides the perfect scenery for the Dubai boutique's collection.

Lola incorporated the gorgeous blues and greens of the

water with the earth tones of the sand for the color palette. Glittery Swarovski crystals embellish the bras, panties, slips, and evening wear pieces to mirror the glass structures.

This time Roger and Leonie play the roles of dashing billionaire mogul and paparazzi-hounded celebrity. Their holiday is fraught with dodging photographers with high-powered lenses while on their megayacht to being chased through the streets after a night out.

Not much different from reality my reality…

"*Oui!* It's as though we're experiencing our everyday lives!" Leonie giggles as she looks over the photographer's other shoulder at the photos.

Roger grunts and adds, "Right. Well, if it gets as extreme as this storyline, you're getting security."

Leonie opens her mouth to respond. But Sebastian cuts in, holding up his hand to stop her.

"I agree with Roger completely. You are carrying the next generation of Steeles. And as the eldest of this line, it is my responsibility to protective everyone. Period."

Malcolm leans over and whispers in my ear, "And you thought I was overly protective…"

Now I know how Lola must feel when Sebastian enacts his Alpha Dom. He's so commanding, I'm about to say, *yes Sir* to him, too!

Leonie turns to Lola, and she shrugs. Outnumbered and understanding their concern, Leonie nods in agreement.

"Words, Pretty Kitty. I will have your words," Roger demands.

"*Oui,*" she answers.

Roger, Sebastian, and Malcolm reply excellent in unison, and Lola smiles as she wraps her arm around Leonie's waist.

"Get used to it, Hot Mama. There's nothing that will stop these cavemen from taking care of their loved ones."

I can't deny they're more than right on this one…

WHEN THE CAMPAIGN IS COMPLETE, we stay in Dubai while Lola and Leonie round out this city's trip with marketing efforts. Malcolm had meetings he couldn't reschedule. So he flew to Brussels a few days ago.

The girls host private viewing parties for the city's VIPs and dinners at STEELE Dubai. They take part in interviews with local fashion magazines and lifestyle television shows. Social media takeovers increase followers for the business and their personal accounts. The results satisfy the public relations and marketing teams.

Thankfully, we're on our way back to Paris. Roger and Leonie sleep in the bedroom of his private jet while I stretch out on the sofa converted into an additional bed. Sebastian, Lola, and Blair head to New York City on his jet.

It exhausts everyone after the month of non-stop travel. But it was well worth it. The early shots are incredible, as predicted. The sales team expects great numbers in revenue and an increase in brand awareness.

But I told Leonie it's time for a hiatus when we arrive in Paris. She giggled when I added, *time to rest up, Haute Maman!*

"This is a fantastic facility right smack in the heart of Paris! Who would have thought a gym in a gem of a building in a prime area of a top arrondissement?!"

I exclaim once we finish the tour of Norman Green's Elite Training Facility Paris.

Anita beams with pride at my compliment of her husband's luxury gym. She nods her head as her jet black curls bob around her heart-shaped, honey-colored face.

"I know! Can you believe we're still in the city's bustling business district? The location proves the ideal spot to attract high-powered titans of finance, real estate, media, and other industries as members. The waiting list for membership stands at four months long," she says.

She tells me how the idea came about over four years ago when Roger met Norman in Las Vegas at a party at STEELE LV after his final KO match. He told Roger he promised his girlfriend, now wife, Anita he would stop with that fight. He was at the top of his game with no more to prove. Norman said it's better to leave on high than get carted away low.

Roger offered him the opportunity to open his chains of branded gyms through STEELE's Entertainment Properties Division. One for underprivileged youth and another as exclusive elite training facilities for the über-wealthy and star athletes.

Born and raised in Harlem to upper middle-class parents, Norman understands the importance of giving back to the community. A mentor taught him boxing after school and his career took off. As a celebrity athlete, he understands the need for specialized training and the demands on the body. He didn't hesitate and agreed to the deal. A perk for Roger is he became his first client.

When Roger moved to Paris, he and Anita came with him and opened locations in the city, London, and Madrid. The States has several besides the New York City flagship including Las Vegas, Los Angeles, Austin, Chicago, and Miami.

Morgan, Sebastian, and Malcolm are pleased with the profitable revenue stream. Especially since the membership and assorted fees of the elite facilities pay for the community ones. Norman can continue in the sports world and add even more to his multimillions. It's a win-win business partnership for all.

Then Anita expanded upon it after she finished culinary school at Le Cordon Bleu and started a meal plan delivery service. Norman added her customized plans to the paid offerings of the elite facilities and complimentary healthy snacks to the youth. She also took over the food services in both chains. They're a dynamic couple who raise the bar in the fitness industry.

In addition, she teaches classes and private sessions here in her eponymous full-service yoga studio—each Facility location includes one. We ended the tour in her private room. I admire the quiet-energy vibe.

"My man knows his stuff! He knows a good thing when he sees it—including me!" Leonie laughs.

Anita and I join in as we settle on the mats spread out on the bamboo floor.

We spend the next hour going over Leonie's health history, current level of activity, and goals, then we develop a practice plan. I take Leonie through a session I designed for her to give Anita a chance to observe Leonie's skill and comfort levels. It pleases me to see Anita take notes throughout our conversation and Leonie's session.

"If you don't mind… I'd love to join in on your yoga *nidra*," she says at the end of Leonie's asanas portion of her session.

She laughs and responds, "*Absolument!* It's my favorite part. No offense, Starr *chérie*! It's so just relaxing and *Haute Maman* needs her rest. Just doing as you say!"

The studio fills with our giggles, then quiets while I tuck them into warm blankets and place lavender-scented pillows over their closed eyes. A smile plays on my lips as I take a seat and begin their relaxation process.

Once the time ends and we recount their journey, we head to the locker room for quick showers. The spa for body treatments and massages comes up next on our Girls' Healthy Day. I'm looking forward to the body polish and a deep tissue massage with Anita's proprietary blend of essential oils for rejuvenation. My body needs recovery, too!

Afterwards, we meet upstairs on the rooftop for lunch. It's a clear sunny day. So the staff withdrew the retractable glass roof into its casing. The sounds of car horns, people's voices, and sirens drift up the six stories to remind us we're in the city and not drifting in bliss.

I don't mind it. With a sigh, I lift my face to the sky, enjoying the sun on my freshly scrubbed and moisturized skin.

"Well, hello there, ladies!"

We turn to see Norman striding over to our table.

He's six feet, five inches, solid two hundred-fifty pounds of muscle who moves with the grace of a gazelle and the speed of a cheetah. His extraordinary physique proves he can go a tenth year and knockout his ninth opponent with ease.

Norman is a fine chocolate bear of a man, but Malcolm has my heart.

Anita grins at her husband as he bends over to kiss her cheek. At five feet, three inches, he towers over the petite beauty seated in her chair. Her tawny brown eyes shine with love.

"Norm, honey, meet my friend, Starr Knight. She's the yogi from Beverly Hills I spoke with you about who teaches Leonie virtually. Starr, meet my husband Norman," Anita says.

"Nice to meet you, Starr," Norman replies as he shakes my hand in his sizable one. "Hey, Leonie, how are you feeling, little mama?"

Leonie giggles and pats her babies bump with motherly affection.

"The three of us are doing wonderful, Norm! Thanks for asking," she responds.

"Your facility is impressive, Norman—"

"Call me Norm, like my friends," he interrupts with a warm smile.

I nod and tell him how much I enjoyed myself and will visit his location in Los Angeles when I return home. He tells me he'll add me to the VIP VIP member list so I can access all locations. Then he leaves us to our meal.

We turn our attention to our delicious salads with grilled salmon or chicken made from fresh, locally sourced ingredients. Anita crafted the tasty dressing from her recipe. She tells us more about the meal plan side of her business and her goal to expand it to other wellness companies. I agree SLFW will partner with her, and she squeals with excitement.

"That's great, thanks so much!" She claps. "We can draft the contract before you leave. Then you can show it to your legal team when you return to Beverly Hills."

"Sounds good! Supporting one another is the yogi way!" I tease.

Leonie nods and lifts her glass of iced lemon ginger tea to add, "Here's to our friendship, health, and success!"

Anita and I lift our glasses of citrus-infused water to join in her toast.

"Hi, Angel, how was your week in Paris?"

I cuddle deeper under my blankets in the President's Suite at STEELE Place Vendôme and pull my iPad closer to me. Malcolm's handsome face fills the screen.

"It was great, baby. Leonie is happy with the plan for Anita to teach her. Anita and I worked out a partnership with her meal plan and food service company to run SLFW's café and offer food delivery for members. I did some shopping, naturally…" I laugh. "Tell me, how's London?"

He pauses, then bites his suckable lower lip between his front teeth.

"What?" I ask, curious as to the cause for his hesitancy.

Malcolm's lip pops out, and he sighs.

"I have to stay longer than expected, so I can't give you a ride to New York City as we planned. But it would be better if you flew over here and stayed until I leave. I miss you," he responds gruffly.

Now it's my turn to pause.

My mind goes over my schedule for the upcoming week: some business meetings, privates, and classes; a friend's housewarming party; Sunday dinner with my parents. Adrienne can arrange for teacher coverage; I'll send a gift; they'll understand—especially since they've grown to like Malcolm. Hell, I rarely take a vacation. I deserve some time to myself after years of growing my company!

My delay proves too much for him.

"I'll make it worth your while," he adds with a seductive smirk.

"Well, in that case…" I purr.

MALCOLM

I pace back and forth impatiently for the STEELE London Sikorsky S-92 Executive helicopter to land on The Tower's roof. A glance at my precise Patek Philippe watch shows the helicopter is two minutes late. Where the hell is My Angel?

Wind whips my hair as the sound of the helicopter's blades fill the air surrounding me. I lift my hand to shade my eyes, then sigh in relief when I see My Angel waving from the window above. With a grin that lights my heart, I wave back.

I don't wait for the pilot to stop the blades. Instead, I duck my head and rush forward to the door. Just as the helicopter settles, I reach for the door's handle. Before I can open it the flight attendant pulls the exterior door open.

"Good afternoon, Mr. Steele," he says with a slight nod of his head.

"Good afternoon," I respond, biting back the urge to push him aside and enter the cabin.

Not necessary at all.

"Hi, baby! I missed you!" Starr cries as she leaps into my arms and wraps her long legs around my waist. Her inner thighs tighten, and my cock hardens.

"I missed you, too," I growl into her mouth as I take her lips in a savage kiss.

Without missing a step, I pivot and walk back towards the interior door. No need to put on a further show for STEELE staff, I chuckle to myself. And a show it will be. Guaranteed.

My hands grip her lush ass over the tailored pants she wears. Damn. Why didn't she wear a skirt, I wonder when I get us inside of the empty stairwell and kick the door shut.

My Angel's slim fingers tangle in my thick, ebony hair to pull at my scalp. The zap of pain makes my balls draw up tight. Her soft coos as I dominate her tongue sets me on fire.

I need to be inside of her. Now.

As though hearing my demand, My Angel unwinds her legs and stands to open her pants. She only gets one leg out before I'm on her again.

Her back slams against the concrete wall, and an oomph bursts forth from her parted lips. Undeterred, she tugs at the hem of my shirt as I wrestle my cock free from the now tight confines of my trousers. Not waiting to check—but knowing she's dripping—I align my weeping mushroom head to her pussy and ram it home. Deep.

We groan as one as our bodies merge in our carnal connection.

We share no dirty talk or words of love. We fuck hard and raw. Starved for the other.

My balls swell with my seed, ready to fill my woman's womb. One more passion-driven thrust combined with My Angel's quivering pussy walls, and I blow my load on a groan. I swallow her scream as her orgasm detonates with mine.

I lean my damp forehead against hers while we catch our breath. My semi-flaccid cock remains inside of her channel, happy to never leave her tight, wet heat.

"Well, I guess you really missed me after all… Now, when are you going to make it worth my while?" My Angel quips breathlessly.

I chuckle and nip her neck.

I'm a fucking goner. Worse than Sebastian and Roger. Damn…

"—THE expansion plans for the Kuala Lumpur property are on track for an early completion date by three months. The technology team will install their equipment two weeks ahead of occupancy to allow for full system testing…"

I'm in the weekly status meeting with my Entertainment Properties Division, but my mind drifts back to the night My Angel and I had at LEVELS London. My cock stirs at the reminder. I shift in my plush leather chair for a more comfortable position. Then I almost laugh out loud when I recall My Angel whimpering as she couldn't hold her position on the Sybian Saddle.

I kept her on the masturbation device for twenty minutes as punishment for her smart-ass remark after I blew her mind in the stairwell.

Sweat dripped between her jiggling, D-cup tits as I increased the speed. The short, but extra-thick dildo I attached to the saddle kept her full and sopping wet the entire time. After the first five minutes and she realized I wasn't letting her off, tears ran down her reddened cheeks.

I sat back in a chair and stroked my engorged cock as I watched her go from ecstasy to pain to relief and back again with a flick of the remote control. She never knew what to expect. But her body loved it.

Flushed face; pointed nipples; quivering belly; trembling thighs; juices flowing; hands fisted, bound behind her back.

Yeah. My Naughty Girl loved every minute of it.

When I took her off of the Sybian and fucked her ass until it gaped for me, she climaxed four times in a row screaming my name.

I held my release back until she was writhing, blubbering, and mindless. Then I let loose.

My balls ache for release now. Surreptitiously, I adjust my junk beneath the conference room table. Then I glance at my watch and the meeting's agenda. Three more presentations; forty-five minutes more.

Fuck.

. . .

"Hi, baby! How was your day?"

My face splits with a broad grin when I spy my woman sitting in one of three salons of the STEELE Kensington's Presidential Suite. Unlike Sebastian, I don't bother with a mansion in London. I'd rather stay at one of the Presidential Suites of a STEELE hotel or resort when I travel for business or for pleasure.

"Long and hard. Sounds familiar?" I smirk.

Her contagious laughter tinkles around us. I join in as I swoop her off of the sofa and into my arms. I kiss her silly until she moans and grinds her bare pussy against my eight-pack abs.

As I decreed after she arrived: no panties and no bra shall come between her body and mine and only dresses worn.

No barrier keeps my fingers from entering her always-wet-for-me core. A second digit follows the first as they flex and curl to stroke her G-spot and prepare her for my entry.

"Malcolm, ohhhhh... Right there... Oh fuck... There, there, THERE!" My Angel explodes.

I allow her to ride out her orgasm on my fingers, knowing I'll have her cum a few more times before I seek my release.

She whimpers in my arms.

I slip my dripping fingers from her pussy and put them in her mouth. She licks them clean while she stares into my hooded eyes boldly.

The Temptress.

I stand her up and pull the coral-colored strapless cashmere maxi dress from her body—another of my favorites from the Lola's Coterie Collection. It brings me much joy to buy her lingerie and loungewear. Even more joy to rip it off.

My Angel stands naked before me. Her mouthwatering body ripe for my taking. It's like a magnet for my dick as it tents my trousers.

I shrug out of my suit jacket and vest, then remove my silk tie. When she reaches to help me, I put up a finger to stop her and shake my head. She will watch me undress and appreciate my body as much as I salivate over hers.

My striptease continues with the unbuttoning of my custom-tailored dress shirt. Slowly, I open it to reveal my hard chest and happy trail of dark hair leading to my erect cock. I tug the shirt hem from my pants and toss it to the ground.

Never do I remove my eyes from her face. But her heated gaze drifts to my bulging crotch.

Bingo.

I glide my hand over my taut abs to reach the buckle of my belt and the button on my trousers, then unzip them. They fall to my feet in a puddle. One step, two steps and I stand in my black boxer briefs and shoes only. My hand strokes my turgid length through the soft material and tug on the silver balls of my Prince Albert piercing.

I hiss.

My Angel licks her full lips.

My cock weeps.

I rest my hand on my bulge until her eyes come back to mine. Now that I have her attention, I put my thumbs in the waistband of my boxer briefs and pull them down. Then I toe out of my shoes and yank my socks off.

My Angel's nostrils flare as she inhales deeply. Undoubtedly she can smell my pheromones and her feminine wiles yearn to mount my dick.

She will. Soon.

My cock stands out straight towards her, dripping with pre-cum.

Her fingers twitch to touch me.

I beckon with my finger.

She drops to her hands and knees and crawls to me. Ass high, head low. Just as I taught my little sub.

When she reaches me, she kisses each of my feet and sits back on her haunches, hands clasping opposite elbows behind her back, eyes downcast to await my next silent command.

I fist my cock at its thick base and tap the tip on her wet lips.

She opens.

In my cock goes to the back of her throat with one thrust of my hips.

She gags. Tears fill her eyes. She whirls her tongue around and sucks.

I hiss. My head goes back, and my eyes roll to the ceiling as my toes curl.

Fuck. Me.

My Temptress works my cock like her favorite ice pop, slurping up the juices, never letting them fall from her mouth.

I cum on a roar as I grip her head and piston my hips, driving my dick down her relaxed throat.

After I can see again, I lower my gaze to hers.

Tears stain her cheeks.

I kneel before her and lick them.

"Good girl," I praise her.

She mewls.

My day is complete.

STARR and I wait for the FaceTime call from Roger and Leonie, where they'll add in my siblings and sister-in-law. We're all impatient to know The Twins' gender since Leonie had her eighteen-week scan today. She and Roger wanted to wait until we were all gathered on the call or at a restaurant in Paris.

Our parents flew over yesterday afternoon, eager to hear the news in person. They and Leonie's parents Guy and Josy Beaulieu wanted to go to the doctor. But the couple decided to have dinner instead for their big announcement.

"Well??? What are The Twins?" Lola demands.

"Boys!!" Leonie cries. "See for yourselves!"

Dutifully, Roger passes out copies of images from the ultrasound to those gathered. While Leonie holds up one for the FaceTime group.

"Holy cow! You can see their faces and everything!" Harris exclaims peering closely from his iPhone.

Haley claps and adds, "They're absolutely incredible! Roger, they look like you!"

We laugh at the folly of her comment since they don't have true distinguishable traits yet.

"Fantastic, bro! We see what you made," I say, giving Roger a virtual high five.

Starr grins, "Can't wait to see you, little munchkins!"

"Mini Steeles in the oven!" Sebastian laughs, then glances between Leonie and Roger. "In all seriousness, we're so happy for you both. Congratulations, Mommy and Daddy!"

Leonie and Roger thank us all and prop the iPad on the table where we can see them.

Once it's quieted down, he turns to Leonie.

"My love, this is a day I want you to always remember" —he takes a flat black leather case out of the breast pocket of his suit jacket—"this is for you."

Leonie peeks up at him, then presses the sapphire-studded closure. She kisses his lips.

He removes the platinum necklace and place it around her neck. The three large, pear-shaped sapphires styled like her *toi et moi* ring settle against her heart. The intense, velvety, deep royal blue colored stones are the rarest and most valuable—just like the three males in her life.

"Oh, Roger, this is beautiful. *Merci, Mon Cœur*," Leonie says as she fingers the sapphires sliding along the chain. "All three of my boys close to my heart."

Tears fill her eyes as she cups his face and kisses him. Then she wraps her arms around Roger to bury her face against his neck.

He rubs her back soothingly.

"The heavenly blue of sapphires signifies the epitome of celestial hope and faith. Believed to bring divine insight, prosperity, and safe keeping according to the ancient and medieval world." Guy says from his worldly knowledge. Everyone comments on his words and the gift's beauty.

The wait staff enter with bottles of Taittinger Comtes de Champagne Blanc de Blancs. They bring Leonie iced lemon green tea in a flute. I hand Starr a flute and take one I poured before the call started.

Her laughter bubbles like the champagne when she spies her cocktail.

"*À votre santé*!" She says standing with her hand on her babies bump as she leans into Roger's side.

"Cheers!" We follow, raising our crystal flutes in the air with hers.

Lola has meetings in Paris. So she and Haley arrange to go together to see Leonie "live and direct." Harris tells us he'll create the best baby monitoring system ever with all the high-tech bells and whistles available. Starr says she's only a plane ride away from her doula duties. We chat some more. Then Roger ends the video call so they can eat.

I turn to Starr and pull her into my lap to kiss the top of her curls. I rest my lips against their silkiness as I ponder what it would be like to have a baby with My Angel.

MALCOLM

"*B*ro, this shit is fucking insane! I almost knocked the teeth out of some paparazzo on our way in."

Roger looks up to see me striding into his STEELE Paris office, followed by Harris. Sebastian is in a meeting in his offices down the hall.

He, Lola, and our parents have been here for the last two weeks to support Leonie and Roger. Harris, Haley, and I arrived this morning. We'll work from our offices here, too. However, Haley will work remotely from *Le Beaulieu Manoir*—Leonie's family's ancestral home with her parents. She wants to stay close to her sisters, Lola and Leonie.

Le Manoir offers the most secure residence for Roger and Leonie while the media goes wild over the pretrial. It's on the westernmost part of the outskirts of Paris in Neuilly-Auteuil-Passy. The majestic property features manicured park-like grounds, stables, tennis court, swimming pool and cabana, and a palatial French Rococo mansion. A part of the 16th arrondissement, it's in the wealthiest neighborhood.

They built the hamlet between the thirteenth and seventeenth centuries. Later, during the reign of Louis XV, it became a fashionable country retreat for French elites. The Beaulieu's twenty acres of land border Bois de Boulogne with parts of the acreage awarded to their ancestors by the monarch.

Roger smiles, thankful for our love and support. It's typical of the Steele clan to drop it all to rally behind one of us. This time, it's for my younger brother.

Fuck!

It's been a nightmare. More negative media coverage. More comments from "sources close to" blah blah blah. More absolute bullshit.

My experience isn't the worse of it.

Roger took my advice and followed my lead with Starr's security. He implemented a detail for Leonie when a reporter harassed her after leaving a baby boutique with our mothers. Eric Vogel—their driver—had to intervene and knocked the reporter to the ground for pushing her in his eagerness to get a shot of her in distress.

Like I did at Starr's mansion, Guy hired additional security for the *Manoir*. Some paparazzi scaled the wall to get photos of them on the grounds and in the mansion. Fucking drones circle overhead at all times of the day and the night. Federico Fellini said it best in his interview with *Time*: "Paparazzo… suggests to me a buzzing insect, hovering, darting, stinging." How apropos. It's an invasion of the worse kind.

Roger even upped the ante at STEELE Paris. Obviously to no avail based on my encounter.

He calls the vice president of security to update him and to request additional precautions. When he rings off, he nods at us and goes to the drinks cabinet for some waters.

"It's a pain in the ass. These fuckers are like sharks with one drop of blood in the vast ocean," he says as he tosses bottles in our direction.

We stretch out on the sofa and club chairs while he fills us in on the latest developments. Just listening makes my blood boil with rage. *The Enforcer* in me wants to handle it. My way. These fuckers know no bounds, again like with My Angel. Particularly since Leonie is visibly pregnant. They don't give a fuck.

"Man, I'll look into some type of tech to help—"

The ringing of Roger's mobile interrupts Harris' comments. Roger strides to his desk to retrieve it.

"Hi, babe. What's up?" He asks.

He physically sags with relief, as though it's good news and not something dreadful.

"Yes, they're here, and they wanted to surprise you. Surprise!" He laughs genuinely.

"It's good to see you smiling, bro," I say when he ends the call.

His gaze shifts from his mobile he was staring at with a goofy grin to me.

I smile just as wide and tip my water bottle to Roger in salute.

He returns my gesture and ambles over to talk some more with us.

"You know what time it is, don't you?" I ask, leaning forward and rubbing my hands together as I stare at Roger.

A smile quirks the corners of his mouth as the water bottle pauses midair. He cocks his head to the side and raises his eyebrow. An expression of *oh boy, here it comes from The Rebel* flashes across his face.

I chuckle wickedly, knowing I have Roger hooked. And Harris, if his sitting straighter in his club chair, serves as a sign of his interest.

"Guys' Night Out! Tonight. The Jackson boys are in town along with Borya, and of course Luc. Call your buddy Joel Bailey. We'll meet at Jackson Smoke&Scotch Lounge Paris. Nine o'clock," I declare. "And I will not take no for an answer."

Harris whoops and punches the air.

"Yeah, baby! Count me in!" He exclaims.

The smile on Roger's face spreads to a full-on Cheshire Cat's grin. His slate gray eyes shine. With a nod, he brings the bottle to his mouth and chugs the water.

Harris eggs him on as though it's a shot of tequila—or more appropriately, Scotch.

I chuckle and wink before I finish my bottle.

The cure to the blues: family and friends.

"HERE'S TO GUYS' Night Out and the support of my boys!"

Roger lifts his Baccarat crystal snifter of Jackson Reserve Scotch in a toast.

We're in one of the glass-enclosed tasting rooms at Jackson Smoke&Scotch a new lounge Lucien opened nine months ago on Rue Saint-Honoré.

The legendary Place Vendôme/St. Honoré area is the place to see and be seen. Where money is no object for the people it attracts. Old society, fashionistas, and celebrities frequent the nearby high-chic spots to shop, drink, and dine.

It's the latest addition to Jackson Corporation's luxury establishments created by *The Sexy Chef*, as legions of his female followers dubbed Lucien. They slated locations in London, New York, and Los Angeles for over the next few months. Another hot property for the Jacksons to add to their list.

I rarely smoke, but tonight I take a long draw on my Jackson Cuban cigar and settle back in my leather club chair. The tasting notes of the spicy, earthy, and woody flavors linger on my palate. They blend well with the smoky, dark berries flavor of the Jackson Reserve Scotch. Its trademark bite drags along the back of my tasting.

My mind drifts back to our first night at the Lounge with Sebastian, Roger, Joel, and Lucien. Baz teased me about my encounter with My Angel at his wedding.

"Damn, it must be in the water!"

"Hell, as long as it's not in my Jackson Reserve, I'm good. Let those three keep the water!"

"I'll drink to that, bro!"

Everyone laughs at Lucien's and my banter.

"Funny, you were chasing after Starr Knight at my wedding,"

Sebastian says as he blows out smoke from his Jackson Cuban Cigar.

All heads swing to me, curious to know who sparked the interest of the Dom playboy enough for me to give chase. It's the reverse—I can't keep women from their pursuit of me. My face flushes and I take a swig of my Scotch.

"Fuck off, Baz," I mumble an answer with the snifter at my lips.

"Pardon... Say again? We didn't hear you, Lover Boy, er, playboy..." Sebastian teases me relentlessly as only an older brother can.

Now recovered, I cradle the Baccarat crystal snifter in my palms as I smirk at Baz. His gray eyes flash with devilment.

"I don't know what you're talking about," I scoff. "You must have been floating in the clouds, struck by Cupid's arrow." I respond as I make goo-goo eyes and bat my eyelashes coyly at Sebastian.

We crack up, Baz included. His cheeks even redden with embarrassment. Poor guy. I got my big brother down pat.

"Say what you want, Hettie and I have a good thing going... As it is. No signs of marriage on our horizon," Joel states with a decisive nod between puffs of his cigar. "I'm way too young to commit for the rest of my life."

Lucien and I clink glasses with Joel, adding robust cheers and here, here.

Roger shakes his head and chuckles. Now that he's back with Leonie, he's as bad as Baz.

"Laugh all you want. I was just like you. Probably worse," Sebastian starts, eyeing each of his hecklers. "It'll happen to you, too. And I'm going to be the one yucking it up."

Lucien's, Joel's, and my eyes widen at Sebastian's proclamation. Then we burst out in hysterical laughter. Lucien wipes his eyes while Joel doubles over. Sebastian and Roger can't help but to join us...

Now let's go to the scoreboard: Sebastian married... Check... Joel married... Check... Roger engaged... Check... Malcolm head over fucking heels in love with none other than said Starr Knight... Check Check Check!

I chuckle and sip my Scotch.

"Private jokes, bro?"

Laurent's question pulls me from my reverie.

I glance at the youngest Jackson, who's four years my junior. Like me, he's the rebel of their clan, the one who marches to his own tune. And doesn't give a fuck. After Lucien, he's my favorite cousin.

"Just recalling how I was adamant not acknowledge my attraction to Starr Knight—you know Lola's yogi friend from her wedding—when the guys gathered her nine months ago. Now, I claim her and have to admit I'm in the same goo-goo world as Baz and Roger were then and still are today," I respond with a chuckle.

Laurent nods his head and smirks, "Yeah, I remember her, the brown-eyed beauty with the banging—"

I growl at him, and he raises his hands as he laughs.

"Whoa, cuzz! No disrespect to you or your woman," Laurent says. "She must be someone really special for you to go all caveman on me. However, I don't blame you, she is fine as fu—"

This time I chuck the pillow from my club chair at his

head. He ducks and laughs uproariously. His emerald green eyes flash with mischief.

Instead, the pillow hits Borya on his back, and the former MMA champion spins ready to beat his opponent.

"*Kakogo cherta?!*" He growls *what the hell* in his native language as his glacial blue eyes spit icy daggers.

It's my turn to put my hands palms up in surrender.

"Pardon, bro! I meant that for mouthy Laurent," I chuckle.

Borya flicks his glare to him and says sternly, "Stop fucking around, *rebenok!*"

Laurent may not be a *kid*, but he's suitably chastened by the massive Russian.

Everyone laughs, then goes back to their discussions on sports, business, and typical guy talk.

Lucien and I update them on the latest with Jackson Hole at STEELE's construction. Then I tell them about Starr's SLFW Resort grand opening at STEELE St. Barth's coming up. Baz lets us know about an idea he has for a new retail opportunity that extends our brick-and-mortar offerings. Lachlan found an old recipe for one of the first Scotches Jackson Corporations's founder had hidden. Luc's Banque Montaigne just bought another, so he's added more to his billions. Our businesses thrive.

"Excuse us, gentlemen, but would you mind sharing with us what has your undivided attention?"

All talk ceases as every head turns toward the sultry, Spanish-accented voice. A stunning brunette with olive-colored skin and sable eyes smirks at us. Three other women stand in the doorway with her—another Spanish beauty and two blonde bombshells. Their faces flushed from the Scotch in their glasses or from the lust in their eyes.

Each takes her time gazing at one then the others of us. The women take our pause as an invitation to step inside of the room. One blonde sidles up to Sebastian. But he raises his left hand and wiggles his finger with the unmistakable platinum wedding band. Joel does the same when a brunette approaches him. Roger backs away with a firm shake of his head, his intense stare offers no chance of the affirmative.

When the initial brunette sashays to sit on the arm of my chair, I rise and shake my head no, too. Then gesture for her to sit, since Laurent has a gleam in his eyes for the stunner. She inclines her head and settles in my vacated seat.

I join Baz, Roger, Luc, and Joel at the bar.

"No thanks, I have my own brown-eyed beauty," I tell them with a laugh. "Besides, she'd have my balls if I flirted with another. Even though My Angel isn't here, I know what I do. And that I cannot do to her."

Baz grins and slaps me on the back.

"If I recall correctly, it was within these hallowed walls I told you what would happen when you teased me about Lola… *'Laugh all you want. I was just like you. Probably worse. It'll happen to you, too. And I'm going to be the one yucking it up.'* So…" Baz doubles over with laughter. His dove gray eyes fill with tears as he cracks up.

The fucker was right after all.

STARR

"Oh, Leonie! Cheer up! Think how much nicer your wedding will be once this shit is over! You don't want to reminisce and have a cloud of negativity shrouding your big day, do you?"

She glances over at Lola and raises her eyebrow.

It's a few weeks later and we're on a Girls' Getaway to Arachon, France. The trip is in lieu of Roger and Leonie's wedding. All thanks to Delia Shaw, an intern at STEELE Paris and former classmate of Leonie's at the Paris American Academy, and her bullshit sexual assault and harassment lawsuit against Roger.

"Hey! I'm not taking sides. But Roger *The Responsible* is right," Lola adds. "That's the best solution. Now you can wear your choice of gowns without a big ole belly bump!"

She balls up her Hermès beach blanket and puts it under her tunic. Then grabs Leonie's and includes it to make her pseudo-bump larger.

Leonie rolls her eyes and walks faster towards the

chaise lounges. But can't help laughing when Lola waddles past her, pretending to walk down the aisle.

"I hate you, Lola Steele!" Leonie calls after her best friend.

Lola puts her hands on her lower back and exaggerates her movements even more than before. Her snorts of laughter trail behind her.

"Some BFF, huh?" I ask Leonie.

She shifts her gaze from Lola to me as I loop my arm through hers. Despite my attempt to maintain a serious expression, my sorrel-brown eyes twinkle with mirth. When Lola sumo squats to sit on her chaise and the towels fall to the sand, I can't help but to burst out laughing. My dimples deepen in my face.

Although Leonie must think I'm acting the devil now…

"Oh, don't tease her—so badly," Billie chimes in as she cracks up.

Haley nods, "Well, you know Roger, he'll do what he thinks is best no matter what. However… I most definitely agree with his decision. For once, one of my overbearing older brothers is correct."

Anita, Bair, and Hettie Fuchs—the fiancée of Roger's friend Joel—stand firm with Leonie's fiancé, too.

Reality set in. She'd rather have her fairytale wedding than a blight on their big day.

Plus Roger arranged this Girls' Getaway to make up for the delay. A chance for Leonie to get her mind off of the pretrial madness and hang out with her closest friends for a fun time.

"Ha, ha, ha, Loser Girl!" Leonie says as she lowers herself down onto the chaise lounge next to Lola's.

"Remember to engage your pelvic floor, Leonie," says Anita.

Leonie nods, then puts her legs up and giggles to herself.

"I can't believe I've never been here before after all these years of living in France. It's spectacular!" Hettie exclaims.

Roger didn't want Leonie to go too far—no more than an hour's flight time from Paris. So her father suggested the seaside resort town of Arcachon on the southwest coast of France, known as the *Côte D'Argent* or the Silver Coast. Off the Atlantic Ocean, the luxury spot is south of Bordeaux's Haut Medoc vineyards and famous for its delicious oysters and seafood.

The stunning unspoiled sandy beaches, like the one we're on, make the change in wedding plans worthwhile. The magnificent villa we rented sits on the seafront and is only a brief ride to this beach.

Roger insisted Eric and a STEELE driver along with Leonie's security detail escort us. They drove from Paris in Roger's and Sebastian's Cullinans ahead of us. Then met our group at the heliport. Roger refuses to take any chances with The Twins and Leonie's safety because of harassment caused by the pretrial.

We arrived last night and just chilled at the villa. It's a marvelous architectural piece of history. The slate tile roof and stone facade with pale blue trim are ornate. With three floors and a large parcel of land on the seafront, it's a sizable property. Each of us has a suite of rooms with private baths.

After changing into Lola's Coterie loungewear, we met in the eat-in kitchen for a simple dinner prepared by the chef. She made several platters of freshly caught seafood, herb chicken, and roasted vegetables. We ate the tasty dishes buffet style around the table.

Later we stretched out in the media room and watched a movie while we stuffed ourselves with the variety of pastries the chef made from scratch. The rest of us enjoyed aperitifs while Leonie had her iced lemon ginger tea. We spent more time chatting than we did watching the latest chick flick. The drama in our lives proved more entertaining than the anything the characters faced!

This morning we headed to the beach. I chose a leopard print triangle bikini. It's sexy and fierce. A white mid-thigh length caftan, flip-flops, and a woven Kenya bag round out my outfit. I lift my glamour girl shades to peer at Leonie.

"Girl! Don't let Lola's antics get to you! If you didn't turn to the side or face us, we would never know you had a giant beachball for a stomach!" I say laughing.

"Nice compliment… I guess!" Leonie says as she tosses a pillow at me.

I lay my colorful Hermès beach towel over my chaise lounge then sit back to take in the view of the white sandy beach and deep blue-green Atlantic Ocean. The air is crisp with the saltwater scent as seagulls call out to each other. The sun is warm on my skin. Its warmth is a luxurious sensation after being in clothes for so long. I tilt my head back against the chaise lounge and close my eyes as I absorb my surroundings.

Peace and serenity.

"Great idea! Let's have a five-minute meditation session," Anita says when she spies my hands formed in a mudra on my thighs.

"Yes! Wonderful way to embrace all of this natural beauty," I respond.

Opening my eyes, I find everyone gathered around, settling on to the two chaises on either side of me. I smile and make room for Anita to sit at the foot of my chaise. We face each other cross-legged.

She leads us through a guided meditation that reflects on our connection with nature. Her melodic voice enchants us as we're led on the mind-body-surroundings journey. She ends with a chant and namaste.

When I reopen my eyes, my thoughts are clear, and I feel lighter. So far, so good.

"Tomorrow morning we should come down and do a flow class on the beach. I'd love to start my day with a sunrise session," Billie suggests.

I nod, "I have a new sequence I'd love to share with you. Leonie, I can modify it for you. Although I must say, your strength shows in your movements. You can probably teach it!"

She laughs and thanks me for my words of encouragement, but declines.

"I'm not ready for prime time! I'll leave the teaching to you and Anita, *merci!*"

"Well, I'm all for morning yoga tomorrow. But right

now, I'm getting in that glistening water!" Haley announces as she stands and takes off her Missoni tunic.

"Me, too! I can't wait to dive in," Hettie adds as she takes off her Norma Kamali sarong-style midi skirt. "I won't say last one in is a rotten egg because you smell nice, Leonie!"

Everyone laughs, agreeing she would be the last one in the water. Lola helps Leonie to her feet and links her arm through hers as they walk to the water's edge en masse.

The security team keeps a distance. But stay near since the beach is busy with other visitors, vendors with trinkets, and waitstaff. They're discreet in swim trunks and t-shirts. Only their clear earpieces hint at their purpose.

Leonie acknowledges them with a slight nod.

When we reach the water, the girls dive and jump in and Leonie wades in right behind us. The buoyancy makes me feel even lighter than the mediation session.

"The water is perfect! I'm so glad your father recommended Arcachon. Who knew France had Caribbean-style beaches!" Blair says as she floats over to me.

"We used to come often when I was younger. A simple trip my parents enjoyed since you get the beaches, the wine region, sailing lakes, and pine forests. The variety of activities kept us busy. The visits increased my interest in architecture with the historic homes of Ville d'Hiver," Leonie responds, smiling at the memories.

"I know it's early. But I can really go for some more of those oysters. They were delish last night!" Anita says. "They made me miss Norman!"

She adds with a wink.

"Why are you grinning like the Cheshire Cat?" Billie asks as she raises her elegantly arched eyebrow at Leonie.

She laughs out loud at being so busted for private jokes.

"Oh, let me guess… That fine ass man of yours and oysters?" Billie says grinning.

"Maybe, maybe not!" Leonie responds, then ducks away, averting her face.

"That's a definite maybe!!" Yells Billie at her retreating form.

We giggle and taunt the blushing Leonie.

We spend the rest of the time enjoying the sun, sand, and surf for a relaxing day at the beach. When we return, I check in with Adrienne on Starr Light Fitness & Wellness happenings, then send a text message to my man while the girls go about their business. Lola, Blair, and Billie get in some work for the boutiques. I told Anita I'd record Instagram videos for our thousands of followers for a crossover challenge. Haley geeks out on her computer where she's working on some top-secret project she's cagey about when asked. Hettie works on some legal cases for her clients. We're Independent Women who work hard and play harder!

"LEAD the way to the baccarat table, *merci*!"

I reply when the general manager for the Casino D'Arcachon greets us and asks for our favorite games. My eyes twinkle in glee as I clap my hands in anticipation of a night of gaming.

We decided to glam it up big time tonight in all red

outfits. I chose a cutout crystal-embellished crepe mini dress that reveals a sparkly sequin and crystal-embellished bra cup. Lola flaunts her toned legs in a smock exaggerated pussy-bow hammered silk mini dress with ruffled shoulders and elasticized cuffs on the breezy sleeves. Haley goes for the sparkle with a crystal and paillette-embellished tulle mini dress. Blair picks a new piece from Lola's Coterie evening wear collection, a contoured lace-up satin mini dress with contrasting lace-up detail and underwire cups. Billie's elegant outfit of a strapless filigree-like appliqué crystal-embellished mini dress. Hettie goes for a 90s style in a slinky, open-back chain-mail mini dress. Anita does a take on the classic tuxedo with a crystal-embellished satin-trimmed halter-neck mini dress. Leonie rocked her babies bump in a stretchy, one-sleeve ruched mini dress with an asymmetric skirt detailed and adjustable drawstrings on the shoulder and hem. We're all flowy hair, tan skin, and high strappy heels!

"*Absolument mademoiselles!* Please follow me," he says with a chuckle at my enthusiasm.

We walk through the 19th-century Château Deganne, where the casino is located. The impressive Neo-Renaissance-style mansion on the edge of the beach harkens to the grand times the area experienced. It's elegance similar to the Casino de Monte-Carlo reminds me of a James Bond from the time.

"I'm going to try my hand at blackjack," Hettie announces when we pass the table.

Anita nods, "Oh, me, too! I love pushing as far as possible without going over twenty-one."

Blair and Billie join them as the rest of us set up at the baccarat table.

A crowd gathers around our table to cheer me on my winning streak. Our laughter rings out above the excited din of the rooms.

"Come on, baby, let's make that money!" I laugh.

"This is such a blast! Who would have thought this little gem of a town would have a casino?" Haley giggles as she picks up her winnings from another bet. "This may become a regular spot for me!"

Lola and Leonie nod in agreement.

"STEELE should open a property here or take over this casino. I'm sure Malcolm would take it to the next level," Lola whispers so only we can hear.

I'm too absorbed in the game to pay them any attention —even if it is about my man. My laughter when I win yet another round makes them laugh, too.

"Girls, I'm on a roll! You better put your money down and get in on this streak!" I turn to my friends and say with a wink.

"Hey, I'm all in on this one!" Leonie answers, putting her chips on the table. "What's the saying, 'Mama needs a new pair of shoes,' right?"

They laugh as she rubs her belly in emphasis.

"*Oui, mademoiselle.* But your shoes seem more than good to me."

She glances over her shoulder, then tilts her head back to meet the eyes of the stranger. He's around Roger's height, handsome with aqua blue eyes, and a smooth baritone voice. His smile widens when their gazes meet.

Is he flirting with her? I wonder as I pause my game to face the attractive stranger.

"*Merci, monsieur*. How kind of you. My fiancé would agree," she says as she rubs her belly with her left hand, the giant stone shooting sparks in the light.

The stranger glances down and nods slightly.

"Lucky man, your fiancé," he replies. "Well, I shall leave you to enjoy your evening."

He bows and strides away just as Leonie's security detail moves into position behind him, ready to handle the situation.

Lola bursts out laughing, "Okay, MILF Alert! Roger better be careful!"

I nod in agreement.

"He needed to go. I don't want any bad vibes around my game!" I add with a scowl.

We crack up and get back to baccarat.

After a late dinner at the casino, we call it and head to the SUVs. The night is full of wins and losses, but all fun.

* * *

"GIRL HUSH, don't give the surprise away, Billie!"

Blair says when we hear Leonie walking towards the villa's living room entrance.

Roger called Lola to tell her he was coming down to surprise Leonie since today is the original date of their wedding. He also told her it's the one-year anniversary of Leonie and him being back together.

It the last night of our Girls' Getaway, and we were

supposed to go out to dinner at this great restaurant the house butler recommended. We know Leonie was feeling down today, and now we're puttering around in pajamas while throw her off. She'll never guess the truth!

"Hey, why aren't you guys dressed yet?" she asks as she walks into the living room to find us lounging about with the television on and eating ice cream.

"Oh, don't you look lovely!" Lola says sitting up. "Can you do me a favor and hand me my tote from the foyer?"

Leonie frowns and cocks her head questioningly.

Lola raises her hand to stop her from speaking.

"Come on, Leonie. You're already standing, and it's just around the corner. Please?!" She says with puppy eyes.

Leonie rolls hers and about-faces, grumbling to herself.

She probably thinks now we haven't even dressed, and we're going to be later than expected—considering she's ten minutes late as it is.

We jump from our seats to peek into the foyer where Roger waits for the love of his life. Leonie gasps when she sees him and starts to tremble. He embraces her, and she melts against him. With sighs of happiness for our dear friend, we turn away to give them privacy for such an intimate moment.

Ah, pure love. The Girls' Getaway just got even better! No need to think of the nasty pretrial. Only love.

MALCOLM

"*R*oger! Why did you sexually assault Delia Shaw?"

"No means no!"

"Roger Steele! *Honte à toi!*"

"Leonie! How can you marry a monster?"

"Leonie! This way!"

Fuck!

This is a damn media circus combined with a protest that's beyond fucked up. And this is only day one of the pretrial…

Albert Perry—STEELE Paris' General Counsel—and his legal team take the lead up the steps of the pretrial courthouse. Their mood is no nonsense and all business. They set the tone for us.

Sebastian and Roger flank Leonie, holding her arms as they move through the crowd held back by their security detail and the police. Despite how nasty the crowd behaves, she keeps her head high and her back straight. Leonie is no shrinking violet who simpers in the face of opposition. She's a fierce *Lion*.

The rest of our family and friends follow them. All Steeles; Starr; Guy and Josy; Lachlan and Lucien; Luc; Joel and Hettie; Blair and Billie; Norman and Anita came out in a full force of support. Françoise Faucher—Roger's long-time assistant—along with several other STEELE staff members join us in solidarity. Their presence is a comfort for my younger brother and Leonie.

No one speaks while we proceed to the courtroom. The halls are full of people who turn in our direction as we pass. Our pace doesn't slow. We want to get in and settled quickly.

A flash goes off to our left. Followed by more as the media within the building take notice of our group.

More catcalls fill the already tense air.

It pisses me off. These people have zero knowledge of the facts. Yet they judge and condemn my brother. The state of the world today assumes the man is guilty automatically. Some may be. But Roger is not. The immediate castigation of him angers me.

Starr must sense my inner turmoil. She squeezes my hand as she peeks up at me with concern in her gorgeous sorrel-colored eyes.

I nod and squeeze her hand in acknowledgment of her support. What would I do without her?

She's been a total trooper the past couple of weeks. She's helped Leonie as her doula to lessen her stress with the upcoming birth of The Twins. Along with continuing to do meditation and yoga *nidra* with Leonie and Roger to ease their nerves. All on top of My Angel's other work with her company and the upcoming grand opening. She's even put off going to St. Barth's for a site visit to spend time with a close friend. That's my woman—selfless and loving of others.

Finally, we reach the doors to the courtroom. More police officers stand guard to maintain control and to prevent overcrowding. They allow us to pass with nods.

Upon entering, we see the lying bitch Delia Shaw at the claimant's table. She shifts in her seat to glance at some asshole guy next to her. Then faces us when he indicates with the tilt of his chin our entrance.

For a brief moment, the real Delia shines through with a sneer directed at Leonie. The fleeting expression reveals her cocksure attitude and devious intent. In a blink, it's gone, replaced by a chaste, eyes downcast countenance. Then she widens her eyes and covers her mouth on a sob before she turns away slowly. The guy standing behind Delia pats her shoulder comfortingly and whispers in her ear.

If I hadn't seen her glare at Leonie, Delia's performance would have been believable—and the Academy Award for Best Actress goes to…

Sebastian huffs in response to Delia's dramatic behavior.

I agree and growl under my breath.

My Angel squeezes my hand again, and I relax at her reminder to keep my cool. She made me promise this morning while we were getting dressed. Ever seeing the bigger picture, My Angel reminded me Roger didn't need any interference that would sway the judge's decision.

Now, I nod again.

After I help her into her seat on the bench between behind my parents and Leonie's mother and father, Roger joins Perry and the legal team at the defendant's table and faces forward. Not a glance at the liar.

Game on.

At the call to order, the din of voices quiets and everyone stands. When the judge enters the courtroom, the solemnity of the situation hits me in the chest like a Mack truck.

This woman can cause my younger brother to go to an abysmal French jail for years all over her lies. This is beyond fucked up.

The proceedings start with an opening statement presented by Judge Favre as a summary of the claim and the parties involved. The magistrate outlines the timeline for the proceedings. He plans to convene eight times after today on alternating days over the next month. Today will give both sides the opportunity to make opening statements. With the investigation set to begin next week.

Delia's legal team presents their opening statement. They drone on to paint me as a sex maniac who preyed on Ms. Shaw—an innocent, trusting university student who earned her position as an intern. Her only mistake was being in the division run by a monster...

Her appearance would support her claim of purity with a navy blue conservative skirt suit, severe bun, and no makeup. Her curves no longer on display and her vivacious personality hidden behind a sorrowful persona.

It's hard to get a read on the judge. He sits stoically on his bench. Periodically during the claimant's statement, his eyes flick to me with an analytical stare.

Perry rises from his seat.

He presents Roger's statement in a succinct, factual manner. Unlike the claimant's attorney, Perry completes his opening remarks in less than fifteen minutes. Even the judge seems to appreciate the brevity of Perry's words as Judge Favre's face relaxes a fraction.

He thanks both sides for their opening statements. Then he reminds everyone we will re-convene next week. He rises from his bench and exits the courtroom as we stand.

We wait until Perry and his team gather their paperwork before we leave.

In a show of support, Leonie kisses Roger on the lips in full view of everyone. The sound of cameras clicking fills the room. She knows how to play the game, too.

We make our way back out to the waiting cars. Sebastian and Roger flank Leonie again as we move through the crowd. More insults and questions come at us from all directions. Fuckers.

At last we get inside the four Mercedes-Benz Sprinters and pull away from the courthouse in formation. Perry suggested we lease the souped-up vans instead of driving our personal vehicles since strangers would view the license plates. We certainly don't want stalkers finding our homes. The damn drones and paparazzi are bad enough.

We take a roundabout way back to the *Manoir* to avoid being followed.

We wait until we reach the *Manoir* and sit in the living room before we discuss the investigation. Perry gives his feedback along with his team. They pulled a report on the judge and found him to be stern and only interested in facts, not emotions. The statement made by Delia's legal team was full of emotion. While Perry's was all facts. He says it's a score for Roger.

Our father and Roger ask more questions. But there's not much to go on at this point. The real action will occur next week. Perry suggests we enjoy the weekend, rest, and return ready for the tough part. He and the team leave, declining an offer to join us for an early dinner. Françoise also leaves and offers words of encouragement before they go.

The rest of the group heads to the dining hall—the larger eating area that harkens back to *Le Manoir Beaulieu*'s days of entertaining royalty in the larger space. The staff serves the meal prepared by their chef. Josy cooks on the weekends when she gives them the days off.

We dine on the scrumptious dishes and wines from their ancient cellar. No one discusses the proceedings. We opt to have a normal conversation with Harris teasing Haley about some mysterious project she's working on, and Hettie recounting Joel's time at their cake tasting with his allergic reaction to almond paste. Norman regales us with stories from his most renown matches, and Anita tells how he's a softy for their daughter Antonia. It amounts to a good time with loved ones.

* * *

"YES, SIR!"

My Sweet Sub's cry of anguish as I stroke her clit engorged from my suckling makes me want to skip the demo and fuck her now.

We took Perry up on his recommendation to enjoy the weekend. But our idea of rest probably isn't what he had in mind… It's LEVELS Paris.

Tonight is Demo Night, where members experienced in various acts of BDSM offer to show their skills to others. Masters of play including sensory deprivation, edge, electrostimulation, flogging, and my favorite—suspension bondage and submission.

Shibari—my preferred method I learned under the tutelage of a Japanese Master—requires the utmost skill on the Dom's side and trust from the sub. Since the sub is partially or fully suspended in the air by their body parts, suspension bondage is intense, and it comes with significant risks. A Dom must use great care and maintain an absolute focus on the sub's responses to understand and to heed them. Years of training during which I was a sub to a Japanese Domme taught me the beautiful art of rope play.

I would bare any other sub completely to the eyes of the LEVELS members during our demonstration. And I—not one to shy from anything—would show my face.

But not tonight and never with My Sweet Sub.

Not one individual will ever glimpse Starr Knight naked. For. My. Eyes. Only.

With her eyes covered by a white silk blindfold, she lies

supine on the table beside the white silk ropes. I chose them to contrast with her skin tone nicely and to remind her of my body wrapped around hers. I bound her heavy breasts with more of the soft material to form a narrow bandeau top and a strip of silk covers her smooth pussy.

I move the scrap of material back in place before I rise to my full height.

Completely clothed in a black long-sleeved shirt open to reveal my muscular torso, custom-fit black leather pants, and black leather boots, I'm the opposite of My Sweet Sub. Her black on my white. A full mask to maintain my anonymity finishes my outfit.

Now that she's primed and at ease, I help her to a kneeling position where her lush ass rests on her haunches and she grasps opposite elbows behind her back. I rub my hands along the tops of her thighs—just as silky as my ropes—letting my thumbs glide inward to soothe her. Then ask if she's ready. My Sweet Sub takes in an excited breath, then whispers yes against my lips as she nods her head. I nip her plump lower lip, and she yelps.

Playtime!

I turn to the members gathered around the primary stage in the Cellar and bow to signal the start of our demonstration. Through the holes in the mask, I see their excited faces, eager for the show. I smirk and face My Sweet Sub.

I skim the silk rope bundle over her heated skin. The cool touch of the sumptuous material causes another fluttery inhalation. I waste no time in unwinding the coil and setting to work binding My Sweet Sub.

An erotic pattern develops as I loop the silks around her arms to pull them closer to her back and make her chest rise so her ample tits jut out. Rope around her long, delicate neck exposed by her curls slicked into a topknot, then down between the valley of her tits to bind above and below the mounds. Encased in the white silks, her nipples peak and I can't help but to lean down to suckle them.

"Aaahhh, Sir…" My Sweet Sub moans.

I nip her and growl, "Silence, Naughty Pet!"

We agreed she would remain quiet since she's very vocal when we fuck. No need to risk her slipping in ecstasy and saying my name, revealing my identity and thus hers since the media photographed us together often. The global media spotlight cast on Roger has widened to the rest of the Steeles and those around us by association. We appear more than we prefer in the tabloids and news these days.

My Naughty Pet bites her lower lip and bows her head.

I leave a substantial length of rope to the side and help her lie back with her knees bent, feet flat on the table. Then I pick up two additional coils. A few loops around each thigh and calf pull them flush to the corresponding body part. I leave another substantial length of rope on her left thigh. The binding done, I squeeze her knees to signal we're ready for the next stage: suspension.

Once again, I ask My Sweet Sub if she's fine with phase two. This time I place a trial of open-mouthed kisses along her flat belly up to her luscious mouth. She moans a yes as I press my lips to hers.

I turn to our rapt audience, the hush in the room louder

than the usual sensual cacophony of moans, groans, and cries of pleasure and pain in the BDSM dungeon. Even more members gathered while I focused on My Sweet Sub. Not one person present in the Cellar glances away from us.

With a nod, I pivot and stride to the metal ring suspended above the stage. For the third time, I check the ring, the chain, and the lever to ensure their sturdiness. Satisfied, I return to My Sweet Sub and push the table beneath the ring.

Then I attach the extra length of the two coils to the ring and another piece from her left thigh to both lengths to form a triangle. Only her right leg is free from the ring. Before I push the table away, I recheck the knots and go to the lever to hoist My Sweet Sub into the air.

My Angel hovers above the table, captured in my silks. Beautiful.

The ginormous bulge in my constrictive leather pants demands release. I stroke my length. Soon.

Striding across the stage, I move the table swiftly, then stand behind My Angel and do a Vanna White move with my hands to reveal her to the audience.

They clap, impressed by her nubile form. With her long limbs flexible and sculpted by years of yoga and Pilates, My Angel is an incredible sight to behold. She is a work of art. My work of art.

Mine!

With that thought in mind, it's time for her reward. I move to stand by her bent legs and grasp her bound thighs. She moans in anticipation.

Yes, My Sweet Sub, time to fuck you as you fly.

In a blur, my zipper opens and my cock springs free, already aimed at her sopping wet pussy as illustrated by the wet patch on the strip of silk. I swipe it aside and slide my girth into her ready channel.

Fuck yes!

My Sweet Sub arches her back at the carnal invasion of her body. Her mouth hangs open as she swings sideways on the ring rope attached on the left half of her body. Like a pendulum, she keeps coming back to sheath my cock in her tight, wet heat.

The rippling of her inner walls lets me know she's close to climax. Now after eight months, I trained My Sweet Sub, and she knows not to cum unless I give her permission.

And permission I am ready to give to her, along with my seed.

I redouble my efforts and grip her ass to keep her steady. My hips snap to jackhammer inside of her again and again until she's wailing with each brutal thrust. When her pussy clamps down on my dick, I'm gone.

"Cum for me, Little Pet! Cum for me. Now!" I command.

A shudder wracks through her body, and a keening sound comes from the depth of her soul.

"Oh, fuck… Fuck… Fuck… MALCOLM!!!" My Sweet Sub screams as her climax sends her over the edge to the erotic bliss of subspace.

Well, I guess she blew over cover now…

"Oh, baby! This is incredible! I can't believe how much work they did since I saw the last status video! Thank you so much!!"

My Angel's eyes glitter like the Caribbean Sea as the sunlight dapples its turquoise surface.

We're in St. Barth's for the first site visit of her new Starr Light Fitness & Wellness Resort at STEELE St. Barth's. We came for the topping off ceremony. In construction, it's the Viking practice of topping off a building with an evergreen tree on the peak to celebrate the completion of the major structural components of a building.

In SLFW's case, we put a palm tree on the roof and toast with My Angel's favorite Krug Clos d'Ambonnay Champagne. The construction crew completed the two-story building's foundation, outer walls, interior walls, and roof. Phase two of the project focuses on the interior systems and the exterior finish. The last phase for the interior design and external landscaping appears on schedule in three months. The grand opening celebration will occur a week after a soft opening.

"Yes, Starr! How fantastic is the view of the Caribbean!" Adrienne exclaims as she shields her eyes from the bright sun.

Her comment draws Anton's attention. He can't keep his eyes off of the green-eyed feline beauty.

"*Da*, and what a spectacular view," he growls thickening his Russian accent.

Adrienne may not respond with words to his call, but she shivers visibly and gulps the champagne in her crystal flute.

My Angel chuckles and wraps her arm around my waist as she reaches up to kiss my cheek.

"I can just picture Beach Barre out front on the warm sand. Or, or Moonlight Yoga on the roof deck! I love it!" She says.

My heart slams against my chest. Fuck! I thought she was about to say the L-word about me. I stiffen, then relax when I realize I'm not averse to it after all. Not now. Even though I haven't spoken the words, the last few times we made love or spent time together, I attempted to express them with my actions. Hey, like they say, actions speak louder than words and all that.

She must have felt my knee-jerk reaction because she moves away from me. But I slip my arms around her from behind and clink my flute to hers.

"I'm glad you love it or me if that's what you meant," I tease, brushing my lips against the shell of her ear before I nip the lobe.

A little pleasure and pain to lighten the mood.

"So arrogant, Mr. Steele," My Angel replies. "Huh… Putting words in my mouth."

"I have more than words to put in that sweet little mouth of yours, My Angel," I smirk.

Just as I hoped, she giggles and pushes me off of her.

Disappointed from the loss of her curvy body, but thankful she's not pissed, I'll take it.

We spend another hour in discussions with the project manager and his crew. My Angel and Adrienne ask questions, and they satisfy their concerns with sound answers. Anton speaks with them to complete the timeline, then we head back to the main resort for lunch.

It's only a six-minute walk or two minutes in a property golf cart. We wanted guests to have easy access to the center. Its prime beachfront location will serve My Angel's business well.

She and Adrienne walk ahead of Anton and me as they chat about the new location.

My Angel looks cute and feminine in what she calls a playsuit. The shorts length suits the Caribbean heat and the red floral-print reminds me of tropical flowers. But it's the vision of her long, toned, sun-kissed legs squeezing my ears that makes me grin.

Her curly pony hair bounces with each step, beckoning for me to wrap it around my fist and use it like a pair of reins while I ride her all night long. Moonlight Yoga won't be the only thing pumping on the rooftop deck. We'll have to christen each room for prosperity. Now that's the Malcolm *The Rebel* Steele version of a topping off ceremony!

"DON'T YOU LOOK SEXY, My Angel."

She spins around and the layers on the linen and silk mini skirt she wears flares out, showing off her long, flawless legs. When she faces me, my eyes travel up her body to the white cotton cropped tank top. It molds to her luscious tits.

I marvel at the way her nipples plump up under my hooded gaze. I lick my lips, and she bites hers. I feel her teeth on the tip of my cock.

"Thank you, baby," she says with an extra sassy twirl. "You look hunkalicious yourself."

The wink she gives me makes my cock twitch. It's need for her increases constantly. Damn.

But it's the sight of my collar around her neck that gets the blood flowing to my groin in earnest. My Sweet Sub wore her day wear version. The diamond-pavé letter S in its platinum mesh center brings out the caveman in me. S for Steele equals mine, all mine.

If we hadn't agreed to dinner with Anton, Adrienne, the project manager, and his wife, I would drag My Sweet Sub by her curly ponytail to bed and never let her leave it. Rawr!

She must sense my growing desire for her, and she smirks.

"This way, Mr. Steele, duty calls now, playtime later. That is, if you are a very good boy and deserving of a treat…" My Angel teases, looping her arm through mine and heading for the villa's front door.

"Watch yourself, My Naughty Girl, or playtime will become punishment time," I rejoin with a carefully placed swat to her sits bones.

My Naughty Girl yelps and skips from the unexpected smack.

I chuckle wickedly as we exit the villa.

We hop into the golf cart and drive to the resort's beachfront restaurant. Anton waves us over to the bar where he stands next to Adrienne. The hulking, blond Russian dwarfs the green-eyed, buttery pecan-colored skin beauty as she sits on a bar stool.

"Hi, there! You should have one of these cocktails. The bartender made it for me especially," she says, casting a sultry smile at the mixologist.

I chuckle when Anton's fists clench and his nostrils flare. Oh boy…

My Angel giggles and reaches for the glass the bartender places in front of her. Then rolls her eyes when I growl in her ear possessively.

Mine!

Fortunately for the mixologist, the project manager and his wife appear and distract Anton and me from explaining how close to dangerous ground he treads.

Instead, the hostess leads us to our table by the beachside railing.

I help My Angel into her chair and take the seat beside her. We order a tantalizing seafood tower for our appetizer and an array of mouther-watering meat and chicken entrées. Conversation flows freely as we chat about everything from island life to the benefits of coconut oil to the best restaurants on the closest islands.

The project manager regales us with stories of him catching a great white shark by mistake when he went night fishing. He has us cracking up when he describes it landing on the shore and him running out of his sandals when he recognized the apex predator.

His wife chimes in with how her husband left out the part where he swore the shark flew out of the water with its mouth wide open, ready to devour him, and he ran screaming. Like a baby, she adds for emphasis as she laughs hysterically.

My Angel's carefree giggles and her shining eyes make my heart soar with affection. She makes it harder and harder for me to deny the level of my attraction to her. And I'm not sure if I want to ignore it any longer. Even if I admit it to myself only.

I lean over and kiss her cheek, not giving a damn it's PDA in front of a STEELE staff member.

MINE!

Later that night, I show My Angel just how deep my emotions for her go as I make slow and deliberate love to her. I worship every part of her delicious body. From the tips of her toes I suck to the kisses I place on the backs of her knees to the special attention I pay to her supple breasts. By the time my mouth covers hers for a soul-stirring, passionate kiss, she trembles beneath me and widens her legs as an invitation to fill her with my aching cock.

I slide into her with ease as her hot, soaking channel envelops my turgid length. My thrusts alternate between slow and deep and shallow and fast until she writhes as she cums over and over. I draw the maximum orgasms from her I know her body can handle before I seek my release.

As her core quivers from her last climax, I propel my cock forward, aiming to fill her womb with my seed until it spills from her pussy to trail between her thighs and the crack of her ass. I plan to mark My Angel as I claim her all night long.

* * *

"How's it going, bro?"

My Angel is in the office of the beachfront villa at the resort working with Adrienne on plans for SLFW Resorts, so I place a call to Roger. The pretrial is still happening and not being there to support him is working on me. But as he told me when I said I had to go for business, STEELE needs us as much from us as our family members. He said with the rest of the clan in Paris along with Leonie's parents and Luc, they have plenty of support.

Starr and I will return after she heads to Beverly Hills and I go to New York City to handle some in-person work. Even though she's Leonie's doula, she told Starr to focus on her business first, there's plenty of time before Leonie gives birth.

"As to be expected. She said, he said, blah, blah, blah. Let's give it a rest for now. Tell me about Starr's venture," Roger responds wearily.

Fuck, my brother really doesn't need any bullshit with Leonie ready to pop and her concerns for a healthy delivery. Fucking Delia Shaw!

I fill him in on the status and he offers some valuable advice. He says it's good to focus on STEELE and not the pretrial. Then he hits me with an unexpected question.

"Have you told Starr you love her, yet, *Rebel*?" He asks.

From the tone of his voice, I can tell he has an intense expression on his face. Roger has always been the responsible one of the siblings—Roger *The Responsible* Steele. As the middle child, he worries about the rest of us as much as Baz does as the eldest.

I take a moment to consider his question and how best to answer it. True, I have feelings for My Angel unlike any other woman before her. True, she makes me behave as I never have in the past.

But I sense she's holding back from me, and it bothers me more than I want to admit. I know she still has reservations about how quickly she's picked up on being a submissive and on balancing her Independent Woman. Even as free-spirited as she is—and not falling in line with convention—My Angel still struggles to give in to a D/s relationship completely.

And I've let it evolve into a vanilla relationship of boyfriend-girlfriend to help her ease into things. But I want it all with her, the BDSM and the vanilla rolled into one.

Fuck, who would have thought?

So I don't know how to answer Roger truly.

I do feel deeply for Starr. But I hold off on saying those three words. If I'm honest with myself, it's because I fear she doesn't love me as deeply as I've fallen for her. I use my bravado to hide my fear. So far, it works. Just like earlier when I teased Starr to keep her from getting upset. How much longer will that work?

"Who says I love her?" I ask, falling back on my rebel playboy bravado with a chuckle. "We're just in the here and now, bro. Not all of us are ready to run down the aisle to the love of our life!"

A noise behind me makes me shift in my chaise lounge on the deck. I see My Angel in the doorway behind me. A fleeting expression ghosts across her face, but it's too fast for me to decipher it.

My stomach drops.

Fuck! I sure as hell hope she didn't hear my callous remark about loving her and marriage. That would be a major blunder. Damn.

Then she smiles.

I can't tell if it reaches her eyes because they're covered with giant sunglasses.

With a hope for the best, I smile back and hold my hand out to her.

She sashays over and sits between my legs with her back resting against my torso. I twine our legs and place my hands on her lower belly. She stiffens a bit, but relaxes with a sigh when I kiss the side of her neck where it meets her shoulder.

I chat with Roger a bit more—after changing the subject—then end the call.

"How'd your plans go?" I ask to test the waters.

Starr nods and tells me some of their ideas.

We talk through them, and I make suggestions. Then she asks me about Roger and Leonie. I fill her in, and she says she'll go back to Paris after she handles some affairs at home. After a while, we fall silent.

The sound of the water lapping on the shore and the seagulls' cries lull us into a nap. When I awake, Starr is gone. For a moment I panic, thinking she heard me after all and left me. Fuck!

When I rush from the chaise lounge calling her name, I spot her on the beach.

She's practicing her asanas.

I watch her for a while, marveling at her poise and strength. The way she can contort her body with ease amazes me. She's so flexible.

That's how I need to be—allow myself to just go with the flow. Not try to fight the norm for a change. No more need to prove how I can stand apart and do things my way,

I wouldn't mind the relationships Baz and Roger have with their women. The loves of their lives. My mind plays scenarios for My Angel and me: love, happiness, marriage, children, BDSM...

Why can't I have it all?

Haven't I always gotten what I wanted? And I want my brown-eyed beauty. Forever.

My Angel finishes her practice with a bow of her lovely head. When she stands and faces the villa, she notices me on the deck watching her. She pauses and appears to gather herself. Then she lifts her angelic face and waves at me.

I stand and walk down the steps to the seawall to embrace my love. My future. My Angel.

I can't believe what Malcolm said to Roger! Just as I came to terms with this whole D/s thing—me, an Independent Woman with a successful business and satisfying life.

While I laid next to Malcolm in bed at his private suite in LEVELS Paris after his—I mean our—demonstration with the ropes, I thought if I could do that for him, I must love this man. Hell, I mean I let him tie me up with ropes with nothing but bits of cloth covering my tits and pussy, hang me from the ceiling by said ropes, then fuck me delirious while I screamed his name all in front of a crowd in a damn BDSM dungeon!!! Without a doubt, the world now knows who we are and my addiction to submission!!!

Even the extreme sports we did—water jetpacking, cliff diving, zorbing, and OMG BASE jumping—excited me. He turned me on to the idea of thrill seeking and to cutting loose for real. Being an actual free spirit...

I've put up with mad shit from Vicky Reynolds: public

embarrassment, gossip, and fucking with my business! And for what? For what?!?!

ARGH!!!

Really, Starr??? You lose all cool points for falling for a man who gives ZERO fucks about you!

Does he?

Yeah, dummy... Didn't you hear what he told his own flesh and blood?!?!?! He has no reason to lie to his own brother... "Your Dom... Man" sure as hell didn't sound as though he were joking!!! For fuck's sake he was LAUGHING. ABOUT. YOU!!!

True, so true.

Now look at me! This man has me not only talking to myself, but responding for a full-on conversation!

My wise great-grandfather used to say, "It's all right to talk to yourself, but just don't answer. Then you worry!"

Okay, so I'm very, very, I mean very worried right now…

I couldn't let Malcolm know I heard his words. Instead, I pasted a smile on my face for the rest of the three days we stayed. Even when he made lo—I mean fucked me or held me close to him. Not only was I in shock, but I had to save face and handle my business—even if he didn't know I love him.

* * *

"Leonie, honey, your mind wanders."

Softly, I speak when I notice her fidgeting during her evening yoga *nidra* session.

When I did a video call to check on my friend after I

returned from St. Barth's, she appeared so glum. Not at all like the sparkly Leonie or the fierce *Maman*.

She recounted her OB-GYN's words to her, *"Leonie, you have a noticeable increase in your blood pressure. It's not from your pregnancy, as you have no other signs. It's stress related. How are you holding up with the investigation?"*

I flew to Paris a few days later. All thoughts of arrogant Malcolm Steele set aside. My focus shifts from wallowing in self-pity—and a quart of Häagen-Daz Belgian Chocolate ice cream—to Leonie, The Twins, and Roger. Time to step up my doula duties.

Now, I sit beside her on the chaise lounge Roger added to her yoga studio at *Le Beaulieu Manoir*. It's easier for her to settle on her side on the piece of furniture than to lower herself to the ground at nearly thirty-six weeks pregnant.

He cares so much for his fiancée. Unlike his brother for me...

I give my head a firm shake to dislodge the negative thought. Focus, Starr!

Leonie opens her eyes, and a tear slips from a corner. A pitiful sob follows.

Sensing she doesn't need words, I gather her into my arms and rock her gently. I think of positive thoughts: Roger and STEELE International cleared of any charges; the healthy birth of The Twins; her upcoming wedding to the love of her life.

Put in the Universe what you want; ask and you shall receive; give thanks. Every tenet I can think of to surround Leonie with peace and tranquility, positive vibes.

After a few minutes, she sniffles and raises her head. A

small smile of gratitude blooms on her tear-stained face. She nods, and I help her sit up with the pillows behind her back.

"*Merci, chérie.* You are such a comfort, Starr," Leonie says, now smiling fully.

"You're more than welcome, my dear friend," I respond with a grin.

As I rise to get a tissue for her, her next words stop me in my tracks.

"What's happened between you and Malcolm, *chérie?*" She asks quietly.

Caught off guard by her question and by my visceral reaction to his name spoken aloud for the first time in days, I shudder.

"Starr?" Leonie asks.

I scoop up the tissue box and walk back to her, avoiding her amber eyes.

"I don't know what you mean," I hedge. Surely he hasn't mentioned I've not responded to his voicemails and text messages.

Yeah! What does he care?! Pipes up my inner warrior.

I have to stop myself from telling her to shut it. No need to freak Leonie out as I hold a conversation with myself...

"He told Roger you're avoiding his calls," Leonie responds, watching me closely.

I shrug, going for denial.

"No, not at all!" I exclaim brightly. "I've just been so busy with work. You know the grand opening of the Resort's first location at STEELE St. Barth's happens soon."

Leonie nods, but I can tell she doesn't quite believe me. So I launch into the things I'm doing and plans for the new center along with others. Better to expound on the truth than to lie.

Re-directed, Leonie lets my non-answer go, and we stick to safer topics.

Besides, the last day of the pretrial happens tomorrow.

She needs to relax tonight since she's insisting upon going to the courthouse to support her fiancé. The purpose of our evening yoga *nidra* is to ease the day's troubles from her mind and prepare it for a night of peaceful slumber.

After a while, Roger enters the studio to collect his wife. He bids me good night, and I return to my guest suite.

Hopefully, I'll have peaceful dreams, too.

"Leonie, come sit here, sweetheart."

I stop speaking with Lola and shift my gaze at Shelley's words to the door where Leonie enters the pretrial court-room with her parents, Guy and Josy.

"*Merci, Maman Aussi,*" she answers as she double kisses Shelley's cheeks in greeting.

Leonie takes a seat between her parents and Morgan and Shelley, then waves at her family and friends. Lola, Sebastian, and the rest of the Steele clan, the Jacksons, Joel and Hettie, Norman and Anita, Luc, Blair, Billie, Françoise, and some STEELE employees gather in support.

Moments later, the bailiff calls the court to order, and the judge enters the room.

I close my eyes and send a silent prayer to God and every deity in every religion's pantheon for Roger and STEELE cleared of these false claims.

Delia Shaw just wants attention and money. None of what she said holds an ounce of truth. It's absolutely terrible!

I choose to ignore the liar and keep my eyes stay riveted on Judge Favre as he reads his summation of the case.

He's so slow.

Mentally, I push him to read faster. Just give us the answer already!

"Because of the testimony provided by both the plaintiff and the defendant, the evidence brought forth, and of my careful deliberation, I determine Roger Steele and STEELE International, Inc. should—"

"*AAAH... MON DIEU!!*"

"*Qu'est-ce que—*"

"*Oh, Mon Trésor!!*"

"Leonie!! What's wrong?!" I cry at her scream.

Pandemonium breaks out.

I jump up and rush to her side just as Roger springs over the divider.

We reach Leonie at the same time.

Her water broke, and she's having contractions.

Sebastian shouts orders, and everyone moves.

He and Roger carry Leonie between them while their other brothers, male friends, and security detail clear a path for them. Lola leads the way for us to exit out the back of the courthouse. Then we hurry into one of the

Mercedes-Benz Sprinters Roger leased to transport everyone during the pretrial.

Meanwhile, I call Leonie's OB-GYN, Dr. Pierre Berger. I confirm he's on his way to the hospital as the five of us speed off. I do my best to keep Leonie relatively calm during the ride.

Once at the hospital, Dr. Berger arrives with his team. An anesthesiologist, two pediatricians—one for each Twin —two labor and delivery nurses, an OB tech, and a nursery nurse follow him into Leonie's suite.

They prep her for pre-labor—in twin pregnancies, it can take up to thirteen hours for her body to be ready for the actual delivery. He expects the first Twin within two hours after and the second Twin less than twenty minutes later.

Leonie appears less fearful now that she's in the hospital's safety and under the doctor's care. Her golden caramel complexion flushed rosy from the sensations overtaking her body. Her feline amber eyes glower, while French curses spilled from her lush lips.

Lola and I fuss over Leonie. I put her long mahogany waves—once pulled in a sleek ponytail—in one thick braid down her back.

Roger and Sebastian hover around her bed. Soon the rest of their family and friends arrive. Josy and Shelley hurry to her side, hustling Roger and Sebastian out of their way. Haley joins us at the foot of Leonie's bed as she massages her feet and calves to comfort her.

Surrounded by the most important women in her life, Leonie braves the birth of their twins.

Despite her snarls, cursing at Roger in French, and swatting him away when he attempts to comfort her, she gives birth to two healthy, identical boys. Rodolphe Beaulieu Steele and Gaspard Beaulieu Steele enter our world. With gray eyes and black hair, the Steele family traits continue.

Later that night, I return to my guest room next to Leonie's suite at the hospital. I'm so happy for my friend and grateful for her successful birth and new little family. She and Roger are beside themselves with joy!

So engrossed in my doula duties, I didn't have time to think about arrogant Malcolm Steele. Since I spent all of my time at Leonie's side, he and I didn't interact. Until moments ago.

"Hi, Angel," he said tentatively. "Crazy day, huh?"

Trapped in the hallway heading back from the nurse's station, I couldn't avoid him. So I nod and try to go around his massive frame.

He sidesteps to block my path again.

We do a shuffling dance that Haley interrupted inadvertently. As soon as she asked Malcolm a question, I dodged the entire scene and fled to my room. I could feel Malcolm's penetrative stare on my back, but I rushed on.

Now I shoot a quick text to Roger and Leonie to let them know to call my room since I'm turning my mobile off. Already Malcolm is blowing it up with messages. With a sigh, I shut it down.

Unfortunately, shutting my mind down proves more difficult. Dreams of mini Malcolms play on repeat: swaddled in blankets held in my arms; smiling up at me as I breastfeed them; coos as I talk to them. All the while, his magnetic presence hovers on my periphery. Watching his sons, me.

* * *

"THE NEXT GENERATION of Steeles is born! May they carry on our clan name and STEELE and Beaulieu forever!"

Declares Morgan as he holds his day-old grandsons proudly.

"*Oui, Mon Trésor* extends her family's line with males, one for Beaulieu and one for STEELE!" Guy adds proudly as he plucks Gaspard from Morgan's arm.

Leonie shakes her head and smiles.

Roger slips his hand in hers and dips his head to kiss her lips.

She whimpers and buries her face in his neck as she sobs.

"Let's give them some privacy—" Lola suggests.

With fresh resolve, Leonie faces us.

"*Non, non,* stay. Don't mind my blubbering," she says as she dabs her face with Roger's handkerchief. "You do not understand just how much I love and appreciate you. It's been a trying time. But new life brings great joy."

Her mother goes over to the bed and clasps their hands before she kisses them.

"*Mon Trésor,* never make excuses for your emotions! Your body is going through a lot"—she turns to Shelley and gestures for her to join them—"I may have had only one baby, but I know how you're feeling. Shelley, who's had five, will agree."

Roger's mother smirks and strokes Leonie's cheek.

"Yes! And you thought you had some choice words for Roger. Well, let me tell you, I laid Morgan out each and every time!"

The room fills with our laughter, Morgan's chuckles loudest of us all.

"I agree! Norman may have been the champ in the ring. But I won by a TKO when he dared to utter one word while I was in labor," Anita says from the sofa.

Norman feigns the impact of a crushing blow and collapses against the armrest. The same king of the boxing ring who plays dress up and has a tea party with his toddler daughter.

Again, the tough guys are always the softies at heart.

I feel Malcolm's stare from across the room. I can't help but to meet his gaze.

His forlorn face almost breaks my resolve. Noticing my lingering look, his eyes brighten, and he starts toward me.

Quickly, I avert my eyes and chat with Anita. Out of the corner of my eye, I see Malcolm slouch back against the wall with a frown marring his handsome face.

Good. Leave. Her. Alone! My inner warrior growls.

Funny how it's her I want to kick out of my life.

"WHAT TIME IS IT? Have you heard anything, yet? I'm worried sick—"

Leonie stops speaking when she sees Roger standing in the hospital suite's doorway. Her eyes widen and her mouth forms a perfect O before she claps her hands over it.

"Hello, my love," he says gruffly as he steps into the room. "It's over."

Leonie gasps and closes her eyes as she falls back against the pillows. Her body shudders as her sobs increase in her hands.

Roger glances at Josy and me, barely. His sole focus is Leonie as he rushes to her side and pulls her into his arms, kissing her face as he murmurs words of love.

Josy smiles at her daughter- and son-in-law, then turns to me and nods at the door.

I nod back and follow her from the suite with a smile on my face.

"Oh!" I exclaim as I bump into a wall of muscle when I close the door behind me with a click.

My head tilts back to see Malcolm glowering at me.

Without a word, he takes me by the elbow and ushers me next door to my guest room. He cocks his eyebrow at me wordlessly demanding I unlock it for him.

I do.

Once inside, he grabs my face between his sizable hands and crushes my mouth with his in a possessive, toe-curling kiss. Malcolm doesn't let me catch my breath before he hoists me up and slams my back against the door.

Automatically, my legs wrap around his waist and lock at the ankles. My hands seek out his thick, silky hair.

He rips at my wrap dress, pulling the hem up to my waist. The sound of his zipper, then the feel of his Prince

Albert piercing's balls jewelry against my pussy lips brings me back to reality.

I push him away.

My palms against his broad chest offer no help to dislodge me from his clutches. I squirm in his firm hold and try to get down.

Malcolm laps at my tongue with his as he continues to breach my core.

"RED!!!" I scream against his mouth.

At once he lets me go and steps back. His gray eyes darkened to obsidian with lust, now peer at me dazed and questioningly.

Despite my body's betrayal—flushed face, pebbled nipples, swollen clit, wet pussy—we can't, I can't. My eyes close and I take a deep cleansing breath to settle my racing heart. Then I smooth my dress before I bring my gaze back to Malcolm.

He scrubs his hand over his face and runs his fingers through his hair. He too takes a deep breath and shakes his head to clear it. The wild look leaves his eyes as he stares back at me.

I break the silence.

"Malcolm... I... You told me we could explore one another. That it will have no negative impact on our business. You swore to uphold your promise to me for our business to proceed, no matter the result of our 'interaction.' I hope you are a man of your word," I say and pause for his confirmation.

His mouth opens and closes, then opens again.

I hold up my hand and ask, "Yes or no?"

Malcolm cocks his head to the side and raises his eyebrow as he studies my face intently.

I hold my ground, lifting my chin to stare back at him.

His face shutters, and he grows taller, aloof.

"Yes," he responds.

A part of my heart cracks. I had hoped he'd argue. In his Dom voice tells me he won't let me do this to us. Then spank me until I saw the light. But no. No fight for me, for us.

Told you!! My inner warrior says gleefully.

I ignore her.

"Good. I no longer wish to pursue the D/s relationship with you. However, I intend to continue as planned with Starr Light Fitness & Wellness' partnership with STEELE International. Agreed?" I ask.

Without hesitation Malcolm responds coolly, "Agreed. Anton will continue as your contact. Goodbye, Starr."

"Goodbye, Malcolm."

STARR

*H*i Starr. *I'm on my way to LA and want to see you. Come by my place at 8 tonight. I'll be on the rooftop.*

My heartbeat speeds up faster than Malcolm's Koenigsegg Agera RS as I read the text message from him.

It's been a month, and as we agreed, no contact between us.

At first I thought he may take part in the SLFW Resort meetings. But only Anton showed up. The most recent site visit without him was hard when I stood on the completed rooftop deck and remembered him teasing how he planned to christen it for prosperity before the other areas.

In the weeks that passed, I realized I should have given him a chance to explain himself rather than cut all association. When he didn't blow up my mobile or send flowers as he had in the past, I gave up on my wishes, hopes, and prayers for a reconciliation with Malcolm.

But this text message—albeit out of the blue—makes me tingle and in all the right places. Heart and pussy.

I'm not saying we'll jump back in bed together or restart our D/s relationship right away—although I do miss his domination. But I do want to hear what he has to say for himself.

Despite my I will do nothing but talk mindset, I go to the spa at SLFW to pamper myself. A body polish followed by a hot-stone massage, manicure and pedicure have me walking on air when I head home to change.

I opt for a simple white silk slip dress that brushes the tops of my knees and flaunts my curves and flesh-tone mules. I leave my hair out in a cascade of curls to the middle of my back. Before I leave, I dab on pink lip gloss and coat my eyelashes with waterproof mascara. Perfect to entice Malcolm with my shiny full lips and no chance of raccoon eyes should my gag reflex kick in. Just saying...

Girl... just stop, you mean! My inner warrior chides.

I snap her shut like the clasp on my Chanel clutch handbag and stride out the front door.

In no time, I arrive at Malcolm's West Hollywood penthouse. I park in his extra space, then head up on his private elevator. I smile to myself when the old code still works.

Ha! He trusts me. Probably because he expected we'd get back together.

Well, maybe we will, I giggle to myself as I fluff my curls and reapply my lip gloss while gazing at my reflection in the reflective surface of the elevator doors.

When they open, I glide off the elevator and pause in

the entry foyer to inhale the scent of Malcolm's cologne, John Varvatos - Dark Rebel Rider. The name says it all. It's all about the biker, the man who doesn't give a damn, the man who's out to make his way no matter what. The orange, balsam, leather, and amber fill my nostrils. Fearless. Sleek. Unconventional. Just like my man, dark, masculine, and sexy! How I've missed his smell.

I walk through to the stairs that lead to the rooftop deck. With a smile on my face, I climb my stairway to heaven. When I open the doors, I almost call out to him. Instead, I stare, a bit confused.

Ahead of me is a naked woman straddling a naked man on a chaise lounge. His back is to me. But she faces my direction. The sounds of her moans and his grunts, their skin slapping skin fill my ears.

My vision tunnels on them. Everything else fades out of view.

I step closer, my mind attempting to process what my eyes see before me and my ears pick up distinctly.

When we're only yards apart, the woman tosses her long blonde mane of wavy hair over her shoulder and pins me with her blue eyes. Her mouth a moment before contorted in a cry of ecstasy now morphs into a wicked smirk.

She leans back and her large breasts bounce from the man's brutal upward thrusts into her pussy. Then she leans forward—never taking her eyes from mine—and cups the man's face. Her red manicured fingernails poke through his ebony waves above the back of the chaise lounge.

"Oh, God, Malcolm, baby! You feel so fucking good! I missed you so much, too!" She cries out.

* * *

Malcolm & Starr's Story Continues: *Embrace My Desires*

Turn the page for the Steele Family, Author's Note, and a Preview of *Embrace My Desires*

THE STEELE FAMILY

STEELE INTERNATIONAL, INC

Multigenerational, multibillion-dollar business luxury real estate
development and management corporation

Headquarters & Family's Primary Residences:

The STEELE Tower, New York City

A modern, gray-tinted glass fifty-seven story mixed-use
skyscraper on southwest corner of Fifty-Seventh Street and Fifth
Avenue within Billionaires' Row

Global Offices:

- The United States of America (New York City, New Jersey, Chicago, California, Miami, Las Vegas)
- The Caribbean (St. Maarten, St. Barth's, St. Lucia)
- The French & Italian Rivieras (Nice, Cannes, Positano, Capri)
- Monaco (Monte Carlo)
- The United Arab Emirates (Abu Dhabi, Dubai)

STEELE FOUNDATION: A STRONG AND SUPPORTIVE HOUSE

Builds and manages attractive, affordable housing for urban, lower-income families

Available for download at https://bit.ly/SteelePintables

Author's Note

Thank you for reading Part I of Malcolm and Starr's sexy, sizzling romance! I hope that you enjoyed the start of their passionate love affair. If so, I'd love to hear your thoughts, please share a review at **amzn.to/2Lnvu52** and tell your friends.

Click below for what's up next for this darling duo:

Embrace My Desires Malcolm & Starr Part II

At **CharmaineLouise.com** take the *Four types of lovers. Which are you?* **Quiz** to match your Sexy Fantasy: sub, Voyeur, Dominatrix, or Dominatrix sub Switch.

Follow me on social media including my CLBooks Coterie Fan Club or on your favorite channels below and subscribe to my newsletter **bit.ly/CLBooksSubscribe** for a **Free Book**.

Fulfill Your Desires.
xoxo
Charmaine Louise

BB bookbub.com/authors/charmaine-louise-shelton
f facebook.com/CharmaineLouiseBooks
instagram.com/charmainelouisebooks
g goodreads.com/charmainelouisebooks

STEELE International, Inc.
A Billionaires Romance Series Book 8

Embrace My Desires Malcolm & Starr Part II

Click on the link below or visit books2read.com/u/b5lDe1
to get your copy.

Embrace My Desires Malcolm & Starr Part II

Books in the Series:

Discover My Desires Sebastian & Lola Prequel
(Available Exclusively to Subscribers)

Fulfill My Desires Sebastian & Lola Part I

Heighten My Desires Sebastian & Lola Part II

Ignite My Desires Roger & Leonie Part I

Stoke My Desires Roger & Leonie Part II

Justify My Desires Roger & Leonie Part III

Deepen My Desires Sebastian & Lola Part III

Capture My Desires Malcolm & Starr Part I

Embrace My Desires Malcolm & Starr Part II

Cherish My Desires Malcolm & Starr Part III

A Trilogy of Desires Sebastian & Lola Parts I-III

A Trilogy of Desires Roger & Leonie Parts I-III

A Trilogy of Desires Malcolm & Starr Parts I-III

Series Extras

Series Playlist

COMING NEXT: EMBRACE MY DESIRES MALCOLM & STARR PART II

1 *Month Ago*

"I DON'T KNOW. She fucking ghosted me, bro... No, I have no idea what happened. One minute we're dancing at the STEELE St. Barth's beachfront club. The next, she's ignoring me. Not answering my calls, texts, emails. She even had her collars hand delivered by courier to my West Hollywood penthouse. So yeah, you tell me, Sebastian."

My frustration with my wayward sub-cum-girlfriend hits its limit after weeks of her MIA action—or lack thereof...

Starr Knight, my beautiful woman with the face of an angel and the body of a sinner. When she smiles, dimples dot her sculpted cheekbones the color of warm chestnuts and her wide, sorrel brown eyes shine. I smirk at the memory of fisting her long, curly dark brown hair as I lose myself in Starr's sexy AF body—five feet, six inches, fit, curvy. Her submissive behavior—after eight months of being together—trained to match my Dom needs. Perfect. For. Me.

As a multibillionaire bachelor, women flock to me with the goal to gain a hunk of ice on their left ring finger. Visions of dollar signs float before their eyes, right along with my striking visage. Arrogant, maybe, but true.

Starr? No.

My Angel is a boss. Stanford University undergraduate degree in economics then continued on to the B-School for her MBA. She earned multiple fitness certifications, including her specialty in yoga. Followed her passion for health and wellness combined with helping others and opened Starr Light Fitness and Wellness Beverly Hills seven years ago at 25 years old.

Her initial goal achieved lead to a partnership with STEELE International, Inc. to expand into worldwide fitness retreats at luxury resorts and to add a second center location in the Caribbean. Beautiful, bodacious, smart as hell, and a self-made multimillionaire. Boom.

Fortunately for me, I head STEELE's Entertainment Properties Division as the president and First VP of the Board. I oversee our casinos, hotels, and resorts. My division generates the most revenue for my family's multigenerational, multibillion-dollar luxury real estate development and management company based out of The STEELE Tower in New York City.

SLFW falls within my milieu.

Another stroke of luck came in the form of Lola Lewis,

now Steele. My sister-in-law met My Angel at her first international fitness retreat in Fiji on the private Laucala Island. Lola raved about her experience and how cool My Angel is as a yoga instructor. Then she acted as a matchmaker. Well, that is for a business partnership…

Lola insisted I contact My Angel to discuss the opportunity. I agreed. But it was at Lola's wedding to my older brother Sebastian that I first met My Angel when she bumped into me. My eyes fell onto her gorgeous face, and sparks flew when my fingers brushed her soft skin as I balanced her on those fuck-me sandals.

Unbeknownst to me, the angel at my feet who shocked me to my core was Starr Knight, Lola's yoga teacher and close friend. It wasn't until the morning after the wedding I learned they were the same—Starr Knight, My Angel. Then she proved elusive.

After using my wiles to orchestrate a trip to STEELE St. Barths' instead of a boring conference room for potential partnership discussions, our mutual interest in the other led to us being in a Dominant/submissive relationship for the past eight months. A relationship I thought was on the cusp of a permanent situation.

Unlike my previous D/s relationships I had based on contracts for no longer than three months, the one with My Angel morphed into much more.

Within a month of being together, I took her to dinner with my parents, Morgan and Shelley. The Steele Matriarch knew My Angel from Lola and Sebastian's wedding preparations, then caught my interest in her at the festivities, naturally. My mother didn't disguise her pleasure in

My Angel being in our family as more than Lola's close friend.

My mother's expressive brown eyes lit up at the sight of My Angel approaching the restaurant's bar. She's a striking woman in her mid-fifties with shoulder-length, wavy black hair. Compared to my father from whom my siblings and I inherited various shades of his gray eyes, thick ebony hair, and six-foot-plus height. Except for our baby sister, Haley, who's two inches taller than our mother at five feet, eight inches.

She's the fraternal younger twin to Harris. Roger was the youngest until the twins were born—a double surprise for our parents. Then there's me with Sebastian as the eldest.

Each sibling works at STEELE International and has a board position: Sebastian recently took over the helm from our father as CEO and Chairman of the Board while he remains president of the Retail Properties Division; Roger, president of the Residential Properties Division and Second VP; Harris and Haley, fraternal twins, co-founders of the subsidiary STEELE Technology and Cyber Security and Members. Each of us head divisions best suited to our knowledge and interests.

I'm the most appropriate sibling to take on the Entertainment Properties Division. My wild ways of pushing the envelope and my love of the challenge extreme sports triggers prepared me for the role to lead our division focused on pleasure and thrills.

I thought cave diving and heli-skiing pumped my

adrenaline. But the pleasure and thrills My Angel gives to me beats them all. And I can't get enough.

It was on to the next level when we had dinner with her parents after being together for two months.

In their city, but on my ground at Spire 70 and Restaurant 69 in STEELE Rodeo Drive. Despite the initial annoyance of meeting Quinn Peters—her ex-boyfriend—unexpectedly My Angel and I had a good time with Peace and Sun.

Yeah, her father Peace Knight and mother Sun Knight—Jordan and Belinda originally.

They're brilliant environmental law attorneys who take on the most challenging cases against big businesses and win billions. The law firm—Knight & Knight LLP—her parents founded years ago after they met at a music festival while at Stanford Law School ranks in the top five of the United States. With offices in LA, Seattle, Denver, Chicago, Houston, New Orleans, Miami, New York City to represent cases in the top environmentally focused cities. They may be hippies, but they're sharks in the courtroom.

Needless to say, I succeeded in making a good impression on her parents.

Now, the big question: is Starr still My Angel?

My head spins as I rattle off the last few weeks of no contact with My Angel to Sebastian. I need Baz's advice as a fellow Alpha Dom for whom Lola is his sub and wife.

I know it's selfish of me, so absorbed in my life while Roger faces a crazy ass pretrial for sexual assault and harassment and STEELE International is the co-defendant. The baseless case brought forth by Delia Shaw, an intern at STEELE Paris and former classmate of Leonie at the Paris American Academy. Leonie *The Lion* Beaulieu gorgeous megamodel and then girlfriend of Roger, now fiancée and mother of his twin boys. He refused to pay Delia Shaw any attention, and now this bullshit.

Just as the pretrial judge was announcing his determination, Leonie cried out in the courtroom. Her water broke. The stress of the media frenzy and pretrial caused her to go into labor early.

Morgan, Shelley, Leonie's parents, Lola, Sebastian, and the rest of the Steele clan, the Jacksons, Joel Bailey and Hettie Fuchs, Norman and Anita Green, Luc Montaigne, Blair Thomas, Billie Chandler, Françoise Faucher, and some STEELE employees who gathered in support left the courtroom en masse.

Hours later, after Leonie gave birth, I caught up with My Angel, finally. She was so engrossed in her doula duties she didn't notice I followed her down the hallway as she headed back from the nurse's station. We hadn't spoken since the slight nod she gave to me when she entered the courtroom. Then she spent all of her time in the hospital at Leonie's side, so we didn't interact until the hallway encounter.

And what a dismal encounter…

"Hi, Angel," I say tentatively. "Crazy day, huh?"

She couldn't avoid me. So she nods and tries to go around my massive, six-foot-four-inch frame. I tower over her by ten inches.

I sidestep to block her path again.

We do a shuffling dance that Haley interrupts inadvertently.

As soon as she asks me a question, My Angel dodges the entire scene and flees to her guest room next to Leonie's suite.

As she hurries away, I watch her retreating back. Once Haley finishes, I call My Angel's mobile and send text messages eager to speak with her. No. Fucking. Answer.

I finish my sad story and glance over at Baz.

He doesn't show any judgement on his face that mine resembles. At only two years apart, I'm his absolute doppelgänger: same six feet, four inches in height; gray eyes; black hair; clean shaven or 5 o'clock shadow covers a firm jaw. People often confuse us or think we're twins.

It used to drive me crazy as a teenager. I strove for my own identity, hating being in Baz's shadow. It resulted in my rebel ways for years. Now we're good, and I see Baz as a confidante and not as a competitor. Still similar driven and dominant playboys—well, not anymore.

Baz gave up his one fuck and done ways after he met Lola. I gave up the sub contracts after I met My Angel. Call us reformists…

"I get how frustrated you must be, given how Lola iced me out of her life so abruptly. Did you do or say anything that may have upset Starr? Even if you don't think it bothered her?" Baz asks as he frowns.

A moment passes while I consider the last few times My Angel and I were together. Nothing untoward comes to mind. Hell, I was planning our next trip!

"No, bro, nothing. Not a damn thing," I respond as I stroke my five o'clock shadow thoughtfully.

Baz nods, then pulls out his mobile. After a finger presses on the screen, he lifts it to his ear.

"Hey, babe. Are you near Starr? Okay. Question, what's she saying about Malcolm?" His gaze remains on my questioning face while Lola speaks. Then he ends the call with an *I love you, too.*

Lucky fuck.

"Well, Starr has mentioned nothing to Lola. And she doubts Starr said anything to Leonie or she would have told Lola," Baz starts, then runs his fingers through his hair. "Either Starr doesn't want to interfere with Roger and Leonie's moment, or Starr isn't ready to disclose anything to them yet."

I nod in agreement.

"So, just leave it for now. Give her a couple of days once she's not as busy with Leonie"—he claps me on the back, and angles us toward the door of the waiting room—"Go to your President's Suite at STEELE Place Vendôme, shower, and eat a good meal. Then come back to the hospital refreshed. You need to clear your head, bro."

I take his advice and head out after I check in on the new parents. My heart swells with love when I see them holding Rodolphe and Gaspard. Could that be My Angel and me one day?

* * *

"THE NEXT GENERATION of Steeles is born! May they carry on our clan name and STEELE and Beaulieu forever!"

Declares our father as he holds his day-old grandsons proudly.

"*Oui, Mon Trésor* extends her family's line with males,

one for Beaulieu and one for STEELE!" Guy—Leonie's father—adds proudly as he plucks Gaspard from Morgan's arm.

The rest of the conversation fades into the background as I lean against the wall, watching My Angel across the room. Fuck if I don't feel like a lost puppy hoping to be reunited with its loving owner.

When at last she raises her gaze to mine, my heart thuds in my chest. At last!

Then it crashes to the ground, cracked.

She averts her eyes and chats with Anita—the wife of Norman Green, the former world heavyweight champion, STEELE's partner in his eponymous chain of luxury fitness facilities, and Roger's personal trainer.

My feet no longer propel me towards My Angel. Instead, I slouch back against the wall with a frown marring my face. Okay, this shit will not fly for much longer. Enough.

I am far from one who bows in defeat when I want something. No matter the challenge, I stand firm and get what I want. And I want my brown-eyed Angel back in my arms and writhing beneath the sting of my palm and the pounding of my ten-inch cock.

* * *

"OH!" My Angel exclaims as she bumps into me when she closes the door behind her to Leonie's suite at the hospital with a click.

Her head tilts back to see me glowering at her. It's been

two days since Leonie gave birth and one since our hallway encounter. Yesterday I resolved to put an end to this limbo.

Without a word, I take My Angel by the elbow and usher her next door to her guest room. I cock my eyebrow at her wordlessly, demanding she unlock it for us to enter. This intervention requires privacy.

She does.

Once inside, I grab her heart-shaped face between my sizable hands and crush her mouth with mine in a possessive, toe-curling kiss. I don't let My Angel catch her breath before I hoist her up and slam her back against the door.

Automatically, her long, toned legs wrap around my waist and lock at the ankles. Her hands dive into my hair, tugging at my scalp.

The pressure of her warm pussy against the front of my shirt coupled with the pain from her frantic tugs makes my cock jump to life. It's been too long since I buried it balls deep in her tight, wet core.

With a growl, I rip at her wrap dress, pulling the hem up to her waist. The sound of my zipper, then the feel of my Prince Albert piercing's balls jewelry against her pussy lips drive me to the brink. Only to be jerked back from the edge of carnal bliss.

My Angel pushes me away.

Her palms against my broad chest offer no help to dislodge her from my firm hold. She squirms in my arms and tries to get down.

I lap at her tongue with mine as I continue to breach her pussy.

"RED!!!"

My Angel's scream against my mouth jolts me—her safeword.

Fuck. Me.

At once I let her go and step back. My gray eyes darkened to obsidian with lust, now peer at her dazed and questioningly.

Despite her body's betrayal—flushed face, pebbled nipples, swollen clit, wet pussy—she wants me to stop. My Angel closes her eyes and takes a deep cleansing breath. Then she smooths her dress before she brings her gaze back to mine.

Meanwhile, my heart continues to race.

I scrub my hand over my heated face and run my fingers through my mussed hair. Now I tug in frustration. I too take a deep breath and shake my head to clear it. The wild look leaves my eyes as I stare back at My Angel.

She breaks the silence.

"Malcolm… I… You told me we could explore one another. That it will have no negative impact on our business. You swore to uphold your promise to me for our business to proceed, no matter the result of our 'interaction.' I hope you are a man of your word," she says and pauses for my confirmation.

My mouth opens and closes, then opens again as I remember my words to her so many months ago. I try to formulate an answer. One that will get us beyond this line of questioning.

She holds up her hand and asks, "Yes or no?"

I cock my head to the side and raise my eyebrow as I study her face intently.

My Angel holds her ground, lifting her chin to stare back at me. Her sorrel brown eyes defiant, no longer filled with passion or submission. Or us.

My face shutters, and I grow taller, aloof. So be it. Malcolm *The Enforcer* Steele begs no one.

"Yes," I respond blandly.

"Good. I no longer wish to pursue the D/s relationship with you. However, I intend to continue as planned with Starr Light Fitness & Wellness' partnership with STEELE International. Agreed?" She asks.

Without hesitation, I respond coolly, "Agreed. Anton will continue as your contact. Goodbye, Starr."

"Goodbye, Malcolm."

That answers my question: Starr Knight is no longer My Angel.

***

Click the Link Below or Visit books2read.com/u/ b5lDe1 For Your Copy

Embrace My Desires Malcolm & Starr Part II

I dedicate this novel to the thrill seekers, rebels, and free spirits. Keep doing your thing, baby!

Fulfill Your Desires.

xoxo
Charmaine Louise

WELCOME TO CHARMAINELOUISE — THE SENSUAL LIFESTYLE

GLITZY. GLAMOROUS. STEAMY.

CharmaineLouise New York, Inc. invites you to indulge in *The Sensual Lifestyle* through **CharmaineLouise Books** and **CharmaineLouise Intimates**. CLBrands immerse you in *Sexy Fantasies* with CLBooks contemporary romance novels and give you *Sexy Under Things & Loungewear* with CLIntimates.

Charmaine Louise Shelton the Founder, CEO & Author of CLNY loves all things classic, elegant, feminine, and of course with an erotic edge! Favorite outfit of choice is a cashmere cardigan, leather pencil skirt, and seamed silk stockings with stiletto heels. Sexy Fantasy Type: sub with a dash of Voyeur. When not writing and designing, Charmaine Louise travels and spends time with her Maltese buddies, ZIGGY and Jynger.

CharmaineLouise — *The Sensual Lifestyle*

~ Visit online at **CharmaineLouise.com**

~ Subscribe to **CharmaineLouise Newsletter**

~ Find us on Facebook **@CharmaineLouiseNewYork**

~ Instagram **@CharLouNY**

CharmaineLouise Books *Sexy Fantasies* launched summer 2020. Sizzling, contemporary romance with your soon-to-be favorite Alpha Doms, Powerful Billionaires, and the women they lust after and love for second chances, insta-love, enemies-to-lovers, and more.

Want to chat it up and share your thoughts with other CLBooks Lovers? Read our blog, join our Charmaine-Louise Books Coterie Fan Club and follow us on my author pages and social media to be in the know about the book release dates, exclusive content, giveaways, contests, and more!

~ **Purchase your eBook and paperback novels from my Author Page by clicking here!**

~ Read and subscribe to our blog ***The World of Sex***

~ Connect on **Amazon Author Page**

~ Goodreads Author Profile

~ <u>BookBub Author Profile</u>

CharmaineLouise Intimates *Sexy Under Things &* *Loungewear* debuted in 2003. Inspired by the sensuous sirens and sylph swans of the past and present, the hand crochet cashmere and silk collections are for the sexy: hence, the line names Ginger — Bombshell; Diana — Showstopper; Jackie — Timeless; Lena — Classic. Also known as The Movie-Star from Gilligan's Island; Ms. Ross The Boss; Mrs. Kennedy Onassis; Ms. Horne.

Do you thrive on seduction and being sexy lounging at home? Read our blog and follow us on social media to receive the tips, the latest additions to the collections, private sales, and more!

~ Read and subscribe to our blog ***The Art of Seduction***

~ Find us on Facebook **@CharmaineLousieIntimates**

~ Instagram **@CharmaineLouiseIntimates**

Fulfill Your Desires.